This gift provided by:

The
Seattle
Public
Library
Foundation

CAMERON BATTLE AND THE HIDDEN KINGDOMS

CAMERON BATTLE AND THE
HIDDEN KINGDOMS

JAMAR J. PERRY

BLOOMSBURY
CHILDREN'S BOOKS
NEW YORK LONDON OXFORD NEW DELHI SYDNEY

BLOOMSBURY CHILDREN'S BOOKS
Bloomsbury Publishing Inc., part of Bloomsbury Publishing Plc
1385 Broadway, New York, NY 10018

BLOOMSBURY, BLOOMSBURY CHILDREN'S BOOKS,
and the Diana logo are trademarks of Bloomsbury Publishing Plc

First published in the United States of America in February 2022
by Bloomsbury Children's Books
www.bloomsbury.com

Bloomsbury books may be purchased for business or promotional use.
For information on bulk purchases please contact Macmillan Corporate and
Premium Sales Department at specialmarkets@macmillan.com

Library of Congress Cataloging-in-Publication Data
Names: Perry, Jamar J, author.
Title: Cameron Battle and the hidden kingdoms / by Jamar J. Perry.
Description: New York: Bloomsbury, 2022.
Summary: When Cameron and his best friends are magically transported through the
pages of an ancestral book to the fabled West African country Chidani, they find a
kingdom in extreme danger and have to find a way to save the Igbo people.
Identifiers: LCCN 2021032192 (print) I LCCN 2021032193 (e-book)
ISBN 978-1-5476-0694-8 (hardcover) • ISBN 978-1-5476-0695-5 (e-book)
Subjects: CYAC: Magic—Fiction. I Mythology, Igbo—Fiction. I Friendship—Fiction. I
African Americans—Fiction. I Books—Fiction. I LCGFT: Novels.
Classification: LCC PZ7.1.P44773 Cam 2022 (print) I LCC PZ7.1.P44773 (e-book) I
DDC [Fic]—dc23
LC record available at https://lccn.loc.gov/2021032192
LC e-book record available at https://lccn.loc.gov/2021032193

Book design by Jeanette Levy
Typeset by Westchester Publishing Services
Printed and bound in the U.S.A.
2 4 6 8 10 9 7 5 3 1

To find out more about our authors and books visit
www.bloomsbury.com and sign up for our newsletters.

To my mama, Tiffany Evans,
for giving me books to love

To Emily Timbol,
for teaching me when no one else would

To Michael Strother,
for making my dreams come true

CHAPTER ONE

I forgot my umbrella.

My best friend Zion hadn't.

Raindrops splattered all over my jacket, pants, and my favorite all-red Converse Chucks as I scrambled off Grady Elementary's school bus. "Hey, Zion. Let me underneath your umbrella? I don't have mine."

"Nope!" Zion said, falling into step with me as we walked the neighborhood streets leading to Grandma's house. "I told you to bring yours this morning when you called me. You decided not to listen. Your fault." He removed a small package of Skittles from his pocket and popped a green one in his mouth, laughing as he did. His stomach poked out from his light jacket.

I rolled my eyes. "Come on, Zion. *Please?*" I faked a sweet smile. "Don't forget, I'm wearing your favorite pants today." We wore each other's clothing often.

Zion sucked his teeth, his brown curls bouncing as he shook his head. "Nope!" His curls were damp, as opposed to my soaking wet, coarse hair. "And you mean . . . *your* pants now that they're drenched."

Groaning, I took off my jacket and wrapped it around my head. Grandma had told me this morning, with a far-away look as she stared out the kitchen window, that it might rain, but I hadn't listened to her or Zion. I was under the false impression that summers in Atlanta meant constant sunshine, not thunderous rain for days on end. "Things are changing, Cam," she had said. "Our home ain't the same as it used to be."

Boom. Thunder rolled in the sky, the clouds opened even more, and the steady sheets of rain became a flood. It was almost like the weather had heard my thoughts.

"Great last day of school, huh?" Zion said. The water almost obscured his brown-skinned face, just a touch lighter than my own dark walnut-brown skin. Droplets of rain marred his black-rimmed glasses. I swatted water from my eyes, trying to see the neighborhood. Grandma's house was set back on a dead-end road, so it was easy to miss it, especially when the weather was bad.

I squeezed my soaked shirt with my left hand.

"It doesn't really feel like summer, does it?" Zion asked, shivering a bit and popping another Skittle in his mouth. I had to agree with him. The last few weeks had been nothing but miserable outside, forcing us inside. Everyone knew that summer came early to Atlanta, but the weather lately had been more like winter, raining for almost a full month, the sky a constant dark gray, almost black. I even thought I had seen snowflakes drifting down to the ground just last week. I ran to show Grandma, but by the time we stepped outside into the backyard, it had all mysteriously disappeared. After that, Grandma made Zion and me stay in the house, a worried look crossing her face every time she caught us sneaking out to the woods surrounding her home.

To be fair, it was Zion who had convinced me to slip away, but she was quick enough to catch us every time.

"It hasn't felt like summer in a long time," I responded as we walked. "Did you text Aliyah about the sleepover?"

Zion looked annoyed. "Why did you have to invite her? This was supposed to be a Zion and Cam weekend sleepover. It's been that way since we were six."

A sigh escaped my mouth. "We've discussed this, Zion. She's our friend, too. We all got close this year, so don't act like you don't love her, either. You're always over at her house—*without me*, I might add—playing video games."

"Yeah, whatever," Zion muttered, shifting his backpack on his shoulders. "This is *tradition*. You don't break tradition." A hurt look bloomed on his face, but I ignored it. He'd get over it once Aliyah finally showed up; we were all the best of friends, but we hadn't invited her to our weekly sleepovers yet until now.

Grandma and I lived in Underwood Hills, a neighborhood in Buckhead in Northern Atlanta. The small, cozy homes rose on each side of the sidewalk as we passed by. Kids jumped off school buses, spilling into the road and onto the pavement, talking in groups as if thunder hadn't just sounded in the sky. When we got to a stop sign about three hundred feet from our bus stop, we turned left.

A sly look passed through Zion's hazel eyes. "Speaking of tradition, we might as well—"

"Nope!" I said, mimicking Zion's high voice. "You know the attic is off-limits."

"It wasn't off-limits when—"

"It is," I said, cutting him off. "And we're not going up there, either."

"But why?" he whined. "We used to read *The Book of Chidani* all the time, you know . . . before. Remember the queen, her sister, and Chidani? It almost seemed . . . real every time we read it."

"I *know*. And remember the demons, the gods, the palace?"

"Please, please, Cam? It wouldn't hurt to just take *one* look."

We hadn't been to the attic in two years, not since I'd lost my parents to a car crash. What would a quick peek hurt? But still, Grandma had forbidden us to go up there. "No, Zion."

Zion grumbled underneath his breath. "Party pooper."

Grandma's brick house appeared at the top of the hill.

4

I touched Zion's shoulder and turned him around, ignoring the rain. "Listen. Don't bring up the *Book* with Aliyah. I'm serious. Grandma was clear when she locked it away."

"But reading it was our friend thing."

A twinge of sadness pierced my chest as I thought about Mama and Grandma reading it to me when I was younger. When I met Zion, he had joined in. It was something that had connected us even more. "I liked reading it, too. But rules are rules."

"Rules are meant to be broken, though," Zion said.

"I—" *Sizzle. Pop!*

Lightning struck the ground near where we stood, next to the apple tree in Grandma's backyard. We both jumped and screamed, covering our faces as the light filled our eyes. *What the . . . ?*

"What was that?" Zion said, clinging to me. A crack appeared in the sidewalk where the lightning had struck.

A dark shadow ran across my vision as I stared at Grandma's house. The rain shower stopped falling, as if someone had pressed Pause. The apparition took on a monstrous, humanoid shape right next to the old shed in the backyard. It was dark, tall, and obscured by shadows.

"What is that—" I said, but my voice caught in my throat as the figure started to move toward us. I let out a squeak of fear as a memory tingled in my mind, but I wasn't able to fully capture it before I made a grab for Zion and yelled, *"Run!"*

My arm grasped only air as I ran toward the woods

surrounding Grandma's house. Zion ran far in front of me. I pumped my legs, burning with my every step, as a hissing sound came from behind me. *Don't look back, Cameron. Don't look back.*

I looked back anyway. The shadowy figure grew in size, surrounding me in smoke. As soon as I hit the covering of the trees, my sneakers became slick with grass and dirt, and my leg twisted on a branch. I yelped as I fell, the shadow moving closer as I grabbed at my leg. I tried to stand.

"Zion!" I cried out as the shadow *grew* legs, running toward me. I thought I could make out the word "book" coming from its nonexistent mouth as it barreled my way. The memory tingled again, so close yet too far away. The shadow got closer, and I shut my eyes, sure this was the end.

Pressure built under my armpits as I was pulled across the wet dirt. "Cameron, Cameron, Cameron!" Zion was saying. I struggled with the pressure, trying to fight as much as I could. I sent a punch upward.

"Ow! What did you do that for? Open your eyes!"

I sat blinking and took in my surroundings. Zion had moved us deeper into the woods, right near the pond behind Grandma's house. It had started to rain again, but at least the trees gave us some cover. I scrambled upward, looking around, breathing hard.

"Where is it?" I asked. "Where is it?"

"Where is what?" Zion asked, anger blossoming on his

face as he straightened his glasses and pulled out a cloth from his pocket. "You didn't have to punch me!"

"What do you mean, *what*? You saw it!"

"Saw what?" Zion said. "I didn't see anything. You said *run*, and that's all I had to hear. You never, ever ask questions when someone tells you to run, especially when it's coming from your best friend."

I gestured around us, my heart still hammering. "I could've sworn I saw a shadow, smoke, something. It was running from Grandma's house."

By this time, Zion had cleaned his glasses, straightened them, and put them back on. "It was probably just a glare or the sky getting dark because of the rain. You really gotta stop this, Cam."

"Stop what?"

Zion pushed past me toward Grandma's house again. "You know you can be weird about these types of things. You *always* think something is happening that's not."

I huffed behind him, slightly embarrassed. "I am *not* a conspiracy theorist. I just use my mind in creative ways—at least that's what Grandma says."

"Yeah, uh-huh."

We broke through the cover of the trees. By the time we got to the back door, I had convinced myself that maybe the shadow was a trick of light, an illusion created by the rain. *Yeah, it was just created by the rain. That's it.*

I couldn't help, though, the flesh bumps that rose on my arms.

Grandma opened the door as soon as we got close, her gray hair tied with bobby pins and piled on top of her head, cotton house shoes flopping in the air, still wearing her night-gown. She had been waiting for me lately, every time I got off the bus. Sometimes, she would even make the trek all the way down the street to walk me home. Her dark-brown face, usu-ally calm and inviting, was lined with concern. In the two years since I had lost my parents, she had seemed to grow much older, not moving as fast as she used to, always hovering over Zion and me.

She grabbed us both and hugged us tight. "I told you to come straight home! You know things are changing . . . I thought the worst had happened. I don't know what I would do if . . ."

"Grandma," I whined, extricating myself from her arms. "It's just a little rain."

The faraway look appeared in Grandma's eyes again as she stared at the backyard. "Yeah . . . just a little rain."

Zion fished in his pocket again as Grandma ushered us inside. He pushed something toward me.

"Skittle?"

CHAPTER TWO

After we'd dried off, Aliyah texted Zion that she'd be over in a few minutes. She was struggling with her seven-year-old younger brother as they emerged from her father's car. I was in the front yard watching her, ringing dirty water out of my Chucks.

"Give it back, Kendall!"

"But I just wanna play with it!" he was whining.

Her dad sighed as he rummaged in the back seat, removing Aliyah's things. "Kendall, we don't have time for this. Give it back to your sister." Aliyah snatched the Switch handheld console from her brother and wrapped the book bag her daddy handed her around her shoulders.

"Hi, Mr. Banks," I said, thrusting my hand forward.

He squeezed it hard. "Hey, Cameron. How's it going? Grandma okay?"

Aliyah groaned and pushed her braids over her shoulder. "Dad, I told you—"

"She's doing fine, Mr. Banks," I said, interrupting her. "Aliyah, you ready for the weekend?"

"I sure am," she said, placing her Switch in her bag. "I'm so glad it's summer."

Mr. Banks shivered, glancing at the sky. It had stopped raining, but the weather had gotten considerably colder since Zion and I had arrived home. "Sure doesn't feel like it."

Kendall tugged at his father's coat. "Can we go now? It's cooo-olllddd."

"Stop whining," Aliyah said.

"Aliyah, enough," Mr. Banks commanded. "Say goodbye to your brother." Aliyah bent over and reluctantly hugged her brother, who pulled away as soon as he could. I waved goodbye to them all and led Aliyah inside.

"'Bye, Dad! Love ya!" Aliyah called as they drove off.

Zion was lounging on the extra bed in my room reading one of my books, while Aliyah went to browse through Grandma's Netflix account. Something hard and thick hit me upside the head as I placed my Chucks near the window to continue drying. I turned around. Zion was trying to stifle a laugh.

"Ow! What was that for?"

"You're daydreaming again," Zion said, shifting his glasses on his nose. "I didn't do nothin'. You just got scared."

"Don't be mad because I have an imagination, something you clearly *don't* have," I said, gazing at the carpet as I spoke.

"And seriously, there was no need to throw a book at me to get my attention." I saw my battered copy of the first book in the Percy Jackson series on the floor.

"I didn't throw anything at you," Zion said.

I looked back up at him. "You can't just throw Percy Jackson! Do you know what those books mean to me?"

Zion gestured to what he was reading. "I didn't throw anything at you, bro. I'm reading book two. Calm down."

I narrowed my eyes at Zion, then turned toward the TV. "Did you find something to watch?" I asked Aliyah.

"Your grandma's done a good job with the parental controls," Aliyah responded. "All I see is kiddie stuff. What kinda summer are we supposed to have if we can't watch anything above PG-13? *Stranger Things* again?"

Zion shivered. "I *hate* that show. It's scary. We shouldn't be watching it anyway. We're not thirteen yet."

"We can watch that again . . . ," I said, smirking at Zion as he closed his book and headed over to my bookshelf. "Make sure you turn up the volume."

Crash. Aliyah and I both jumped as my entire bookshelf fell onto the floor, spilling all the contents on the ground. Zion still held the book in his hand, half-lifted as if he were waiting to put it back where he got it from.

"I promise I didn't do that," Zion said, eyes wide. "I wasn't even close to it when it fell!"

"Come on, man, don't lie," I said. Fear crept up my spine. "A bookshelf can't push itself to the floor."

"I'm not lying!" he protested.

I sighed. Together, we lifted the heavy bookshelf and pushed it back against the wall, then returned the books to their places—Zion handed them to me, and I made sure they were arranged alphabetically by title, just how I liked them.

After we were done, Zion curled up on the spare twin bed. "That's enough exercise for one day," he said. He yawned, and his glasses slipped down his nose again. He acted as if he lived in my house. Which he actually kinda did.

Sometimes, I forgot how long we had been friends. We'd gravitated to each other in the first grade after coming in first and second place in Grady Elementary's school-wide spelling bee. I won, of course, but then I'd found Zion crying after school in the bathroom. When I had asked him why he was so upset, he'd responded, "Because I'm supposed to be the smartest, not you." I think that comment was supposed to make me mad, but it had only made me laugh. Which then made him laugh, too.

"How old are you again?" I had asked. From that moment on, we became inseparable. Now that we'd completed sixth grade, we'd started dreaming about working hard for college scholarships and getting out of Atlanta one day.

"I guess we have to settle for *Stranger Things*." Aliyah sighed, throwing the remote down in disgust. I was glad when we added Aliyah to our two-person crew at the beginning of our sixth-grade year at Grady. She started out as the new girl; she sat alone in class, ate lunch alone while fiddling with her Pokémon cards, and played by herself at recess. Then I introduced myself, and we played a battle with her cards—not before I made a joke about how only older people still played with them. She had tried to cheat by using two of her cards to attack mine, even though the game rules clearly stated she could only use one. She hadn't known yet that Mama and I had played with Pokémon cards for years before she died.

We became fast friends after that. Zion was jealous at first—and in some ways, still was—but he had ended his sulking pretty quickly after she invited us over and he saw her gaming setup. Her father was a video game developer, and she always got the latest games first.

As soon as the remote hit the floor, the lights in my bedroom flickered, and we heard a flash of thunder.

"It's raining again—" I started to say, but this time, the power went out, leaving us in complete darkness. Zion screamed and pulled the covers over his head. Aliyah rolled her eyes; I could see the whites of them in the darkness.

"Here he goes again," Aliyah said.

I crept over to my bedroom door and peeked outside. The hallway was dark, too. "Looks like the power is out in the entire house."

"Do you have a circuit breaker? We can turn the electricity back on easily," Aliyah said.

I stiffened. "Y-y-yeah, we have one." I swallowed hard. "I

mean, I *think* we do." I paused for a second. "What's a circuit breaker again?"

Aliyah sighed. "A circuit breaker holds all the electric circuits in your home, Cam. It's what you use when the lights go out! I bet it's in the attic. That's where it is in my house."

I hesitated. "Yeah . . . the attic's locked. We can't go up there."

Aliyah started to walk toward the bedroom door. "Don't be silly. Come on. Let's go upstairs."

I grabbed her arm before she could take another step. "There's another problem," I said as Zion let out another small, frightened squeak. "I don't know how to use a circuit breaker."

Aliyah twirled her braids. "How old are you again? It's no big deal. Daddy used to be an electrician before he started designing games, so I know how to use them. You just read the names written on each switch and power the room you want. Or it could be the breaker on the whole house, which would be a bigger problem. But come on—let's go check."

Nervousness crept in. "The attic is locked. I don't want to get in trouble if Grandma catches us up there."

Zion shifted the covers so that the only thing showing was his glasses. "Trust me, Cam has a good reason for not wanting to go upstairs," he said, his words muffled.

"Shut up, Zion," I warned.

"What are y'all talking about?" Aliyah said.

"Nothing, Aliyah," I said.

"He's lying," Zion said in a singsong voice. "There's an old book up there. His parents read it to him when he was a kid. They said it came from their ancestors. It's super creepy and awesome." He threw off the covers and puffed out his chest. "We used to read it all the time."

"It's locked, and we don't have a key," I repeated, urging her to change her mind. "There's no way the power has *not* gone out for two years, so the circuit breaker can't be up there."

"You're trying to change the subject," Aliyah said. Her eyes sparkled with interest. "I wanna see this book!"

"No. It's not—" I said.

"It's in the attic," Zion finished. "Grandma has forbidden us from going up there."

"Zion—it's locked."

Aliyah made her way to my bedroom door again, turning the knob and peering out into the hallway. "It's settled. We're going upstairs. I might be able to pick the lock."

"Please, Aliyah. No . . . ," I said. I couldn't help, though, the curiosity that gripped me now.

She walked over, concern in her eyes. "I understand, Cam. I do. You've been through so much. Even though your mother's things belong to you now, if you don't wanna go, we won't go."

She was correct. I had a right to see and read the book my mama had left me. The *Book* was *mine* now that she was gone, but Grandma had been trying to keep it from me. Still, there was no way we could get in the attic without a key, and Grandma always had it with her. And I was *not* going to let Aliyah pick the lock.

"You're right. But first we need—" I stopped talking as soon as I went to the bedroom door, Aliyah following behind. Shining in blue light on the hallway floor was the key to the attic, its head encased in pink tape.

"Hmm, that doesn't make any sense," I said, picking it up from the floor. The blue light disappeared as I grasped it, making me think it was just a trick of the light—or lack of light, actually. "It's the attic key."

That didn't stop the fear, though. *How did it get here? Did I just think it into existence?*

By this time, Zion had joined us, putting my thoughts to words. "Um, Cam, how did the key get there?"

"No clue," I whispered. "Maybe Grandma dropped it on her way to her room?"

Aliyah snatched it from me. "We'll use the flashlight on my phone to see. Let's go."

As we crept up the stairs to the attic, I couldn't shake the feeling that shivered up my skin. *Why would the key be in the hallway?*

The last time I was able to look at the *Book* was two years ago. Grandma and I had snuggled up on one of the worn sofas in the attic a few days after my parents left, right after she had told me they had died in a car crash and wouldn't be coming back. It was a night like this night, stormy and gray. Grandma read about Queen Ramala, the main character in the *Book*, and was showing me her picture when suddenly it glowed golden, and I could have sworn the pictures began to move. The queen's hair, which had been dark brown, started to turn gray before our very eyes . . .

"That's enough," Grandma had said, her voice choked in her throat as she slammed the *Book* shut. "We're done." She dragged me out of the attic, not even giving me a chance to protest, and locked the door behind us. She said, tears swimming in her eyes, "Don't *ever* come back up to this attic, you hear me?" My own tears clogged in my throat; it was like I had lost my parents for the second time.

But now, we tiptoed up the stairs to the third floor, defying her orders. When we got to the attic door, I put the key in and opened it.

CHAPTER THREE

I immediately tripped over an area rug and caught myself on a dresser. As I steadied myself, Aliyah shone the light from her phone, and we looked around. The attic appeared the same as it always had: bookshelves stuffed with books, broken and unused furniture, and multiple mismatched area rugs that covered the ground. There were broken lamps, CD players, boomboxes, worn chests, papers all over the floor, old record players, musical instruments, paintings that used to hang on the walls, all stuff that had been dragged up here in the decades my grandma had lived in the house. A lone coffee table, one of its wooden feet badly chipped, stood in front of the window overlooking the backyard.

Despite how ramshackle and disheveled the place was, I had such fond memories of reading up here with my mama and grandma that it kinda brought tears to my eyes.

"Ooh," Aliyah said, breaking the silence as she walked

across the room, as dim light from the attic window shone through the dark. Zion and I began to riffle through the bookshelves.

"Some help here?" Aliyah said, but my eyes met Zion's. He knew what I wanted to find.

"Are you sure about this, Cam? You remember what we saw the last time we read from it together . . . ," Zion whispered.

"I remember . . . are you scared?" I said, peering at the books so I wouldn't have to look at him.

He grabbed my hand and gave me a mischievous wink. "I'm *always* scared. Never stopped me before."

"The *Book* is *mine*," I said. "My mama gave it to me." I opened one of the chests that was hidden behind a patchy armchair. "Grandma shouldn't have hidden it."

I opened the chest and rummaged through it for a while before feeling something. A familiar roughness. Tears smarted in my eyes as I pulled out the *Book*. It was about five inches thick, its pages worn, frayed, and brown at the edges. Golden clasps wrapped around its front, spine, and sides, protecting its contents and almost obscuring its title, *The Book of Chidani*.

Aliyah joined us then, peering down at the *Book* with her phone flashlight as I opened the clasps. "I couldn't find the circuit breaker."

I handled the *Book* gingerly, wiping my hands across its worn, dark face, feeling every groove, crevice, and ridge. I handed it over to Aliyah and Zion as we sat down on a dusty sofa.

"Here, just look at the pictures," I said. "Most of it is in Igbo."

Aliyah and Zion flipped through the *Book*, gasping as they turned a page and saw some of the fantastical creatures.

"What are these? They look so . . . real," Aliyah said.

"Those are creatures from the land of Chidani," I said.

"Where did this book come from, Cameron?" she asked.

Zion's voice deepened as he spoke the words my mama used to say to us. We knew it by heart at this point. "*The Book of Chidani* has been passed down through the Battle family for centuries."

I smiled as I took up the telling of the tale. "It was smuggled in secret on one of the slave boats during the Middle Passage where our ancestors were kidnapped against their will, to America. It was a way for our people to keep our traditions even when our captors *thought* they had taken everything from us. The *Book* was found by one of the slave capturers and was thrown overboard during the voyage. But it followed its people across the Atlantic and to the Americas."

"It feels almost *alive*," she said.

I furrowed my brow. "That's *exactly* how I felt when I touched it the first time. Mama said it was because part of the lore that is in the *Book is* alive. It . . . changes as Chidani changes."

I thought of how I had seen the queen's hair change color the last time I was up here.

After clearing my throat, I continued. "The *Book* was

hidden in secret by Igbo families—my ancestors—and passed from generation to generation all the way down to my grandmother, my mother, and now me. It's alive because the people who brought it from the Old World could perform the magic of their ancestors. It's part of a rich culture that existed among the Igbo people, a culture of myths and rituals. They kept their traditions despite the fact that they were enslaved. The *Book* was our people's connection to their history, our past. Our knowledge and traditions haven't been lost, and this book is evidence of that."

"That's kinda amazing. But how'd it get inside your attic?" Aliyah asked.

"Legend has it that once the enslaved people reached the plantations in the Americas, the *Book* followed them along the shore until a descendant of the Igbo people, a young girl, found it while swimming in the sea. She brought it home to her mother, who recognized it immediately. Despite the fact that it had been underwater, the pages weren't damaged. The girl's mother sang the history of her people to her daughter, and she became enraptured with the story, much like you are now. Much like I was when my mama first read it to me . . ."

I made sure to repeat the story the same way my mother and grandmother had told it to me.

"After the *Book* was found, the girl's mother saw that chapters had been added. It was almost like as soon as something significant happened in Chidani, a new page would appear, and even though she and her daughter were far away from their ancestral homeland, they were able to keep up with what was happening there. The mother knew it couldn't possibly be real; how were pages being added to the *Book* if no one had placed them there?"

"Magic was clearly the only answer," Zion answered.

"The mother was scared of it being found," I continued, "so she hid the *Book* and cautioned her descendants to do the same. So, it became a relic. Passed down through the generations but always stuffed in an attic somewhere. My grandma gave it to my mother, but . . . I guess it's mine now," I finished.

"It can't be true. I've never heard of a country called Chidani," Aliyah said.

"It doesn't exist on a map. My mom and grandma used to tell me that magic protects it. It's a secret country in Africa, in Nigeria, the land of the Igbo people."

Aliyah raked her hands through her braids. "But the *Book* has always had these pages, right? There's no way it could have been filled through the centuries. It's just a story . . ."

The lights flickered back on, and we all jumped. The *Book* fell to the floor and opened to a page showing Queen Ramala. Her skin was lined and her hair was gray. She looked much older than she should have been. Even older than I remembered . . . I looked away, not wanting to believe what my eyes were telling me.

"Look!" Zion said. The pages of the *Book* started flipping on their own—almost like there was a breeze or maybe a ghost in the room. Zion and Aliyah both gripped my arms, and we watched as words, laced with golden light, appeared on a blank page. The words told the *exact* story I had just told to Zion and Aliyah.

"Cameron! Aliyah! Zion!" Grandma called from downstairs. "Time for dinner!"

"Quick!" I said. I snatched the *Book* from the floor and slammed it shut, then quickly put it back in its hiding place. "She can't catch us up here!"

We rushed out. I locked the door behind us, placed the key in my pocket, and we all ran down two flights of steps until we got to the dining room.

"What's wrong?" Grandma asked, seeing how breathless we were. Her gray hair, usually placed tightly in a bun, was loose and falling across her dark-brown eyes. A crease appeared in her otherwise smooth forehead.

"Nothing," we all responded at the same time.

We sat at the table and ate, trying not to look guilty. Grandma frowned, but she only passed the bread around the table and ladled homemade chicken soup into our bowls. After we were done, Grandma took her plate into the kitchen.

"Grandma, the lights went off earlier, then came back on. Where exactly is the circuit breaker?"

"Can you all help me clean the dishes tonight? I need to rest," she said from the kitchen, ignoring my question.

"Grandma, do we have any photo albums in the attic?" I asked, trying to push her to tell me what I wanted to know. "I want to show Zion and Aliyah some pictures of Mama and Daddy." We needed an excuse to go back up to the attic without running the risk of getting caught.

She came back to the dining room. "Do what I tell you, Cam."

"Yes, ma'am," I responded.

Grandma gave me a little shove toward the sink. "Let's get started on the dishes," she said. "I'll wash, you dry."

Grandma took one of the plates out of the sink, winced, and dropped it to the floor. It didn't break, but my heart beat faster as she bent over slowly to pick it up.

I grabbed her arm. "It's okay, Grandma. Aliyah, Zion, and I can handle the dishes."

"Don't worry," she said, "everything's okay. The plate was just a little hot. But I am tired; I think I will go upstairs for the night."

When I picked up the plate, though, it was cold.

Grandma heaved a loud sigh before making her way to her room. I chewed on my fingernails as I watched her climb. I had already lost my mama and daddy. What would happen if I lost her, too? She was the most important thing in my life, the only family I had . . . It was like all the sadness in the world had been placed on both our shoulders when my parents died, and I didn't think that either of us was strong enough to handle it without the other.

We washed the dishes in silence. I dipped my hands in sudsy hot water and scrubbed the bowls, spoons, and cups clean, then passed them to Zion so he could dry them. Aliyah found places for them in the cabinets and drawers.

Aliyah frowned.

"What's wrong?" I asked, lowering my voice.

"I can't stop thinking about the *Book*," she said.

Zion dropped the plate he was holding.

I shot him a look. "What's going on tonight?"

"It wasn't me . . . it just . . . it slipped . . . Thank God the plates are plastic, right?" he said, laughing nervously.

I dipped my hands in the hot water and pulled the plug out so the sink would drain. I stared outside at the dark backyard, noticing a shadow crossing the yard. My heart thumped in my chest, and I stumbled backward as I remembered what had happened earlier today; the kitchen table stopped me from falling.

"You okay?" Zion asked, concern clear on his face.

Aliyah sat down at the kitchen table. "The story y'all told me . . . was unbelievable."

Zion glanced at the screen door that led to the backyard. We could hear only the rain. I risked a peek out the window. Nothing.

"Yeah, mm-hmm," I said, not really paying attention to her. *Just a trick of the light*, I told myself again. Although what light was anyone's guess, as the sky had only gotten darker. I chided myself for being a fool, and I was about to join her at the table when that same dark shadow appeared again, standing next to Grandma's old shed where I had seen it the first time. It stared right at me with fiery red eyes.

"No—" I whispered, but my voice caught in my throat as the figure walked toward the window. I let out a squeak of fear. It disappeared as soon as I blinked. "Guys, um . . . maybe we should go upstairs?"

"It just felt so real," Aliyah said, still in her own little world.

"It's—it's not real," I said, though now I wasn't convinced. At all. *What's wrong with me?*

We sat at the kitchen table for the next few hours, playing with Aliyah's Pokémon cards, keeping our minds off the changing weather and what we saw in the *Book*. I kept glancing at the window, but nothing else appeared.

"We should go to sleep," I said after the sky had gone completely black. Zion was already starting to nod off.

Aliyah stood and made her way to the living room couch. "I'll see y'all in the morning."

I half pulled, half carried Zion up the stairs to my room, and he collapsed onto the spare bed. As I pulled on pajamas and slipped under the covers, I thought about why I loved Chidani and why I resented Grandma for locking it away from me. It was a place beyond time, a place where people looked like me, a place the brutal history of my world hadn't touched.

I wondered what it would be like to live in a place like that. But as much as I wanted it to be true, I wasn't a little kid listening to his mama's stories anymore.

CHAPTER FOUR

I dreamed of my parents, of the last time I'd seen them when I was ten. When Zion and I had first seen the *Book* change.

Mama wrapped warm arms around me as we settled on one of the couches in Grandma's attic of broken and lost things from years of collecting. Mama smelled of oranges, mint, and warm honey. She opened *The Book of Chidani* and placed it on both our laps, releasing dust into the air. I curled in her arms like a baby would as she played with the curls in my hair.

"Nina, where are you?" Daddy called from outside in his deep voice, walking across the hallway with heavy boots. He opened the attic door and saw us sitting there. Although a long, thick beard framed his dark-chestnut face, it was always soft to the touch. He had said I would grow a beard someday to match his.

Mama gestured at the *Book*. "Oh," Daddy said, placing

a kiss on both our foreheads. "Grandma Battle wanted your opinion on the soup she's simmering, but I won't disturb you."

"Thanks, Lonnie," Mama said. Daddy walked out of the attic then, closing the door firmly behind him. Mama continued running her fingers through my hair, scratching every now and again.

"Do you know how much I love you?" she asked, planting sweet kisses on the top of my head.

I ventured an answer. "A lot?"

Mama's laugh was like sunshine, ever present and neverending. "Yes. A lot times infinity."

She began to read from the *Book* aloud, translating the old language; in those moments, when we were together, I barely paid attention to her words. I always spent that time looking at the pictures of the hidden land of Chidani, from the majestic and colorful gryphons that soared over the land, the dark-skinned people who inhabited the small villages dressed in their dashikis and hunting gear, to Queen Ramala sitting upon her throne with her sister, Amina, standing behind her. They almost looked like twins to me, although Ramala was a bit taller.

The images leaped across the pages, as if they were alive. By the time Mama had gotten to the many Igbo gods who ruled their own kingdoms, I had fallen asleep.

When I had awakened, I noticed Mama had placed an old blanket around my shoulders. I checked my sport watch; more than two hours had passed. Zion was supposed to be here for our weekend sleepover by now.

"Mama?" I yawned. She had the *Book* still open on her lap, but she was whispering to herself now, a concerned look crossing her face. "Mama, what's wrong?"

"Nothing, baby," she said, glancing at me and smiling. However, I could tell the smile was forced, because it did not meet the creases at the sides of her eyes.

"Is Zion here yet?"

"No, no, no," she said. "This can't be true."

"Mama?" I thought she was referring to Zion. "Is he not here yet? Hmm, he's never late."

"No, no, no," she repeated. "Lonnie! Get up here!"

The sound of Daddy's boots on the steps was like thunder as he bounded to the attic. He opened the door, Zion in tow with his clear glasses askew, a duffel bag slung across his shoulder. "His mother just dropped him off," Daddy said to me before turning to Mama. "What's wrong?"

She glanced at me one last time before standing and pulling him to the side, whispering in hushed tones. They stepped outside, making their way down the steps. Zion bounded over to the couch and sat down with me, the *Book* in between us.

I left him and pulled up the attic window, yelling to the ground, "Thanks for bringing him, Mrs. Coleman!" She usually brought me butterscotch cookies on the weekends whenever she dropped Zion off, but I guess she didn't have time to come up today; she was too busy hustling Zion's little brother and twin sisters into the car.

After placing the seat belts around her other children, she straightened and waved at us. "You're welcome, Cameron. Zion! Did you forget your glasses cleaner?"

He groaned. "No, Mom. It's in my pocket."

"Good! Keep them clean, and I will pick you up from school on Monday." She got in the car and drove off.

We went back to the couch. "What's up with your mom and dad?" Zion asked. "Why they actin' weird?"

I shrugged. "How am I supposed to know?"

"Ooh," Zion said, grasping the *Book*. "Y'all were reading this?"

"Mm-hmm," I said. "Well, Mama was reading while I was just listening."

Zion's eyes narrowed as he read. "There's something off, Cam. I don't remember seeing any of this."

"What do you mean?" I scooted closer to him. I didn't see anything different, at least not at first. Mama had flipped back to the page of Queen Ramala on her throne, while Amina stood behind her with no expression. As we watched, the image *moved*, the sisters *moved*, and Ramala disappeared. Amina sat on her sister's throne, a sly smile appearing on her face.

"Whoa!" I said, pushing the *Book* on the floor and standing. "What was that?" My heart thundered in my chest.

"I know, I saw it, too!" Zion said. "The images moved!"

Tiptoeing closer, I peered at the worn pages again. "I could've sworn . . ." The image had returned to its previous state, with Ramala on the throne. Zion peered closer, too, turning the pages. He even picked it up and shook it a bit.

"It's not an Etch A Sketch, Zion," I said.

"Listen, we both saw . . ."

"Maybe it was just . . . our eyes playing tricks on us?"

"Hmm, maybe so," Zion said.

"Hey, I have an idea," I said, grabbing his hand, trying to take my mind off it. "Let's go play *Minecraft*." We placed the *Book* back on the bookshelf near the window and then walked downstairs. Voices stopped us near the kitchen, where Mama, Daddy, and Grandma were.

We heard them arguing. Grandma slammed something on the table, and the whole house felt like it shook. Pressing ourselves to the wall, we angled our ears to hear better.

"Nina, you can't put Chidani before the boy," Grandma said, her voice coated in anger. "He needs you! He can't just fend for himself!"

"Mama, don't you see I'm trying? I can't neglect my duties any more than you could. He knows how much I love him. But even you know that these are times of great peril. Chidani needs me . . ."

"What does that mean?" Zion said.

"Shh!"

I heard Grandma walk away and sigh. I imagined her

staring out the kitchen window over the sink, tilting her face upward so that she'd have a clear view of the backyard.

"Lonnie, you're not going to convince her otherwise?"

The deep timbre of my father's voice pierced the silence, like rolling thunder after a rainstorm. "I must admit that it does seem far-fetched, but you made me a believer the night before I married Nina. She has to do this. We'll be back in just a few short weeks."

"A few weeks? That could be *years* in . . . How can you say that? The boy needs his parents! He needs his mama!"

"Mama, weeks there are just a few hours here. Either way, Cameron is strong-willed," Mama spoke. "Just like his grandma. He'll be okay. The barrier is breaking down—we have no choice but to go. You of all people know this."

I couldn't understand what they were talking about, but we couldn't help but eavesdrop. Zion's eyes had grown big behind his glasses as we listened.

Grandma sighed again. "History has never been good to our people. For decades, Chidani was closed to us, even when we needed it most. Now, the barrier is breaking down. It doesn't make sense. Why is this happening?"

No one said anything else. We heard the scraping of chairs against the floor. It was almost like, although my grandma was right about me needing my mama and daddy, even she knew that whatever they were talking about had to be done. After a while, we heard whispers, but we couldn't understand the words. I gestured to the living room, where Zion and I moved to sit on the couch in front of the PlayStation, lost in our thoughts, completely forgetting about playing our game.

"It's time for bed, Cam and Zion," Grandma said as she came into the living room later that evening. She took us both by the arm and led us upstairs.

"I'm not tired," I said.

"It's way too early!" Zion said.

"Put on your pajamas," she responded in a voice that left no room for argument. I could see tears glistening in her eyes, so I went over to my dresser, pulled the spare pajamas I kept there out of a drawer, and put them on. Zion pulled his out of his duffel bag. She kissed my cheek when I was done and left the room.

"What's the point of coming over here for a sleepover if we can't stay up all night? She usually lets us do what we want!" Zion grumbled.

"Just listen to her, Zion," I said, getting into one of the twin-size beds.

Mama and Daddy came in as Zion continued to mumble under his breath. I stifled a giggle when I heard him say, "This is the *last* time I come back here." They brought in a trunk of clothes and set it on the carpeted floor right in front of the old television set. Daddy picked me up, grunted at my weight, and buried his face in my chest. I laughed, until I noticed that he, too, had tears in his eyes.

"What's wrong, Daddy?"

"Nothing, baby," he said. "Nothing at all."

He glanced at Mama, and then he left the room.

"You be strong, okay? You're gonna stay with Grandma Ana for a while, but we'll be back soon. We promise," Mama said.

I nodded, still not really understanding. Mama helped me into bed and tried to tuck me in.

"I can tuck myself in, Mama," I said.

She knelt down on the floor, smoothing the curls on my forehead. "Remember that you're a Battle," she said. "You have my mother's last name because it has power. It's magic. Always remember your name, do you understand me? And keep the *Book* close to your heart."

I nodded. She gestured to Zion, who got out of bed and curled himself in her arms after she made him kneel next to her. She whispered to us both.

"Remember, you always have each other. If you ever need me, recite this song, and help will come."

As the true Descendant, I command to open
The door to Chidani; it shall be broken

Magic awaits those who seek the queen's peace
And all the suffering you feel will cease

Those who open the histories will hear a sound
What was lost has finally been found.

The door opened as soon as she finished singing.

"All right, all right, y'all have to go, don't you?" A worried look appeared on Grandma's face.

Mama gave me another kiss on the cheek and whispered in my ear again, so soft that only I could hear. "Remember the song, Cam. Remember your friends. And read the *Book* whenever you can. Remember the stories I told you." She rummaged through my trunk and put a picture of her and Daddy on my nightstand.

After she left, I could hear her footsteps on the stairs leading to the attic. I saw a flash of blue light before my bedroom door closed.

"I thought they were leaving. Why are they going upstairs?" I remember asking Grandma.

She hugged Zion and me even tighter than Mama and Daddy had. "They are leaving, baby. But they'll be back soon."

That was the last time I saw them.

Two days later, Grandma told me that they had died.

CHAPTER FIVE

A soft knock sounded on my bedroom door. I opened my eyes and looked around the room until they adjusted to the darkness, my gaze falling on the picture Mama had left for me on the nightstand. I glanced at my alarm clock; three hours had passed. I thought I was just imagining the knock, so I laid my head back down.

But the sound came again, a bit more insistent. I peered at the bottom of the door and could just make out the shape of a pair of sneakers.

"Huh, what's that? Mama?" Zion said from his bed.

"No, bonehead, it's not your mama! It's me! Aliyah! Open the door!" she hissed.

"What? A boy can't miss his mother?" Zion's face turned crimson red.

I got up and pulled on a T-shirt and jeans; then I opened the door. Aliyah was fully dressed.

"I can't stop thinking about the *Book*." She narrowed her eyes. "And *why y'all never told me about it until now!* I just can't shake the feeling that I need to look at it one more time."

Zion turned on the lamp beside his bed.

I closed the door behind Aliyah. "I don't want Grandma to catch us up there. And right now, I need sleep."

Zion yawned and pulled on a shirt. "What could it hurt, Cameron? Your grandma's sleeping. She won't hear us if we're super quiet."

I chewed my bottom lip. On the one hand, Grandma did sleep like a rock at the bottom of the ocean; on the other hand, the dream about my parents made my daddy's deep voice and my mama's firm hand call to me in ways that they hadn't earlier.

"I'm not going back up there. I think the attic's haunted!" I said, remembering how the *Book* had changed right in front of my eyes. It couldn't have been a coincidence that I had just dreamed about it. "You can go, but I don't know how you'll get in without the key."

A sneaky grin crossed Aliyah's face as she grabbed a bobby pin from her hair. "I told you I can pick the lock. Daddy taught me."

"Aliyah!" Zion said.

"What?" she asked. "It's good to know practical things."

Before we could stop her, she ran out of the room.

"Okay, okay." I sighed, removing the key from my pants pocket. I turned to Zion. "We go upstairs and look through the *Book* one last time for a few minutes. And then we go back to bed. Deal?"

"Um . . . deal?" Zion said. But I could tell in his voice that he was as unsure as I was.

As I got to the door, I turned around and heard the shuffling of sheets. Zion was crawling back into bed. "Um . . . I ain't going up there. We've *both* been on the receiving end of your grandma's shoe, Cam. It hurts."

The fear was plain on his face.

"What you lookin' at?" I grinned, trying to lighten the moment.

"Nothing. Just looking at you. From bed, where *you* should be."

I crossed the room and pulled him up. "C'mon. If we do this, we do it together."

He grumbled but followed me anyway. Before we left the room, I made sure to put on my Converse sneaks—there was just something about them—and my jacket. We tiptoed up to the top floor of the house, careful not to step on any creaky stairs.

Aliyah was frozen at the top, staring at the closed attic door. A soft blue light emanated from its perimeter.

"Did we leave the light on when we were up here before?" Aliyah said.

I shook my head. "No. I . . . I don't think we did . . . right?"

"Th-th-that means we shouldn't go in." Zion paused. "Right?"

"No," I responded. "I think this means we *should* go in." There was no going back now. The rain, the shadows, the light, the dream—it was all too much. The *Book* was mine, after all, and I had to find out what was going on.

Aliyah fiddled with the knob, but the door opened easily—like it had never been locked at all. "Um, it's already open."

We walked inside. The door closed behind us; Zion stifled a scream and moved closer to me. *The Book of Chidani* was resting on the coffee table in the middle of the room. I knew that I had placed it back in the trunk earlier.

"It moved from where we left it!" Zion yelled, pointing.

It was shining with that same blue light. The coffee table shook.

I walked across the area rugs and reached for the *Book*. I'd seen this light before—on the night my parents left. I'd dismissed it as a strange memory, but I couldn't deny it anymore. For the first time, I started to think that all the stories my mama had told me might actually be real. Why else would Grandma have hidden the *Book* from me?

Aliyah and Zion stood behind me. I touched the *Book* and felt a jolt of energy like a crackle of electricity running through my fingers, down to my feet, then back up my arm. It was like the kind you sometimes see from static, but brighter.

"Whoa, what is that?" Zion asked.

I didn't answer. I reached out again and opened the *Book* to the first page. When I did, the window behind us blasted open, sending air and rain rushing through the attic. All three of us grabbed the coffee table, trying to keep our balance. It felt like a tornado had appeared in the room. The *Book*'s pages flipped to someplace in the middle and . . . stopped. Familiar words wrote themselves across the page.

A loud crash and bang sounded. The wind continued to wreak havoc on the attic, picking up pieces of old furniture, broken chairs, and worn books. They swirled around the room, then fell to the ground, some breaking around us.

"We have to get outta here!" Zion screamed, but some force had us rooted in place.

I looked down at the *Book* and read the words as Zion continued to scream. They were the same ones my mama had left me with. Zion's eyes took on a look of recognition as I read.

As the true Descendant, I command to open
The door to Chidani; it shall be broken

Magic awaits those who seek the queen's peace
And all the suffering you feel will cease

Those who open the histories will hear a sound
What was lost has finally been found.

There was another unearthly sound. A circle of blue light, crackling with electricity, appeared where the opposite wall met the attic door.

"Wh-what's happening?" Zion stammered.

"We're going to Chidani," I whispered, barely believing my own words.

"I don't think I want to do that." Zion whimpered.

"Me, either," I responded.

The circle of blue light expanded until it covered the entire wall. The wind roared in our ears and pushed us toward the circle of light, which seemed to be trying to suck us in. I grabbed the *Book*, hugging it to my chest with one arm, then fell to the floor. Holding on to one of the area rugs with my other hand, I tried to keep myself in the world I knew.

"Hold on tight!" I screamed at my friends. But Zion slipped and fell, grabbed my leg, and screamed as his glasses slipped down his face.

"Don't let go!" I yelled. He held on even more tightly. Aliyah grasped one of the sunken sofas as the wind continued to pull.

"It'll stop in a minute!" I said. "Just keep holding on."

But Zion's entire body lifted off the floor. My grip was slipping, my hands beginning to sweat. I could feel his fingers releasing.

"Don't let me go in there!" Zion yelled at me. I tried with all my might, but my sweaty hands slipped from the carpet, and we were both lifted into the air.

It was almost like time stopped for a moment. And then we were flying.

I opened my eyes and saw Aliyah reaching for us as she held on with one hand to the sofa. But we were too far away.

One second, we were frozen in midair, and the next, we were sucked straight through the hole in the wall.

The last thing I saw was Aliyah's hands letting go as her body followed us toward the open portal. Fear gripped my heart as we were thrown into the unknown.

CHAPTER SIX

Zion's screams filled my ears as we spiraled through darkness tinged with electric blue light. I held the *Book* to my chest as tightly as I could so it didn't fall into the void around us.

Darkness gave way to stars, and we found ourselves tumbling toward what looked like green grass down below. All the bones in our bodies should have broken when we crashed, but it felt more like we just bounced. I groaned as pain shot through my chest, but it was only from the impact of the *Book* being shoved into my stomach. I caught my breath, sat up, tucked the *Book* under my arm, and looked around.

"Cameron?" Aliyah said. But I didn't have time to turn to her. An unearthly growl drowned out all sound. I stood up, trying to gain my bearings. I felt shaky and nauseous.

"What's that noise?" Zion whispered.

And then I realized what I had seen outside the kitchen window and when we got off the school bus.

"Mmo," I managed to say, my voice shaking.

A thicket of trees surrounded us, and a soft light streamed down from the stars in the sky.

"It can't be," Zion whispered back.

I didn't get a chance to respond. They slithered toward us through the trees as black mist, moving along the ground at first. Before they materialized fully, I opened *The Book of Chidani* and looked for something we could use to protect ourselves. But I couldn't turn the pages fast enough. The words and images were a jumbled mess, things I couldn't understand.

"What are mmo, Cameron?" Aliyah asked, her hands balled tightly into fists.

"The spirits of the dead," I whispered, continuing to flip through the pages. But that wasn't completely accurate. The mmo, from what I remembered, were spirits whose deaths were so traumatic that they were stuck in a sort of limbo that kept them from passing to the afterlife. They could either be benevolent spirits or malevolent demons, depending on who controlled them.

The way the dark smoke surrounded our bodies, I got a feeling these were the angry ones.

Come on, come on. Give me something. The *Book* grew hot in my hands as I flipped through the pages. Too hot to hold. I dropped it to the ground.

The shadows thickened. The *Book* glowed around the edges, the pages emitting a blinding golden light as they flipped and fluttered on their own. Then the *Book* settled on an illustration I had never seen before—a trio of ruby-and-diamond-encrusted swords.

"What are we supposed to do with a picture?" I yelled.

The first group of mmo solidified around me.

The creatures had human features. Their faces, gray and sagging in places, were covered in what looked like dark blood while their noses, long and angular, were almost like rattlesnakes. Their eyes were a piercing red. Their legs were strong, gray, muscular, and their hair was shorn to the roots.

"Ahh!" Zion screamed, running into the thicket of trees.

"Zion!" I called after him, but he had already disappeared. His sneakers crashed through the leaves with heavy sounds.

The mmo reached out with what looked like sharp nails made of smoke, just as a second group of them slithered up the trees and launched themselves toward the opening in the sky we had just fallen through. The one closest to me growled deep in its chest and tried to strike me across the face, but I parried the attack with my arm. The force sent me sprawling across the clearing. I wiped my nose and picked up a nearby branch, striking haphazardly, not waiting for the mmo to hit first. It stumbled backward, made a gurgling noise as black blood rushed from its body, and then disappeared in a cloud of smoke, leaving behind the stench of rotten meat.

Zion screamed from somewhere deep in the forest as I turned to fight the next one. More mmo appeared in the small clearing while Aliyah was battling three of them at the same time. She had also grabbed a branch and was holding them off as best she could. I charged toward her, slicing as I stepped. I kicked one mmo and watched as its head hit the dirt. Before it could scramble to its feet, I struck the branch through its throat. It screamed and dissolved into another cloud of smoke, spraying black blood everywhere. This time, the stench was overpowering.

I gagged but had no time to recover before another mmo kicked the branch out of my hand. I desperately searched but could see nothing resembling a weapon. The creature grabbed me by the throat and started to lift me off the ground. I swiped a fistful of dirt and threw it at its eyes. It gurgled, released me, and stumbled backward.

I picked the branch back up and stabbed the blinded mmo just as I heard Aliyah scream. She fell to the ground, her weapon torn from her grasp. A group of mmo fell upon her, teeth bared.

"Cameron!" she yelled.

"I'm coming!" I said as I made my way to her.

I jumped to close the distance between us and landed with a sickening crunch on the back of one of the mmo pinning her to the ground. It stood and backhanded me, sending me sprawling across the dirt again. I landed on my right arm, and a surge of pain like fire burned through my body. Tears smarted in my eyes, but I got up to jump back into the fight. At least Aliyah was on her feet again now, stick in hand, her face covered in black mmo blood.

"Ahh!" we heard Zion scream again, but this time it sounded closer. He stumbled over to us, slicing a sword through the mass of churning mmo bodies. It glinted silver in the darkness. *What? How did he . . . ?*

But there was no time for any other thoughts. The mmo had backed us all the way to the tree line. We continued to strike at them, but we were surrounded. The smoke around us materialized into more sinister creatures with snakelike faces.

"There're too many of them!" Zion screamed. "Cameron, do something! Get the *Book*! That's where I got the sword from."

"You what?" But I didn't know what to do; nothing in my life had prepared me for this.

The *Book* still glowed on the other side of the clearing, but it was too far away for me to reach it. I heard my mama's voice in my head: *Keep the* Book *close to your heart.* We were helpless, about to die in another world, and I had let go of the one thing that had the power to help us.

Just then, a screech split the air, causing us to look up. A rush of wind swept the clearing. The mmo also stared up at the sky, taking their gazes off us. I stepped forward, bent low to the ground, and started slashing at the creatures' feet while they were distracted. Some of them turned into smoke.

We heard another screech that was so loud, I almost dropped my branch. Three huge birds—at least that was what I thought they were at first—swooped into the clearing. They had the head and talons of a bald eagle and the hind legs and body of a lion. The winged creatures snapped at the mmo, causing them to stumble away from us and lumber toward the protection of the surrounding trees.

Everything became quiet except for our heavy breathing. The *Book* was still shining, now with blue light again. We crossed the clearing, and I picked it up.

"Put your arm out," Zion said to me. "That's how I got the sword."

The imprint of the swords gleamed again, but this time, one was missing. Aliyah and I glanced at each other and shrugged. It was worth a shot.

We did what Zion had told us to do, and magically the two other swords appeared in our hands, swirling in shadows.

"Right. Of course we get the swords *after* we were almost eaten to death," Aliyah said.

"The mmo must have been trying to get into our world," I said, looking up at the rip in the sky. I glanced back at the winged creatures that had saved us. Their eyes were gold-rimmed, their faces smeared with dark blood from the mmo. When they moved from side to side, their lion feet shook the ground with power and force. The pages of the *Book* turned again, showing a bright drawing of the portal in my attic, looking exactly like it had tonight.

I gasped as I recognized Grandma's house. Mama had been right—the *Book* changed as history progressed.

Zion placed one of his hands on my shoulder. Pain shot through my arm, causing spots to appear before my eyes.

I slammed the *Book* shut. Then I looked above, seeing the tear in the sky closing. As it did, the rest of the mmo in the trees and those in the sky vanished into smoke.

"This . . . this can't be real." I hoped I hadn't released some into our world before I closed the *Book*—or even worse, into my grandma's house. I directed my anger at Zion. "Nice of you to join us, scary."

"Listen, I didn't have a choice. In the face of danger, I ran. But it gave me time to think, and then I saved your butt, so I don't want to hear it from you, mister."

I sighed in response.

"Um, Cameron." Aliyah pointed at the winged creatures. "Are they waiting for something?"

"They can't be what I think they are," Zion said. "I remember seeing them so many times in the *Book*."

"They're gryphons, I think," Aliyah said.

"How do you know? I had forgotten the name," Zion replied.

"Do you even play video games?" Aliyah asked, rolling her eyes. "I've seen them in *Fortnite*."

Zion's eyes widened. "We're too young for those types of games!"

"What my parents don't know won't hurt them. Girls mature faster than boys anyway."

"So . . . are we supposed to ride them somewhere?" Zion's voice shook.

I paced across the clearing, swiping at my running nose.

I stopped near Aliyah and checked her face; she had a deep scratch on her forehead, but most of the blood wasn't hers.

I tried to open the *Book* again, but the pages looked blank, while some were stuck together. How was it even possible that we were standing here, in Chidani? I cursed under my breath. *I bet Grandma would know what to do. Although . . . it would have been nice had she told me it was all true.*

One of the gryphons approached me, chirping softly. It bumped its head against my body and clucked, causing me to stumble backward. It struck my chest with its beak.

"They seem . . . friendly?" I said. "Maybe we *are* supposed to ride them. Could they take us to see the queen? If she sent them, maybe they know the way."

"And if she didn't?" Aliyah asked.

"Look, why can't we just go home?" Zion said.

I thumped the *Book* with my hands and gazed at the sky. "I . . . I don't know how to get home. Maybe the queen will know how."

The nearest gryphon stared at me, cocked its head, and then turned around, putting its lion backside right in my face. I swiped my hands along its flank. The gryphon emitted a cooing sound, which I think meant it liked it. Zion and Aliyah cautiously walked over to the other gryphons and followed suit.

"There's a saddle here," Aliyah said. "We should be able to ride them."

"I think so, too," I responded. Gathering my courage and

supporting my bruised arm, I walked to the cover of the trees, ran across the dirt at full speed, jumped through the air, and swung my legs up high, landing on the gryphon. I winced at the pain in my arm. The creature chirped and stood. I swayed on its thick back, grabbed on to the feathers along its neck, and looked around for where I could put my feet.

Aliyah placed her foot on the side of her red-colored gryphon in a kind of stirrup, which I had missed, and hoisted herself on its back gracefully.

"You know there are footholds, right?" she called to me. Zion laughed and followed her lead to easily mount his golden-colored one.

"Shut up, Zion. You didn't see them, either," I said, my face growing hot. "Hmm," I said as I placed my feet in the footholds along the side of the emerald-colored gryphon I had mounted. I pointed awkwardly at the sky. "Um, *to the queen?*" I said. My voice was clear but shaky. I had no clue what I was supposed to say.

The gryphons didn't budge. The one I was sitting on just chirped and nicked at the ground with its beak.

"Please?" I begged.

I guess that was the magic word, because they lifted us off the ground with a jolt, and suddenly we were flying.

CHAPTER SEVEN

As we flew through the air, I tried to put on a brave face. I could tell Zion regretted going into that attic with Aliyah and me. I should never have allowed them up there.

My gryphon screeched and flew closer to Aliyah. "Are you mad at me?" I yelled over the roaring wind. We had left the forest behind and climbed so far into the sky that we could see only water splashing below us. It was beautiful but also kind of terrifying.

"No, I'm not," Aliyah said. I stared ahead, trying my hardest not to look at her. If I hadn't agreed to go back up to the attic, we never would have been attacked by evil creatures. Zion and Aliyah could have died, and it would have been all my fault.

"I don't regret it, if that's what you're thinking," Aliyah said. "I asked you if we could go back to the attic. This is on me."

I turned to her. "It's still my fault. The *Book* belongs to my family. I think I'm the only one it really wanted, the only one who should have come."

"So why did it take all of us, then?"

I shrugged and clutched the *Book* closer to me.

My stomach jolted as the gryphons descended in the direction of what looked like a huge city. "I think we're almost there."

The creatures swooped down, and we saw the palace for the first time, looking exactly as it had appeared in *The Book of Chidani*. It was an iron fortress, built right into the rocky facade of a mountain range that stretched as far to the left and right as the eye could see. It also extended high into the air, up through the clouds. Near the base of the mountain were guardhouses and iron platforms that carried people up to the entrance. We saw an enclosure that held more gryphons, screeching at the sky as we passed. Turrets and towers soared into the air like fists, and the entire palace was surrounded by stone walls, protecting its people from the mountain's edge.

I thought through the stories Mama had told me. This had to be Queen Ramala's palace, where she and her sister had lived since Chidani was formed. According to the stories, it was built with magic and was the heart of all power in the kingdom.

We approached a grand courtyard. A large set of doors, from what I remembered, opened to a throne room. We hit the grass with a hard jolt that sent harsh pain through my arm. I gritted my teeth, then watched as Aliyah and Zion jumped off the gryphons and made their way toward the doors. I tried to slowly lower myself down to the ground so as not to hurt my arm again, but it was farther than I thought.

Guards, carrying hefty iron weapons and wearing black armor and thick boots, immediately surrounded us. They spoke to us in Igbo, and they took our swords away from us. I couldn't understand what they were saying. Almost immediately, the *Book* glowed with a light the color of royal blue, spreading from me, connecting with Zion, and then with Aliyah. When the guards spoke again, I realized that I could understand everything they were saying now.

"We don't—" Aliyah managed to say before she was marched off toward the castle doors.

"Aliyah!" I called out. I ran after her, but the cold pressure of a sword at my neck stopped me.

"You follow us, boy," a guard said to me. He was tall, with muscles so big, they seemed to bulge out of his heavy armor. His face was striking, as if his features had been carved by the sharpest angles of a knife. His eyes reminded me of Zion's. His skin was dark, like mine, and his words were harsh. "The queen demands an audience."

We were led up ivory marble steps that looked like they were encrusted with diamonds and pushed through scarlet double doors embossed with gold. I crushed the *Book* to my chest as we walked, determined to never let it out of my sight again, and took a deep breath, trying to ignore my arm's throbbing pain. I snuck a glance to my right and there was

Aliyah. The color was gone from Zion's face when I peered at him.

They led us to another set of doors, where we stopped and waited. My guard rapped on the door. A few seconds later, it opened, and another guard let us through into the Throne Room.

Loud voices and music greeted us. Finely dressed people filtered through the room, talking and laughing with one another. The music came from a harp and flute on the left side of the room, where another group was dancing. Hands raised and connected; then the people turned in a circle to find their next dancing partner. More women milled around the room than men, and everyone had dark-brown skin. The men wore multicolored kaftans, sandals laced with golden string, and crowns made of leaves. The women were dressed in long-flowing gowns that swept the floor as they danced, flowers braided in their hair.

A fluttering sound drew my attention to the ceiling. Small creatures with wings protruding from their backs flitted in and out of the towering ivory and cobalt pillars. They looked like fairies, and like the people, they, too, were dark-skinned. They flew across the room, leaving glittering dust upon the heads of the people below. I stared in openmouthed awe. Could these be the aziza? They were usually found in the Crystal City, which was through the Supernatural Forest. But up until today, all these things had existed only in the tales my parents told me.

I still couldn't believe I was actually in Chidani.

Within moments of our arrival, the music stopped, and all eyes were on us. The guards pushed us forward.

I trembled as we walked down an aisle that had formed, as the people parted to make a path to the throne. It felt as though the world underneath my feet was shifting. I couldn't think, and I was sure that if anyone wanted me to speak, only a whimper would come out. I pinched my arm to make sure I was awake. But it was numb, which was probably not a good sign.

The throne was set on a raised dais at the front of the room, made of the same ivory and cobalt as the columns, but it was embossed with gold that wrapped around the feet of the structure all the way to the top. Alabaster steps led up to where a woman sat.

I gasped. The woman, who I assumed was Queen Ramala, *had* truly changed, just like I'd seen. She was why Grandma had gotten scared and barred me from the attic. The queen's braids, which flowed down the sides of the throne, were speckled with gray, and her brown skin was lined with wrinkles. She was no longer the woman with the gold-rimmed eyes who I had seen as a child. She was also not wearing the diamond crown that was supposed to be sitting on her head.

My skin began to tingle as things I had read about for years came to life around me, a heavy feeling settling in my stomach. I couldn't help myself; as I approached the throne, I used my right hand to cross my heart, almost disbelieving. But believing at the same time.

Beside her stood another woman, so tall that the crown on her head inched close to the top of one of the columns. She was draped in jewels, and her iro was tight around her body, leaving one of her shoulders bare. She radiated a familiar power. I felt as if I should have known who she was.

"Queen Ramala, the children you sent for," my guard said, pushing me closer to the throne steps.

Queen Ramala beckoned us forward. "Ahh yes, the ones who broke through the barrier. Why are you pointing swords at them, Makai? Have you lost all sense?"

Makai lowered the sword from my back and gestured to the rest of the guards to remove theirs from Aliyah and Zion.

"Welcome to the Palacia," the queen said, "my home in Asaba, the capital city. You will have to forgive the captain of my guard. Things have . . . changed in the last few years. Makai is only making sure that no harm comes to me . . ."

Aliyah swayed against me. "I'm scared, Cam."

"I am, too," I said.

Zion couldn't even speak. He was staring, openmouthed, at everything around us.

A halo of snowy white light surrounded the woman standing by Queen Ramala. She reached for Aliyah, towering over her.

Terror gripped me, but then I saw that the woman's face was knotted in concern. "No need to fear," she said. "You are both hurt. Allow me to heal you, my lady," she said to Aliyah.

"But I'm not—" Aliyah said before she gasped. The woman

plucked one of the white lights surrounding her head, then blew it into Aliyah's face.

"Who is that? She looks familiar," Zion managed to croak.

"I don't know," I said. "I remember seeing her picture somewhere . . ."

"I am Agbala, the star goddess," she said. "Daughter and priestess of the Supreme Mother, Ala. I'm Mother's justice on this world. I dole out punishment when necessary and heal those who have been hurt."

The warmth of the magic radiated from Aliyah's body as the gash on her forehead healed. It felt like my father's last hug; it smelled of the peppermints my grandma gave me during Sunday service to keep me quiet and still as the pastor preached his sermons.

Aliyah smiled at Agbala.

The goddess peered down at me, knitted her brows, and sucked her teeth. At the noise, the entire Royal Court quieted. "I will take care of your arm later; we must talk together first."

"I grow tired," Queen Ramala said. I looked past the goddess toward the throne; the queen was hunched over. "I will speak to the children later after they are healed. Makai, lead them to their suites."

Makai prodded us away from the queen, much more softly this time, before I could say anything else. I felt the goddess's gaze piercing my back as I carried the *Book* underneath my good arm. Her magic felt like it flowed through my body, even though she hadn't used it directly on me.

"Wait," I said, turning back to the queen. "Why did you send for us?"

The right side of the queen's mouth lifted. "Because we need you."

CHAPTER EIGHT

We were escorted up two flights of stairs, around a couple of corners, and up another flight. My body drooped in exhaustion. Zion bumped into me a few times, and I didn't push him away, just let him place his head on my shoulder as we continued to climb.

Finally, Makai stopped all three of us at another, narrower stairwell. He nodded to the guards behind us, and three of them detached from the group to stand at the base of the steps. Makai went up the narrow staircase, stopping at double oak doors. He unlocked and pushed them open.

Zion sighed. "Dang, for a minute there, I thought it was all a dream."

"So did I," I whispered.

"I wish," Aliyah said.

As soon as we stepped into the room, Makai closed the door behind us. "You are now the esteemed guests of Queen

Ramala, and you will be treated as any noble would," he said. "If you need anything, do not hesitate to ask. Your guards will be posted at the bottom of the steps, protecting you. Rest well."

"*Esteemed?*" Zion whispered. "And here I thought we were in for it." Aliyah nodded. I had to agree with him there.

Makai left, the door closing behind him.

"What is the queen going to do with us, Cam?" Aliyah said, shivering a bit. "She didn't really tell us anything."

"I don't know," I admitted as I looked around. It was like stepping into a movie as I took in everything I had read about for so long. "It's all real, Zion."

The doors we walked through were made of iroko wood, beautifully abstract with gold swirls etched into them. Richly colored tapestries in shades of blue, ruby, and emerald covered the window openings, drifting from top to bottom, flowing in the wind. Only soft light penetrated through. Each corner of the room had a differently carved three-legged sitting stool, some painted and some not. Images of the gods and fantastical creatures—if I squinted, I could make out an amber-colored gryphon breathing fire painted on one of them—were engraved into each.

Deep, shaggy rugs covered the area. An emblem of a bright sun was sewn into them, a symbol of the highest god in the Igbo pantheon. Fabric fell from the ceilings in shades of violet, tangerine, and turquoise, strung from one side to the other. Large, comfortable-looking chairs covered every inch of the room, some made of metal, others of wood, and others of plush material. Each one held a large pillow fastened to its seat and the back support.

"It *is* real," Zion whispered in awe.

What looked like a rock formation sitting on a tall black chest drew my attention the most, though. I walked up to the stone and placed my hand on it. "Ikenga," I said with reverence.

A person was carved into the rock, a warrior holding a battle-ax in one hand and something else in the other—a smaller copy of that same warrior. In Igbo folklore, as my parents explained it to me, the Ikenga artifact was owned by men and women of noble blood or those who held a high reputation in society. The battle-ax was the symbol of the power that person held, but the small version of the warrior was said to be indicative of one's chi, or their ancestors, the shoulders upon which they stood.

When I looked around the room, I noticed that each stool held an Ikenga. It was said that though gods had power, the Ikenga held a person's entire essence, effectively making them powerful enough to commune with the gods as one if they owned enough of them.

"What human could have been so powerful that they could commune with the gods?" I whispered. A deep part of me knew the answer was mama, but I couldn't acknowledge it at this moment. It would have been too much to bear.

I turned my attention to a wooden table placed in the middle of the room, covered in spiced meat, sweet buns, hot rolls, hot and cold drinks, and desserts, some of which definitely looked like sugarplums. A tablecloth covered it, flowing to the floor. I could just make out an image of Agbala sewn near the head of it, her crown stretching up into the sky.

"Okay, what is going on?" Zion crossed his arms over his chest. "This ain't right, guys. We need to get back home!"

"I don't think that's an option right now," Aliyah said. Her voice trembled.

"It's not," I agreed. "We have no choice but to stay here until we figure out how to get back home."

Zion's awe turned to frustration. "This is all your fault, Cam. I want to be home with my mama and daddy, sound asleep in my bed. They're going to freak if I'm gone for too long!"

He took the *Book* from me and furiously flipped through the pages, whispering to himself. I grabbed him by the arm, but he ignored me.

"Come on, Zion. I—I am scared, too. W-we just gotta—" A lump in my throat cut off my words. I *was* scared. I wanted to go home, wanted to see Grandma again. I sat down on the couch and rubbed my forehead, hoping Zion would find something in the *Book* I'd missed. But I knew nothing in the *Book* would help us right now. We could only wait. And eat. And keep checking out our surroundings.

"What about Kendall?" Aliyah said, fresh tears leaking from her eyes. "How long will it be before our families notice we're gone?"

I started pacing, remembering my dream. "Mama said that weeks here could be hours there, so I think we are fine on that front."

"Being scared makes me hungry," Zion said as he put down the *Book* and walked toward the table of food. "Is anyone going to eat anything?"

"Go ahead. I'll be over in a minute," I said. I stepped to a window as the clinking of plates met my ears. Zion and Aliyah started to dig in.

I opened one of the tapestries and peered down at the courtyard where we had landed. We were in one of the towers of the Palacia, so high up that I couldn't see the base of the mountain. I heard screeches and the flapping of wings and looked up. Gryphons flew around in every direction.

Aliyah walked to me with a plate in her hand. "Do you want a sugarplum?"

I shook my head. The pain in my bruised arm was making me nauseous. "I don't feel hungry right now."

A knock sounded on the door, and we turned to see Agbala strolling into the room. She sat on one of the long couches in front of the fire and gestured for us to join her. Zion gulped down one final bite of meat; then we settled into the large chairs. She looked at us for a while before plucking another piece of white magic from around her head and blowing it our way. The light surrounded my bruised arm. It was warm at first; then it started to burn a bit.

"The pain will go away soon, hero," Agbala said.

"I'm no hero," I said through gritted teeth as the pain intensified. I grabbed at my arm, breathed deeply so that I didn't scream, and concentrated on something else. Like the scent of my grandma's house that I wished we could go back to right now.

"You have the *Book*, do you not?" she said. "That means you are the hero, the Descendant."

I picked it up and placed it on my knees. "It wasn't until today that I found out all of this is real."

"Is it . . . all real?" Zion asked her. He rubbed at his eyes as the goddess's light surrounded his glasses.

The goddess laughed and reclined on her seat. "Are you not here? In Chidani?"

"What is wrong with the queen?" I asked as the pain left my body.

She extended one of her hands, which was covered in honey-colored light. "Give me the *Book*, and I will tell you everything."

I held it out to her, but Aliyah grabbed my hand. "Cameron, no. That's yours. Don't let go of that *Book* again."

"But she's a goddess!" Zion exclaimed.

"Zion's right," I said. "Agbala is in the *Book*. She couldn't possibly mean it harm."

"I created the *Book* and gave it to the Igbo people when they were enslaved," she said.

"*You* created the *Book*?" I said. "Now, I *have* to hear this story." I kept the *Book* on my lap for a few more seconds, sighed, then handed it over to Agbala. As she touched it, white light spread along the tattered edges and rough pages. Soon, it looked as if it were brand-new.

She caressed it lovingly, but sadness filled her voice. "The *Book* has returned to Chidani."

"What happened to the queen?" I repeated my question.

Agbala's sadness intensified. It was almost palpable. "Princess Amina happened."

"Wait, isn't that—" Zion said.

"The queen's sister," Agbala finished for him. "How has the queen ruled for so long?" As if this were a pop quiz.

I couldn't remember that part.

"Let me start from the beginning. Ramala and Amina's parents controlled a divided nation four hundred years ago. Enslavers patrolled the West African coasts, venturing into Igboland and capturing its people as slaves. That caused the four tribes of the Igbo to break into factions, fighting among one another as they tried to rescue their people."

She snapped her fingers, a goblet of steaming liquid appearing in her hands. She nursed it first before gulping it down and continuing to speak.

"It was a grave time, as the former king and queen dealt with an impossible situation. So they prayed to the gods, hoping that we would help them. We did not answer their call, not at first. We couldn't intervene in every human scuffle. But this . . . this was different. The humans we watched over were in grave danger. However, the gods had never before helped the humans without some kind of bargain, an even exchange. I wanted to help the people without one, but my brothers and sisters overruled me. When we presented ourselves to them, the king and queen refused to bargain with us. So, without our help, they went into battle with the enslavers." Agbala sighed as she recalled the memory, her words stricken with pain.

"So they decided to fight the enslavers instead?" I asked.

"Yes. They died along with scores of the Igbo."

"Is that how Ramala became the queen?" I whispered.

Agbala nodded, her eyes closing as she clutched her chest. "I felt their pain as though it were my own. Ramala was crowned sovereign the night of her parents' death, leaving Amina with nothing. Ramala had to figure out a way to unite the four clans as one and protect her people, something her parents could not do. She did not consult Amina with her plans, which was her first mistake."

"Her first mistake?" I said.

"There were several. Ramala ventured into Igboland, finding the most powerful priests to connect with the gods. With their help, she prayed, telling the gods that she would do anything for their protection. Three gods appeared to her: Ala and two of her sons, Anyanwu and Amadioha."

Sparkling tears leaked from Agbala's eyes as she remembered.

"They offered her three gifts—a crown of wisdom, a ring that granted immortal life, and a scepter of thunder and lightning. But before Ramala became all-powerful, there had to be an even exchange. If anyone were to steal the gifts from the queen, the gods would not intervene. That person would become sovereign, and Ramala would die. Ramala also had to agree that her people would pray to the gods for eternity."

"That was the bargain?" I asked. "It doesn't seem so bad. I sit through church every Sunday and it's long, but not the worst."

"For their *eternal* prayers," Agbala said, her eyes narrowing. "Meaning, the humans would be closed off from the larger world, and they would never age. The gods would always exist because prayers would feed them. Ramala's parents believed that a barrier between both worlds that would cause immortality was unnatural, so they would not agree to it."

"The gods didn't actually care about the people Ramala was trying to protect? They just wanted their prayers?" I asked.

"I cared. They did not. The gods are fickle creatures, Cameron. They don't care about the whims of humans. They just want to *control* them. Ramala's prayer made them even more powerful; that's all they cared about."

"So Amina was mad at this bargain?"

"She believed her parents were wise to reject it. With her new power as sovereign, Ramala used the three gifts to unite the people, and the gods closed her country to the enslavers, effectively creating the barrier. Creating Chidani. Only

Ramala could open or cross it. Amina was unhappy with the outcome."

My mind began to race as I remembered the stories Mama had told me. "And that's when you stepped in."

Agbala nodded. "I knew that Amina was plotting against her sister, but I did not know when she would strike. So I created a fail-safe, a loophole. I nearly died using so much power, but I wanted to protect everyone, after they had already suffered so much. I created *The Book of Chidani*, imbued it with magic, and gave it to the enslaved people as they traveled to the Americas so they could remember their lineage. The Descendant of those people could one day open the barrier, saving Chidani from the wrath of Amina if she ever stepped forward. She can't truly beat Ramala and take her throne if the Descendant is still alive.

"I reasoned that I would help the people," Agbala continued. "I wanted to give them their history as they crossed the Atlantic, to give them a connection to what they had lost. So you see, Cameron, it was not just to stop Amina—it was also to preserve the enslaved people's culture in the face of such brutality. I wanted them to remember us."

My eyes began to burn with rage. "So when Mama was summoned to Chidani, it was because Amina finally tried to take over?" The memory of my mama's last day with me tore through me like a sword. It was all starting to make sense to me, but I didn't want to accept it just yet.

Aliyah pulled me close. "It's okay, Cam."

"That is why," Agbala said. "We needed a hero to stop Amina, and as a god, I couldn't intervene directly in human matters. The other gods had seen to that. With your mother . . . gone, that responsibility falls to you."

Horror pulsed through me as the pieces fell into place.

Zion reached out and hugged me, too, causing my face to grow warm again at his touch. I tried to smack his arm, but then I stopped myself. His presence was comforting.

"What are you saying? Mama and Daddy are . . . ?" I said.

"As the centuries passed, Amina grew uncomfortable with her sister's reign." Agbala ignored my question for now. "Amina thought it unfair that Ramala would continue to rule Chidani forever and the enslaved people would have no justice. Amina stole the three gifts in the dead of night and escaped the Palacia, opening the barrier in the process. Ramala has ruled so long that she never thought anyone would dare attack her in such a way."

I winced and thought about our fight with the mmo earlier. Had any of them gotten through the barrier? Was I somehow responsible for that? I thought about Grandma and how I needed to find a way to protect her.

"What's a Descendant?" Zion asked.

"The person who is descended from the enslaved Igbo. The one who has the *Book* now." Agbala stared at me. "Your grandmother and mother were once the Descendant. But now you are the one to save us all."

"What? No!" I said, standing and backing away. "I just

want to go home. I can't save everyone. I . . . I don't have magic. I don't have powers. How am I supposed to stop Amina and save Chidani? I'm just a kid!" My body started to shake. I felt dizzy as my mouth dried. I shook my head in denial, trying not to let the tears fall.

Agbala stood. She didn't walk over to me, but the power coming from her body touched me somehow; it radiated warmth my way. And I couldn't help it; I felt better. Comforted.

"What you're feeling now, Cameron," she said as she stepped toward me, "is what I felt when your mother came here the last time. As soon as I saw you, I knew. Why do you think the queen told Makai to bring you here? These suites belonged to your mother, one of the finest warriors we have ever seen. Your mother's power is yours.

"You will save our people."

CHAPTER NINE

"You knew my mama?" I said, shell-shocked. "And this is where she lived?"

"This is something we should discuss alone." Agbala sent a stern look Aliyah and Zion's way.

"It's okay," I told them. "Go. I need to know this." They left the room, escorted by two servants who appeared seemingly from nowhere.

"I indeed knew your mother," Agbala continued as she caressed the Ikenga around the room. "Only she would have so many of these. A powerful person indeed."

"Tell me everything," I said.

"The barrier broke down when Amina stole the queen's gifts, as I said. Your parents arrived here, and I had this same conversation with them. Your mother did everything she could to save the kingdom, but unfortunately . . ." She took on a pleading tone as she continued, reaching out to me. "You have to understand, Cameron. They both fought valiantly."

A tear fell from the goddess's eyes, and when it reached the table in front of us, it turned into pure gold. I felt nauseous once more. "Please, no. Don't say it."

"I . . . I don't know what else to say. I'm so sorry, Cameron."

"Amina killed m-my mama and daddy?" I felt my own eyes burning with tears.

"We think so. I tried to locate their bodies, but the only thing I found was the *Book*. When I tried to bring it back to the Palacia, it disappeared. I couldn't quite understand what happened, but I guessed that meant there *might* be another Descendant and that it would present itself to the one who rightfully owned it. That's you."

So that's what happened when I saw my parents go to the attic that last night; the *Book* had brought them to Chidani, just as it had brought me.

"And you didn't stop Amina?" I began to shout, crying as I did. "You could've saved them if you wanted to! They died because of you!"

I paced the room. I brushed the tears from my face, angry at my grandma for not telling me the truth, at the queen for losing her gifts, and at my mama and daddy for leaving me.

Agbala hugged me now, which sent more tears rushing down my face.

"I hate to see you hurt," she said. She smelled of a mixture of sugar and honey. "But you must understand—I hadn't a choice. I'm but one god in a sea of many. Their power combined supersedes mine. I'm honor bound by the bargain Queen Ramala made. I did everything I could to help your people, defying the gods and almost losing my power in the process. I tried, Cameron. I did."

She held me for a long while as the tears continued, as the grief I had held for years finally rushed out of my body. My parents had died. And Amina was at fault.

After a time, she pulled back and held my shoulders. "Do you understand the dire situation we are in? If Amina wins, she will destroy the kingdom and take over your world and mine. But, I understand that this may be too much for a young boy. If you want to go home, you can."

I was scared, but there didn't seem to be any other answer. "Yes, I understand. I want to help."

"Then I need to bind the *Book* to your soul, to give you a sliver of its power," she said. "The *Book* doesn't just open the portal; it *is* the portal. If I do this, *you* will become the portal. This way, Amina can't steal it, and you will be powerful enough to stop her. Do you agree? It will hurt. But you must *keep the* Book *close to your heart.*"

It was the same thing Mama had said before she left, so I believed her. "Yes, I agree."

"I am glad. As . . . by my calculations, the queen only has about three moons—three months—to live without at least one of her gifts. That means you have three moons to find them and defeat Amina."

The goddess pressed the *Book* against me as golden tears streaked her cheeks. I screamed as it fused itself with everything in me. The last thing I saw before I lost consciousness was a huge book-shaped depression in my chest.

Then all was darkness.

CHAPTER TEN

I stood on a plain, night permeating everything around me. My toes sunk into dry sand, steeling myself against the unknown; strangely, a sense of peace settled upon my shoulders, my heart, my mind. When the human figures rose from the sand like castles, I did not flee, did not try to run.

Although I didn't know who they were consciously, my soul reached out to them as if I had known them my entire life. A baby, a girl child, sprang from the dirt first, covered in golden light. Agbala stepped from the darkness, her kaftan drifting in the breeze. She smiled at the baby, picking her up and enclosing her in her arms, kissing her on the forehead, whispering, "You'll no longer be enslaved, Nneka. You shall be the keeper of nations."

Light emanated from her lips as she spoke. The goddess stepped back, and the girl grew into a young woman, armor fusing to her skin, weapon in hand, braided hair piled atop her head.

A yellow sun appeared in the sky, and an ocean emerged, flowing from the sand to the north. More figures arose, covered in battle gear; they were darkness personified, the mmo. The young woman jumped into action, destroying them all with fierce accuracy. When she was done, she dropped her sword onto the ground as Agbala approached her. A ghostly imprint of the *Book* appeared on the woman's armor, and she floated into the sky, a smile brightening her face, covering her in gilded luminescence. When she landed on the sand again, multiple figures rose, young men and women alike, some my age, some older.

The young woman sat on a rickety chair now, rocking back and forth as her hair turned gray and lines burrowed into her face. She smiled as her children spread around her. I watched nations and empires rise and fall, waters spring and recede, birds fly and land. The sand picked up and surrounded me, sparkling with reflected light.

I stepped into the eye of the sandstorm. I saw them all, every last Descendant's shape and shadow. As I walked forward, I could hear sounds and snippets of conversation as the centuries changed.

The sand shifted and swirled, forming images like an old-fashioned movie. I watched as the *Book* traveled through the generations. It started in the American South, inside the body of an enslaved girl who had found it alongside the sea, the same girl Agbala had imbued with the history of our people.

The scenes shifted. The *Book* traveled to the American North in the outbreak of the war to a growing city, in the body of a boy on the cusp of high school. His father was a railroad porter while his mother was a homemaker. After, it traveled with identical twin boys as they settled in Europe and Black people gained equality; their parents worked in overseas military service while the twins studied the *Book*'s contents by firelight.

Another swirl of sand and I saw Grandma as a small child, traveling back to America and settling with her parents in Atlanta, when the country was in an uprising once again for civil rights. She read the *Book* on her walks to and from school, unable to ride the school bus. Her dress was clogged with dust as she traveled. At one point, she veered into a puddle of water, soaking her shiny black shoes. She paid no attention to it.

The final scene was of Mama. My breath caught in my throat as I saw her in her pigtails, bounding up and down the steps of Grandma's house, over and over again. "Mama, come on!" she called.

Grandma appeared at the bottom of the steps, shaking her head in mock frustration. "Slow down. I'm coming, Nina." They walked into the attic; it was empty and tidy at this point. The *Book* was displayed on a podium, its pages frayed but full of life. They settled on a couch while Grandma opened the *Book*'s pages.

A figure, smelling of lemon, appeared in the sandstorm as the scenes played in front of me. Agbala tapped my chest. "This is your legacy, Cameron," she said. "These are the Descendants, starting from Nneka. All, except your grandmother, are souls now, but their inheritance lives on inside you."

A deep determination simmered in my spirit as the *Book* responded to her touch. A sense of peace settled on my shoulders as I closed my eyes. When I opened them, souls surrounded me, covered in diamonds, ruby, and pearls. All the Descendants over the centuries appeared, touching me. Everywhere they did, love filled me. It felt like my mother's and father's touch, enduring and everlasting. They whispered in my ear, held my hands, and kissed me on the cheek.

In that moment, I didn't feel like I had experienced loss in my life. I felt whole for the first time in years.

These people were my family. I had become one with my ancestors.

I *wanted* to be a hero.

I had become a hero.

CHAPTER ELEVEN

"Ow, that hurts!" Zion was saying as I awakened the next morning. I was lying on something soft. My eyes were closed as images filtered through my head. I saw pictures of creatures, of gods, of magic; all the information in the *Book* was inside me. I had become part of the *Book* just like the goddess had said.

I opened my eyes. A thick blanket covered me as I lay on a canopy bed. The vision stayed, tinged with shades of gold, crimson, and orange. A heaviness fell upon me when I realized I *knew* everything and that I could recall almost everything about the *Book* from my memory.

Pain lanced my chest as I stumbled out of the bed. I looked down, expecting to see the depression that I saw last night, but my chest looked completely normal.

Zion screamed again, the sound coming from behind one of the closed doors in our room. I marched over to one of them and opened it. The space inside was expansive; a large, deep pool covered the room from left to right. Steam emanated from the water. Cleaning tools lay on the wood floors surrounding the pool. Zion, looking dejected and covered in soapsuds, stood in the middle of it, a comb floating in the water before him.

"Zion?" I called to him. "What's going on?"

"Getting clean, apparently," he said, eyeing the comb with a dark expression. I looked down at my clothes; they were ripped in multiple places, dirt and grime falling everywhere.

Another door opened near the back of the pool. "Lord Cameron," a man said, coming inside the pool area. He wore a sleeveless dashiki and brown cotton pants. A hoop earring was drawn through his nose. "My name is Amir, your personal servant. Would you like to take a bath?"

I sniffed my armpits; they were pretty rank.

Zion chuckled. "Whew, yeah, you need one. I could barely sleep next to you last night because of the smell."

"Yeah, I definitely need to."

"Would you like the enchanted cleaning tools as well to aid you?" Amir asked, gesturing to Zion. "Lord Zion opted for them."

I shrugged. "I guess."

"Um . . . Cam?" Zion said.

"*Ngwa anwansi,*" Amir whispered, then bowed to me. "When you finish, please join me in the dressing area." *Why do those words sound familiar?*

"You don't know what you just said yes to," Zion said from behind me.

Before I could respond, the air whipped around me and my clothes rippled, drowning out Zion's voice. I peeled off my soiled clothes and waded deep in the steaming-hot pool, sighing in contentment. Droplets of water lifted from the pool, twirling around my head. I watched in amazement as they transformed into a comb, a brush, and bars of soap.

"What the—" I managed to say before they all converged on me at once, more tools materializing from thin air. The brush scraped at my back, my neck, my shoulders, and my legs. I stifled a yell as my skin felt like it was being ripped away. This was nothing compared to the pain of last night, though. My hair rose on end and the comb went to work next, untangling it, soapsuds appearing as it cleaned all the dirt away. I yelped as the naps untangled. A small towel was next, hitting me in the face over and over until it found my ears, cleaning them out and then flying through my hair.

"Whoa," I said, as Zion laughed. I caught a glimpse of him being lifted out of the pool by some unseen force, propelling him to the other side where a huge towel appeared out of thin air. It wrapped around him and dried him off.

"Now, this is pretty cool," Zion said.

"I mean—" I said, before another force dipped me underneath the water. Invisible fingers combed through my hair, flipped me over, and massaged the spaces between my toes. When I couldn't hold my breath anymore, I was flipped right side up, and I immediately spit up water.

"This isn't fun anymore!" I screamed. "Stop! I'm clean enough!" When I made the command, the invisible force stopped. I glanced to the entrance to the bathing room, but Zion had disappeared. The wind picked up again, lifting me from the hot water and depositing me near the door. Like what happened to Zion, a heavy towel appeared out of thin air and wrapped itself around my body, tight, drying me off. After, it curled around me like second skin as I walked out of the room.

"Ahh, you look good as new, my lord," Amir said when I returned, bowing again. He stood before a large brass door on the opposite side of the bed. "Time to pick out the clothes you will wear in the pits today."

"Why are we going to the—" I started to ask.

"How did you sleep last night, my lord?" Amir interrupted, his voice lowering.

"I don't know," I said, fingering the tight towel. "I don't remember going to sleep."

"The servants talk, my lord. They saw the goddess walking away from your royal suites last night. Are you—"

"Am I the Descendant?" I finished for him quickly, the words falling out of me like dominoes. *Those aren't my words.* Curiosity blanketed his expression as he regarded me. My head involuntarily moved to the left as a swirl of light appeared on the side of the room. Mama stepped forward, ghostly, but still her, wrapped in a bathrobe as a younger Amir asked her, "Are you really the Descendant? The servants talk."

"Whoa," I said, snapping back to attention as the room shifted from right to left. I fought through the nausea as I turned back to Amir. It had to be a trick that I saw Mama. Maybe I was just missing her.

"Are you all right?" Amir asked.

"I guess I am the Descendant," I responded.

"I'm going to wait outside for you, my lord," Amir said. He pointed toward the brass door. "This area is your dressing room. Another servant is already working with Zion. Once you are finished dressing, Makai will escort you to the fighting pits. And don't worry about the clothes you came here with. They will be washed and repaired for you."

I walked over to the dressing room, trying my hardest to keep the towel from dropping to the floor. The door opened when I knocked on it, and an eccentric-looking man stood in my way. He was dark-skinned, his hair dyed a flaming orange. Gold rings surrounded his fingers, and his muscled arms were covered in diamonds that seemed to be attached to his skin. He had a nose ring just like Amir, but he was much bigger and taller than Amir was. Though he smiled at me, I had a feeling he could snap me like a twig if he wanted to.

"Good morning, my lord," he said in a deep voice. "My name is Damisi of the Onitsha clan. I will be dressing you today. Come in. Lord Zion is already here."

"Why are we going to the fighting pits?" I asked again.

He turned to me. "To learn to fight, of course! Oh, how I miss those days!" Another memory of Mama started to bubble to the surface as Damisi pulled me after him.

I stepped into the white marble dressing room at his prompting, surprised at how big and long the room was. A stencil drawing of a diamond crown encircled by a ring was etched in the middle of the room. Multicolored area rugs were thrown around the room, and there was Zion, standing beside a black raised cushion right beside the sigil, being handed clothing so he could dress himself.

"I think this is a bit too tight, Dabir," Zion said as I was steered toward shelves held by wood columns built right into the walls, covered with clothes, riding gear, and armor. Damisi picked up a few things and then dragged me over to one of the soft, plush chairs in the dressing area.

"Hmm," Damisi said, regarding me closely.

"Hmm," he said again. The pages in my mind rustled, causing me to sit back in my chair and clutch at my head. Having the *Book* in my chest wasn't exactly painful, but it was uncomfortable.

"It's hot here in Asaba, especially in the fighting pits. You will need something that will provide coolness when the hot wind blows," he said, giving me a dashiki and underwear. "I'll give you some privacy to put these on."

"This is so weird," I said to Zion. "But, the magic is cool!"

"What happened last night?" Zion whispered.

I draped my shoulders in the bloodred dashiki; an

embroidery of black roses was sewn all over the front. The cloth was loose on my stomach to allow for cool air to wash over me, but the sleeves were tight against my upper arms, leaving my lower arms free. The memory of Mama surfaced again, making me ignore Zion for now.

"Whoa," I said, leaning forward against the wall.

"Ahh, you're looking better already," Damisi said, coming back in the room and helping me into some dark shokoto pants that fit my legs as if they were a second skin. "We wear short pants only to bed, so sorry, you're going to have to learn to wear long ones here. And—"

"And agbadas and kaftan robes won't do in the pits," I involuntarily finished for him. I opened my mouth again, then closed it.

Confusion appeared on Damisi's face, matched perfectly with mine. The memory was so strong, it almost overwhelmed me. It played out in front of my eyes, as if it were a living thing. I gasped as images rose in the dressing room. It was Mama, hustling around the room as if she owned it. There she was in front of me, her mouth moving so fast that I barely could understand her. She was picking out clothing with someone.

"Descendant?" Damisi said. An image dislodged from Damisi's figure, a carbon copy of himself who busied with Mama in the foreground, helping her pick out her warrior's design.

"Wait," I said, raising my hand.

"Nina, agbadas and kaftans won't do in the pits," the carbon copy of Damisi was saying to Mama as he rummaged through a dresser on the other side of the room. I closed my eyes and shook my head to clear it.

When I opened them again, the scene had returned to normal. I breathed a sigh of relief as I settled into the seat. "I'm . . . I'm okay," I said. "I just . . . need a moment." Damisi frowned and left me for a while.

I couldn't believe it. Not only was the *Book* fused with me now, but it was also giving me flashes of conversations and images that I had not experienced myself. Seeing Mama again was a plus, but it still surprised me. In good ways. In reassuring ways. It was a means of keeping me close to her. But it was still so hard to see her when she was once alive. It was confirmation she wasn't returning to me.

"Are you ready to finish now?" Damisi said as he returned.

"Cam, you okay?" Zion asked, as his servant continued busying with him.

"I am now," I said to him. I turned to Damisi. "Yes, let's finish."

Damisi pushed me back into the chair and tugged at my feet. He squeezed my toes and then placed a metal measuring instrument against them.

"Just as I suspected," he murmured. He placed a pair of heavy, dark boots on my feet and tied the laces.

"Why can't I wear my Chucks?" I complained. "I'm more comfortable in those—"

The incredulous look Damisi gave me shut my mouth.

"Now," he said, standing. "You don't look *exactly* royal, but this will do, at least for the fighting pits."

Before I could take offense, he grabbed my arms and pulled me out into the sleeping section of our suite again, then back through the sitting room where we had eaten last night. Damisi waited in silence until Makai came in, carrying the three swords the *Book* had given us. "The queen's guard still had these from yesterday. You will carry them with you."

The door behind me opened, and Zion joined me, wearing the same clothes I had tried on, except that his dashiki was white with golden stenciling. Another door opened, and Aliyah swept into the room, her dark skin shining with gold crystals, her braided hair tied in a bun at the back of her head.

"You look beautiful," Zion said.

She groaned. "What now?"

Makai gently pushed all of us toward the door and gave us our swords. "Now, you learn to fight. And to fly."

CHAPTER TWELVE

During our walk down to the dungeons, I told Aliyah and Zion about what the goddess had done the night before. How I suddenly knew . . . well, everything. I even told them about the visions of Mama as the Descendant.

"We're going to the fighting pits," I relayed to them, as if I were a walking encyclopedia. "There, we will learn Dambe, a fighting style that is used here." Images flashed in my mind as the words left my mouth before I could even think them. "It's almost like doing magic. You'll see."

"Okay, Cam, you might be omniscient or something, but are you gonna trust some god who pushed a book in your chest? Number one, sounds unsanitary and number two, sounds painful. And evil," Zion said.

"It can't be evil, because why do I feel so close to my parents right now?" That quieted them. I wanted to tell them about the dream I had the night before but decided to keep that to myself.

"So let's make sure we got this correct," Zion said as we traveled. "Ramala became queen, and to save her people, she bargained with the gods? She received three gifts to create the barrier, and in return, they required her people's prayers and their ability to die naturally?"

"And all that ticked off Amina, so Agbala created the *Book* and the Descendant to fight against her when the time came?" Aliyah said.

I nodded. "Correct."

"And here I am, thinking I had *enough* problems with my own sisters," Zion said.

When we reached the dungeons, Makai veered left, walking us down a long hallway until we came to a bolted door leading to the outside. He twisted the huge wheel attached to it, causing sand to fall to the ground. We walked through, and the sun almost blinded us.

In front of us stood an arena-like structure filled with sand. In some places, the sand was smooth, and in some, it had been collected into mounds to make small hills. Swords clinked against each other as numerous soldiers fought. I looked around and saw Agbala floating on a ledge. I felt the pages of the *Book* flip in my mind again until I saw an image of her, surrounded by white light. I turned to Aliyah and Zion, but they didn't seem to have noticed her.

Makai led us to the middle of the sandpits. I clutched my sword tighter in my hand. He whistled and another guard brought out pieces of armor and threw them down onto the sand. I could hear them whispering to each other as if we weren't standing there.

"Captain, are you sure about this? The queen only has three moons to—"

"We don't have much of a choice," Makai responded. "It's either him or our queen dies, leaving us to Amina. I don't want that."

"But they're only twelve!"

"Same age you were when you became a soldier, Bakari. Now, let's do this. The quicker we teach them what they need to know, the quicker we can find Ramala's gifts. We don't have much time."

"So much for confidence," Zion muttered.

Three moons. All we have is three moons. That's what Agbala had told me last night. I couldn't shake the feeling that we weren't up to the task. That *I* wasn't up to the task. How was I supposed to save an entire kingdom? The vision last night had made me proud to be the Descendant, but *becoming* it was an entirely different thing.

Makai turned to us now. "You will each be paired with a soldier. Today, you will learn the art of Dambe. The first thing I want you to do, though, is watch Bakari of the Owerri clan and Halifa of the Onitsha clan fight so you get a sense of what it means to battle in Chidani. Please watch closely.

Amina was well versed in Dambe before she left the Palacia."

Makai fitted us with iron shoulder, knee, chest, and arm guards. Bakari, the guard who had dropped the armor earlier, and Halifa, another soldier who had come when Makai finished speaking, squared off against each other.

I whispered to Aliyah as they circled each other with their swords, magic flowing in every word I said. "Dambe is a fighting style of the Igbo. Centuries ago, it was just simple wrestling, but as the people forged a connection with the gods, the fighting style became something totally different."

"Different how?" Aliyah whispered.

I narrowed my eyes. "Just watch."

As the wind whistled through the arena, the sand picked up around us, sending grains of dirt flying into our eyes. The two soldiers moved so fast that the naked eye could hardly see them.

Halifa jumped in the air, coming down on Bakari with a slash of her sword. Equally fast, Bakari shifted, kicking at the sand as he moved out of the way of her sword, dirt flying around them like a tornado. He moved, crouched to the ground, and kicked Halifa's legs. She fell. A second later, she was up again, moving fast as a bullet, slashing her sword, striking his arm, drawing blood. Bakari yelped but moved away from her attack just as quickly.

The next thing I saw was Bakari on the other side of the arena, as if he'd disappeared in a rush of air. Halifa joined him.

Using the wind to carry them, they both jumped into the air, slamming against each other, then falling toward the ground with a crunch. Halifa jumped on Bakari's chest and, with both hands, placed her sword next to his throat. Laughing, Halifa stood, extended her hand, and pulled him to his feet.

They marched back over to us.

"We're . . . supposed to be able to do that? Are you for real?" Aliyah said.

Zion's eyes had widened like huge softballs. "We can't learn that."

"Yes, you can," Makai said. "The best practitioners of Dambe are children. If you leave Asaba, you will find children younger than you who are well adept at the fighting style. And they don't even have armor."

He looked at us again before continuing. "Now, we will practice until you master it. I will practice with Cameron, Halifa will practice with Zion, and Bakari with Aliyah."

I turned to my friends and shrugged. "Go ahead. We can at least try. This should help us fight the mmo if we ever need to again."

"Oh, you *will* fight them again," Makai said, pulling me away from my friends. "Let's start!"

I heard them whispering as they left. "He seems . . . different," Aliyah said.

"I guess I would be, too, if a book was shoved in my chest and I suddenly knew everything," Zion responded.

"I heard that!" I yelled after them.

Makai led me toward the right side of the arena, to the sand hills. He gestured to my sword. "It's time to be serious, Cameron. The *Book* gave you that weapon because it wanted you to have it. Always keep it at the ready."

"Well, explain Dambe to me. I need to know more."

He circled around me, correcting my posture, moving the sword so that it was flush with my chest, and making sure my feet were shoulder-width apart. "As I said, Dambe is a fighting style. You don't *do* it; you *move* into it. What I mean is that Dambe requires deliberate movement, something you have to call and search for. First, you have to listen to an aspect of nature; then you call for it. It's quite easy to perfect. Once you get it, it'll never leave you.

"There are two things you must know about Dambe," he continued. "Because nature hums at a lower frequency, you must clear your head of all emotions and concentrate on the task ahead. Nature doesn't respond the way humans do. If you have too much emotion, you risk injury, even death, when using it.

"The second thing you must remember is that although it may look like you're moving fast to human eyes, in Dambe, time slows down. That means everything slows down, even pain. There have been soldiers who entered Dambe to escape pain or injuries, only to find their wounds even more pronounced to the point of excruciating pain or even death when they leave. Only use Dambe for fighting and pay attention to any wounds you may receive.

"Now, repeat what I said. How do you use Dambe?"

I took a deep breath before responding. "First, you listen in on an aspect of nature. Second, you call and search for it deliberately."

"And what does it allow you to do?"

"It allows you to fight, to move fast, to do things humans physically can't do. Time slows down for the person who is using it."

"Good." He pointed to my sword. "Now give it your all."

I held it up. "…You want me to hurt you with this?"

Makai smirked. "I'm counting on it."

I stood, feeling awkward as Makai circled me. I felt silly just standing in sand as it gathered around my boots, not knowing what to do. My thoughts were so focused on my own awkwardness that I barely saw his sword hit my armor. I fell down.

He stood above me. "If you pay attention to how you look, you'll never be able to listen for the music of the wind. Now, stand and try again."

I stood. I fell to the ground again when Makai's feet swept under me. I hadn't even seen him move! "Listen, I can't fight you if I don't know what you're doing and if I can't see you!"

Makai shrugged as he spun in a cloud of wind right in front of me. "There's not much to it. Listen and feel the wind. Clear your mind. Close your eyes if you have to."

I closed my eyes, calling for the magic. When I opened them again, he was still standing in front of me, but the sand around him began to move as I focused on it. He blurred ever so slightly as he shifted his feet. This time, I felt the music of the wind, which allowed me to *move* into Dambe; it sounded like chimes emitting a sweet sound.

Swinging my sword around me, I met Makai's, seeing his every movement. I grinned when he fell backward a little bit. "Wait, did I just do it right?"

He raised his sword again as his eyes turned steely. "Almost." He tapped my forehead. "Remember, stay serious. Again!"

The small confidence I'd felt was lost. I recognized the blur in the wind much too late, felt the pull on my shoulders before I saw him. Makai grabbed me and threw me backward onto the sand. I scrambled up, but I was too lost in my own thoughts to see him. In a split second, he was in front of me, punching me in the chest, sending fire through my body. By the time I gained my bearings, he'd reached out, twisted my arm, grabbed me from behind again, and touched his sword to my throat.

"Don't get lost in the triumph of a hollow victory," he hissed. "Amina will *not* back down from you if she sees that you've mastered Dambe. *Three moons*, Cameron."

Before I could respond, he pushed me in the back with a fist, sending me spiraling to the sand face-first. Furious, I spat out dirt. He disappeared in one second and reappeared in front of me, pulling me to my feet.

"How am I supposed to do this if you don't give m-me a chance?" I sputtered.

"Because Princess Amina and her legions of mmo won't give you a chance, either. Once children turn the age of twelve here, they are adults. Act like one."

I concentrated harder, *calling* for and *moving* into Dambe. Makai's figure blurred again as the music of the wind entered my ears. I felt like I was one with the air as I shifted around and stopped the captain's attack by grabbing at his arms. I barely caught the look of surprise on his face before I was gone, circling him as the music built in my ears. I kicked him in the middle of his back, and sent him flying through the air. He stood, but I was gone like a whisper. I threw my sword from the *Book* at him with all my strength.

He grunted in pain. A small smile crossed his lips, but it disappeared as soon as it appeared. I moved again and jumped through the air, feeling like I was flying with sand spraying all around me. But when I fell to the ground, Makai had moved. By the time I turned to him, he had thrown his sword at me. Once I saw it flying, I moved my head to the side, causing the sword to graze my cheek as it passed me.

"Good, Lord Cameron," he said. He went to grab his weapon from the dirt. "Again!"

We continued to spar in our section of the arena until all sound ceased. I took a number of painful sword jabs until Makai stopped me with a flick of his hand. The small victory from before had been nothing but an accident.

We practiced for what felt like hours, but I made only the smallest progress. When I fell on the sand for the thousandth time, Makai took my sword and helped me off the ground. "Looks like we have an audience," he said.

I'm never going to get this, I thought as I saw Queen Ramala surrounded by her Queensguard standing beside the door we had come through. Taking Makai's words to my advantage, I allowed the music to enter my ears again, and I ran. I took my sword from him, wrapped one of my legs around his chest, and pulled him to the ground. The wind shifted, and he tried to take me over, but I was much too fast. I jumped into the air, carried by the wind, sand flowing around me like a tornado, and kicked at him from above. But he grabbed my feet, turned me around, and threw me on the ground.

"Oof," I said as blood filled my mouth.

"Get up," Makai said, reaching out to me again.

"I don't need your hand," I said, struggling to my feet and walking off. "What I need is a break."

"You'll never get better if you don't practice," Makai called after me, but I didn't care. I wanted to be alone, away from his expectations of me. After grabbing a waterskin on one of the sand dunes, I pushed my back against the doors of the arena and watched the other soldiers practice. Seeing Zion and Aliyah, though, did nothing for my self-esteem.

Although a long streak of blood ran down Zion's cheek, a ruthless smirk appeared on his face as he mastered the fighting technique. He whipped around Halifa like a thunderstorm, making her fall to the ground. He pointed his sword at her chest.

But Aliyah was even better at it than he was. She had no wounds on her body as she faced Bakari. The gold flakes on her skin glittered in the sun. She wore dark pants framed by a skirt that opened in a bell shape as she flew through the air, her sword a part of her body as she slashed at Bakari's thighs.

Cameron, just go back. You have to learn. I took a sip from the waterskin, and went back over to Makai, who was talking to another soldier.

"Done whining?" he asked me. I ignored that question.

And so we practiced until the sun reached its apex. Makai was covered in bruises and cuts, but I had still lost the majority of our fights. *I'm never going to get this.* Frustration rolled off me in waves as I sipped more water.

"I'm exhausted," I said, hoping my anger would conceal my fear that I was a failure. "When is lunch?"

"Your work is not done," Makai said. I almost felt like he was trying to mask his disgust for me, but he didn't show it at all. "You've done . . . tolerable today, but you're still not a fighter. We will continue to train. But before that, you must fly.

"The queen only *lent* the gryphons to you when she saved you from the Supernatural Forest," he continued. "You must learn to fly if you want one for yourself."

CHAPTER THIRTEEN

A door opened on the far side of the amphitheater. I gathered my weapon and went after Makai. Aliyah, Zion, Halifa, and Bakari followed. It was dark in this part of the arena, but once we went through the opening, we met soft sunlight.

A group of soldiers waited for us, their horses connected to royal carriages. These carriages were made of carved wood, painted black. The doors were golden with steps placed on the ground in front of them.

Makai led me to one. We strode up the steps, and I sat down, resting on the plush fabric.

"Where are we going?" I asked.

"To the Animal Court," Makai announced as we began to move.

I looked out of the back to see Zion and Aliyah being helped into their own carriages.

"I can't believe this," I said. "Never in a million years did I think I'd have a gryphon of my own."

"You *might* have one of your own," Makai said. "You won't be able to ride one again unless one chooses you."

"What does that mean?"

"The Royal Tamer shall tell you more when you meet him."

While the carriages passed a lake as the walls of the Palacia receded into the distance, I wondered what Makai's problem was. His words and his blows were continuously sharp when it came to me. Was he trying to make me angry by belittling me or was I truly doing terrible? Maybe, in his eyes, I was nothing like Mama or Daddy.

I turned my attention to the window to take my mind off my failures. When we'd flown into the courtyard, it had been too dark to see how the palace stretched between two peaks of the Igbo mountain range. Now I could see how large it really was. We rode past the lake, and I couldn't help but crane my neck to try to look at it. Fish jumped to kiss the sunlight before diving back underneath. A sweet sound, a sound like music that was so beautiful, filled my ears. Waves rippled through the lake first, followed by what looked like shiny tails.

"Mondao," I whispered as I peered out my open window.

"Yes," Makai said, staring with me. "The queen told me you . . . would have an extensive knowledge of our country once you became the *Book*."

I took a breath. "It's more of a mixture between the *Book* and the stories my parents told me. For so long, they were just stories, but for me, they were also a connection to my parents. And I wanted it all to be true. Seeing and experiencing it now is breathtaking."

The songs of the mondao grew louder, but I couldn't understand their words. A flash of a tail appeared again. As I continued to stare, an entire colony of them swam through the water. Soon, the carriage gave me a better view. In the center of the lake sat a rock formation—a small island. Some of the colony swam to the sand and bathed in the sun. They were humanlike creatures, their skin tinged green, their tails brilliant shades of bright colors. They wore chains of gold around their necks, and their hair was black, long, and braided.

They peered at us, and I suppressed the urge to wave at them. The mondao tolerated humans, but they weren't as nice if they felt provoked. They'd appeared to the royals when the barrier was created, right alongside the gods.

"I can just imagine the types of creatures that exist in that lake," I whispered, remembering what I'd read.

Makai grunted. "I don't even want to think about it. The only person who would really know is the Royal Tamer. We go to him now."

I continued to look out the window. In this section of the kingdom, dwellings jutted from the rock face. Some were huge homes with multiple floors, while others were single floors carved into the rock. A few nobles watched us as the royal carriages passed. Battle horses, chariots, and stables lined the base of the mountain. Levers connected the base to the top, where the residences were.

Ahead of us, a bridge connected the two mountain peaks. The soldiers took the carriage to a dirt path that sloped upward; I held on to the closed door as we climbed higher to get to the bridge. We reached it after twenty more minutes of riding. I turned to see Zion almost falling out of his carriage from trying to see everything before Halifa pulled him back. I stifled my laughter as we rode over the bridge.

I tried to look out the window again, but my stomach dropped as I saw how far below the ground was. I could just make out the mondao in the distance jumping back into the lake's depths.

When we got to the end of the bridge, soldiers stopped us at a broad gate. Our escorts got off their horses and spoke to the soldiers; then they opened the gate and let us through. The rock path jutted downward now, and the carriages followed it until we came to an open area. Here, sand spread on the ground for miles. Wind picked up in the clearing as we rode through, causing sand to swirl in the air, stopping me from seeing anything.

"What's going on?" I yelled over the wind.

"We go through the Wind before we reach the Animal Court," Makai responded. "Kali, the Royal Tamer, forbids anyone from training the gryphons unless they have approval from the Royal Court. So we wait until he determines that we have permission."

I watched as sand floated from the ground, whirled through the air like a tornado, and then fell back down.

"I think it's clearing up," Makai said after a while of waiting.

As the sand drifted away, fog appeared. I looked down, realizing the carriage was now resting on a span of gray rock. Makai got out and helped me to the ground. Zion and Aliyah ran up to me.

"It took *forever* to get here," Zion said.

I peered around at the remaining fog. There was no sign of the bridge we had just driven over, but I could see a fuzzy outline of the Royal Court miles away from us.

"Look!" Aliyah gasped. "The fog is almost gone."

The rest of the fog dissipated, and the rock we were standing on led us to the edge of one of the peaks of the Igbo mountain range. Standing there was an older man, clothed in a long golden agbada and sandals. His hands were outstretched as he called to us.

"Welcome to the Animal Court," the man, who must be Kali, said.

Makai nudged us forward. Creatures screeched and flew around Kali's head. *Gryphons.*

The gryphons were truly majestic in every sense of the word. I had never heard a sound like their cries.

"We won't need you during the gryphon training, Captain,"

Kali said. Makai nodded at the Tamer and walked behind Halifa and Bakari as they returned to their carriages.

I was brimming with excitement at the prospect of riding on the back of a gryphon again. The first time, we hadn't had a choice, and my arm had hurt so much that I wasn't able to enjoy it.

Kali paced back and forth in front of us. "I am the queen's Royal Tamer. I take care of the palace's exotic animals. Every warrior must have a gryphon and learn to ride it. Which one of you is the Descendant?"

I pushed Zion. He groaned and pushed me ahead of him.

"Here he is," Zion said.

"Ahh," Kali said, pulling me forward. His eyes were a deep shade of brown. The Tamer had no hair, either on his head or on his face, including the space where his eyebrows should have been. His face was lined with wrinkles, and he smelled like sweet mangoes.

"Yes. You look just like the last one."

I removed my hands from his.

"You knew his mama?" Zion said.

Kali inclined his head as the gryphons continued to fly around us. "Yes, I knew your mother and your father. They both were very brave, keeping the barrier closed for years."

"I . . . I wish I had known them as well as you," I said.

A look of pity crossed his face. "Let's begin." He beckoned

to Zion and Aliyah, who came to stand beside me. The Tamer turned and watched the gryphons soaring in the air, some of them flying near the base of the mountain, others right over our heads, and some of them nothing more than dark imprints against the summer afternoon sky as they flew near the Royal Court.

"Now, gryphons are fickle creatures. But with the body of a lion and the face of an eagle, they are strong allies to have in battle," Kali continued. "The fact that they exist at all is due to magic. Once the barrier was created, they came out of hiding, much like how the gods revealed themselves to us. We train them for riding, to send messages across the kingdom, and for times of war. The relationship between a gryphon and its rider is the closest thing anyone could have. The trickiest part is getting a gryphon to deem you worthy."

"So . . . how are we supposed to ride one?" Aliyah asked.

Kali smiled, his mouth full of bright white teeth. He riffled through his robe and pulled out a blade, then pointed toward the mountain's edge. "One must choose you. Step into the fire."

"How do we know if we have been chosen?" I asked.

"The gryphon will give you a vision."

A line of fire appeared at the edge, and the flame bloomed into the sky.

"Nah, I'm good," Zion said, turning around. "I don't need to ride a gryphon."

Aliyah grabbed him. "Nope, you're staying right here."

"She's right," I said, taking his hand. "Remember, we do this together." He nodded reluctantly.

Kali continued to point the blade to the edge of the mountain. "Step up, heroes. The fire won't hurt you—it's magic. It's how the gryphons know that there is a rider for the taking."

The magic felt cold against my skin even though a roaring fire bloomed in front of us. I rubbed the flesh bumps on my arms and stepped forward. The flame covered me to the point where I was consumed. Then the coolness left, replaced by a steady warmth. It did not burn, and the fear dissipated as a calmness drifted over me. The fire felt like a hug, like Grandma and Mama tucking me in bed at night, like Daddy allowing me to play with his beard, his laugh like a thunderstorm.

"Step up, heroes—the fire won't hurt you," I said, repeating Kali's words. Two images danced in front of my eyes, and I knew who they were. Mama and Daddy, first becoming the saviors I was now becoming. It was a joy and privilege to take their place.

"Cam?" Aliyah asked.

I beckoned them to the fire, where they joined me.

The Tamer threw his hands in the air in a complicated flourish; the trees surrounding the mountain rustled, and the wind vibrated around us. More gryphons peeked their heads out of the trees, then flew into the air, their wingspans long and wide. Suddenly the air was filled with hundreds of the creatures as they screeched at us and flew around the mountainside. Some of them circled over our heads while some flew toward the lake, their wings causing the water to rise in the air. A number of them flew close to the sun.

"How do we ride them?" I screamed over the wind their wings had kicked up.

"Just close your eyes," Kali yelled.

I didn't close mine until I saw Zion and Aliyah do it first. I waited for something, anything. I could only see the backs of my eyelids, but I could hear the rustling of strong wings. I concentrated hard on them, what they looked like, and how it would feel to ride one again. One second, the sounds around me were loud and the wind was oppressive and heavy, but the next second, all sound ceased. I couldn't feel my limbs. I wanted to scream in fear, but nothing came out of my mouth.

I'm worthy enough, I thought. *I'm worthy. I have to be. Don't reject me.*

When I felt like I couldn't take it anymore, a bright light appeared in my mind, a small dot at first, then expanding into a full circle like the sun. A majestic gryphon appeared in the light, a creature whose lion body and eagle face were snowy white. The only color on the gryphon was the dark brown of its beak and the deep blue of its eyes. I reached out to the creature, in control of my limbs again.

I stood on an empty island in the middle of an ocean as I stretched outward, my boots sinking into wet sand. The gryphon screeched in the air before landing and walking toward me on strong feet. I felt no fear now, only awe at the magnificent creature that had deemed me worthy. Actually, I felt relief more than anything; for the first time since coming to Chidani, I'd done something right.

By the time the snowy-white gryphon reached me, I had lifted my arms to it once again. Its name and gender came to me. *Ugo*. The *Book*'s pages fluttered inside me.

"Now, that's cool," I whispered as I touched the creature's beak. "Ugo. The Igbo name for 'eagle.'"

The gryphon chirped and rubbed his head over my arms. I smiled as I ruffled the feathers along his head and on his neck. A tendril of energy shot through my body, causing me to gasp. My soul was connecting with Ugo's in a way that almost made us one. I'd felt that oneness, but in a different way, when Agbala had thrust the *Book* in my chest.

A voice appeared in my head. *It's time to come back*, Kali said. I opened my eyes. The air was still filled with the sound of gryphons, flying back and forth around us. Aliyah and Zion were gone. Kali was staring at me.

"What happened?" I asked. "Did I do it right?"

"You did quite well. You connected with your gryphon. Your friends were successful, too. As you can see, they are already flying."

He reached out his weathered hands to me, and I grasped them.

"Curious," Kali said, staring at me. "Very curious."

That old fear returned to me. "What's curious? Did I do something wrong?"

"No, not wrong. Just curious. Ugo also chose your mother."

I was taken aback. "Wait, what?"

"Yes, your mother rode Ugo all those years ago when she first came here. She rode him with such joy and vigor. When she died, Ugo refused to show himself for years. I had wondered if he had gone somewhere to die. He must have sensed the Descendant's power return within you. I anticipate great things from you, Cameron Battle."

My eyes burned. "I—I wish I had *really* known her. I wish I had really known them both."

He touched my chest. "They live on through you. Ugo wouldn't have deemed you worthy if he didn't sense her presence in you. Now, *jump.*"

I wiped the tears from my eyes. "Wait, what?"

"*Jump off the mountain*, Cameron Battle," Kali said, a smile playing around his mouth. He removed the knife from his agbada again, pointing toward the edge of the mountain. "Ugo waits for you."

If it were any other time, I would have been scared. But now, I knew I had to jump. I turned from Kali, emotion washing over me, and ran toward the edge without fear.

I jumped, letting out a breath as I fell. I didn't have long to wait. With a rush of wings and a loud screech, the white gryphon caught me right when I was about to hit the lake's surface. A spray of water hit me from the gryphon's wingspan. I laughed as Ugo carried me upward, past Kali standing on top of the mountain, and toward the sun.

We passed through the crowds of gryphons until we soared above them. I looked down to see the rest of the creatures diving back into the trees or falling into various rock paths along the mountain range, leaving only the two that were carrying Zion and Aliyah. Zion was riding a beautiful brown one, the creature almost bigger than mine. Aliyah's towered above us both, a bright red color. I whooped and raised my fist in the air, my free hand wrapped around Ugo's reins and my feet in the leather straps at the sides.

Ugo screeched, and I waited as Aliyah and Zion joined me above the Igbo mountain range. We all raced higher and higher until we broke through the clouds and circled one another in the air. Above us was the bright sun. My feet brushed a cloud, sending cold shivers up my leg.

"This is unbelievable!" Zion yelled as we soared next to each other. I couldn't put any of my joy into words; I could only laugh.

"Who would've thought all this would have come from one book?" Aliyah said. Pride warmed me. This entire time, my mama had been preparing me for just this moment. And I had prepared Zion.

"Down!" I yelled at Ugo and he complied, diving through the clouds and soaring across the lake. Zion and Aliyah followed me. We passed the lake, seeing the green mondao swimming as fast as we were flying. We flew past the Royal Court and the Palacia and headed south, toward the Supernatural Forest. Ugo flew so fast that I had to coax him to slow down at certain points so we could see the landscape of Chidani.

Near the Supernatural Forest was a city that glistened with diamonds and crystal. I looked closer and couldn't see anyone inhabiting it, though. Much of it was hidden in shadow.

We flew past it until we came to a desert, barren and hotter than it was at the Palacia. In different places there was sparse grass. As we passed, lions roared. A bridge was built in the center of the desert that connected the forest to a palace that seemed to be constructed from sandstone. People clothed in long robes with scarves covering their heads looked at us as we flew past. Ugo led the way back into the sky. He screeched one last time as we soared to the Palacia, past the Royal Court, deep blue lake housing the mondao, and the bridge that led us to the Animal Court.

As the sand settled, Ugo dropped me on the rock face while Kali looked on in pride. Aliyah and Zion followed suit.

Kali held his arms outstretched toward us as we jumped down from our gryphons. Ugo rubbed his broad head on my arm one last time, and then he was gone in the air again, the other two gryphons following.

"That's enough training for today," Kali said as we ran to him. "The gryphons are yours as long as you remain in Chidani. Now, you must return to the Palacia. I'm sure the captain and the queen will want to hear about your successful day."

We giggled together as Makai and the others brought the carriages to take us back to the Royal Court.

"Now, *that* was awesome," Aliyah said.

CHAPTER FOURTEEN

"Cameron, may I talk to you for a moment?" Bakari asked after we had returned to the sand dunes. We had been chattering this entire time about gryphon training; Aliyah and Zion had refused to ride in their own carriages and had joined me. They talked so much that I couldn't get a word in. Aliyah's gryphon was named Odum, meaning "lion" in Igbo, and Zion's was named Ike, meaning "power."

Makai busied himself with packing up the tools from our training earlier, pushing Zion and Aliyah to help him. I cast a glance his way, but he deliberately ignored me.

"I guess," I said.

"Follow me," Bakari said, placing a flat palm over his heart. "Makai has given me permission." I did as I was told, marching through the sand to a large brass door set on the opposite side of the stadium. Bakari turned the wheel, and we walked outside to a small courtyard. We had been gone for so long that I hadn't noticed the sun had disappeared behind the clouds. A small carriage, pulled by horses, sat on the green lawn. Bakari beckoned me inside, and we drove slowly, the soldier being careful not to get too close to the edge.

"What is this about?" I asked.

His face was a mask. "I have something to show you. I had a feeling about your mother when she was here, but I never said anything. I decided I had to show it this time or I might never get my chance."

I didn't know why I felt comfortable going anywhere with Bakari, but something about him made my nervousness drift away in the wind. I could tell that he was eager to share this with me.

The carriage stopped at a small hut, its roof made of thatched leaves and branches, its base made of sandstone packed smooth with mud and rainwater. It was a modest thing, situated close to the palace, but there was a charm about it. A lived-in feeling. A lone Ikenga stood at its entrance.

"I live here when I'm not training in the guardhouse," Bakari explained, ushering me inside, rubbing his fingers over his Ikenga. Like the outside of the hut, the inside was modest, made up of a fireplace, a mattress, and a few cushions.

"One second," Bakari said, disappearing in a back room. When he returned, it was the first time I had really *looked* at him. He reminded me a lot of myself; his hair was coarse like mine, his eyes dark brown, his face lean and forehead large. His nose matched mine as well, long and broad, nostrils easy to flare. The only difference was that a wound marred his cheek, flowing from his forehead to the stubble dotting his chin. He held a box in his hand, overlaid with bright gems.

His voice caught as he spoke. "This belonged to my family."

"What does this have to do with me?" I whispered.

"A lot," he said, thrusting the box at me. "A priest helped me spell it after the barrier was created. Meaning that no one can open it. But you should try."

Feeling foolish, I grabbed the box and sat on one of the cushions. Bakari joined me. My fingers pressed against the box, feeling for any weakness. They caught on a clasp that I tried to slide open, but it was hard to move. A pressure built in my mind and chest as, in my mind's eye, I saw a young boy who looked just like me. I gasped when the box sprang open, releasing a blinding emerald light. I turned away and looked at Bakari. His eyes filled with water.

"I *knew* it," he whispered. "For years, I didn't think it was possible. But I knew when your mother came to Chidani— you are my relative. A distant relative, for sure."

Confusion gripped me. "This doesn't make any sense." I peered into the box. It contained a blade, a few pieces of parchment rolled up like scrolls, and small trinkets that looked like coins. I gripped one of the pieces of weathered paper, opening it and gasping as electricity bloomed up my hands. It was a simple painted portrait, a small boy with no shoes on in its center. A woman stood behind the boy, gripping his shoulders. The boy looked *just* like me, almost a perfect match. I opened another parchment to see a family tree drawn on it. It was long, but it stopped at Bakari, right before the barrier was created.

"That's me and Mama," Bakari said, pointing. "You can meet her one day. Then we can add your family to our family tree. If you would like."

"You are my ancestor."

"Weird, isn't it?" Bakari said. He reached out with a calloused hand, grasping mine and squeezing. "It's nice to meet you, Cameron Battle. My family."

A sense of foreboding rolled through me like a rain shower as I dropped his hand and scrambled up. "No, no, no," I said. "I can't lose you, too." I wrapped my arms around my stomach, pacing back and forth. "I can't lose you, too."

He grabbed me by the shoulders, stopping me in my tracks. "You're not going to lose me, Cameron. I'm not going anywhere."

"It's just too much pressure," I said. "Not only do I have to defeat Amina in some way, but my mama and daddy are *gone*, Bakari. And what if I fail and you get hurt? How am I supposed to . . . ? How . . . ?"

He stopped me with a hug. "You don't have to worry about me. I'm just happy to meet you. Finally. I never got to tell your mother, and I've felt sadness about that. I never thought I would get another chance. But now it lives on through you." He placed his hand over his heart again. "I will protect you with my life, with all my strength, because that's what you deserve. I lost everyone once. I am not going to lose you, too."

I pulled away from him and stared at an older version of myself. It was uncanny how much we looked alike. A smile brightened my face. For the first time, I felt a little less afraid. It felt good to have family protect me.

He gripped my hand, squeezing it and repeating his last refrain. "Nice to meet you, Cameron Battle."

"Nice to meet you, too, Bakari. My family."

CHAPTER FIFTEEN

The next day, Queen Ramala called for me as we practiced in the sandpits. Well, Zion and Aliyah practiced while I failed.

"Captain Makai, make sure we have soldiers guarding the underground tunnels. Also, I need to see Cameron. There is much we must discuss." The queen's voice was loud and thunderous. What *else* was awaiting me?

Ramala waved her hands in the air as we approached. "Guards, stand down. Cameron can support me, can't you?"

"Yes, I can." I slipped my arm into the crook of hers, and we set off.

We walked through the main floor of the Palacia and past the Throne Room to the gardens. The pages of the *Book* flipped through my mind as I tried to figure out what was going on. The fragrances of flowers and fruit greeted us as we strolled past fountains shooting water.

She gazed at the small wound on my cheek as we continued to walk. "You're hurt."

"Oh, it's from training with Makai."

"He could learn to be a bit gentler."

"He could."

At her words, the aziza I saw earlier in the Throne Room converged around me, sending glittering sparkles down from the sky. Unlike the goddess's magic, the aziza's did not hurt me. My broken skin healed up quickly and easily.

Sighing, Ramala watched the wounds heal. "I don't have much magic left, but at least, when people visit me, I can heal them."

The tiny creatures floated above me and then disappeared in a shower of sparkles as I looked around. Ponds brimmed with jumping fish. The gardens overflowed with lush flowers, trees full of jackalberry, granadilla, pineapple, and mango fruits. Plantains dangled from trees. A crystal structure stood in the middle of a small lake, possibly the arena that nobles used to see performances. Just beyond it was another tall building. We stopped outside.

"What is this place?" I said.

"One of the many libraries of Chidani," Queen Ramala said as she knocked on its door. "I wanted to bring you here alone because there is history here. *Your* history. Your mother and father came here, too."

We waited for a while until a male servant opened the

door, bowing before the queen. The hallway inside was dark and narrow.

"Take us to the map," the queen said. The servant bowed again, then picked up a lit candle in a nook in the wall before we walked up a flight of stairs to a brass door, which he opened.

The room inside, large and all-encompassing, was lined with bookshelves. Every available space was crammed with every type of book: old and weathered, new and glossy, small books that looked more like pamphlets and tall books that had to lean on walls. Some books were bound in leather, and others were nothing more than paper and string.

I followed the queen as she waved to the royal librarians. A few climbed on ladders, bringing books down and dusting them free of dirt, while the rest sat on the floor flipping through weathered and crinkled pages. One librarian lifted his hands to the ceiling, and it seemed as though he commanded books to rain down and soar across the library. Nobles walked through the rows of bookshelves, browsing for books, talking softly with the librarians.

I followed the queen to the end of the great room, where she opened a door. Inside the small space was a single table with a rolled-up parchment on top. The queen reached out and unrolled it. I saw squiggly lines with dots and points but couldn't make out the language it was in.

"What am I looking at?" I asked.

"One of the Maps of Chidani," the queen whispered as she draped her fingers over it.

"Okay . . . I mean . . . I can't really see anything. It's all a jumbled mess."

"Of course you can't see anything yet," the queen said. "Cameron, place your hands on the map to activate it."

I did what she said, feeling foolish. Nothing happened at first, but then the touch of the map caused the *Book*'s pages to turn inside me. My hand glowed with a ruby light as the map shifted. I gasped and removed my hand as the light expanded along the map's edges and then filtered down to the middle.

The lines on the map moved, and the pictures came to life, lifting off the page as if we were looking at a hologram. The queen moved her hand, and the images in the air shifted until we were looking at the Royal Court. She pointed at the floating picture, the castle turning in diamond light, gryphons flying in the air.

"This is where we are," she said. She curved her hand downward, the Palacia collapsed back into place, and the scene changed until I was looking at a familiar outline of a location surrounded by water at its southern border.

I pointed. "That's Nigeria."

The scene changed, and the map floated in the air; then it shifted until we were looking at a spot along the southeastern portion of the outline close to the Atlantic Ocean. "This is Igboland, or as you know it, Chidani. We are hidden so no one can find us. The barrier was created here after I prayed to the gods to protect us from the invaders. This is why Amina stole the gifts from me. She hates that we closed ourselves off to the world when so many of our people needed us."

I didn't have anything to say to that, but the image changed anyway. We soared over the Royal Court, then went southeast to the Supernatural Forest. We saw a number of mmo and other animals as well, including wild gryphons flying around. The image stopped at a clearing.

"This is where you and your friends came through. It is also where your mother and father died. Once Amina stole the gifts from me, the *Book* brought your mother and father here. They stayed for years trying to get the gifts back, but they..." her breath caught before she finished, "ultimately lost their lives."

She spoke of history as if she were detached from it, as if she hadn't witnessed it all. It made me a little uncomfortable, and I couldn't just keep quiet.

"To your sister?" I said angrily.

"Yes," the queen admitted, closing her eyes. "To Amina. That hurt me to my core."

When I turned my attention back to the map, the images changed until I saw four different types of people warring against one another. A woman stood at the forefront of them all.

"There are four different clans of the Igbo," the queen continued. "Onitsha, Owerri, Efik, and Ibibio. They all fought against one another until I gained the throne and united everyone under one rule. We all fought valiantly against the slavers, but we weren't successful."

The scene shifted again, and I was looking at an empty city glittering with gold and diamonds.

"I saw this place yesterday," I said. "I wondered why no one was there."

"The aziza and their queen decided to stay out of the fight," Ramala said. "We didn't even know they existed until the barrier was created. The Fae sent messengers to the Palacia to inform me that they would not interfere with my rule, but they demanded to stay neutral in their Crystal City. Though I've tried to make inroads with them, I have failed. To this day, we can see the city, but we cannot enter it."

"What about the aziza we saw when Makai brought us to you?"

"As a gesture of goodwill, the azizan queen sent them. When Amina stole my gifts, the queen demanded they be returned to her to be safe from bloodshed. I'm afraid the aziza we have left will leave us soon."

The queen moved her hand, and the scene shifted, going from the south to the east of Chidani. I noticed that we passed a small island in the water, but she said nothing about that landmass.

In the east, there was another towering city, but we passed that as well until we stopped at a small village situated along the Atlantic Ocean. These people wore dashikis and cotton pants, while the small children wore nothing more than shell beads around their necks.

"These people are the Onitsha clan," the queen said.

"Why are you showing me all this?" I asked.

"Because I wanted you to see what your mother and father fought for. This is why you are the Descendant of the Igbo. This is why the *Book* was created. It's all to keep us and your world safe. The Descendant has the power to protect us all."

She sat down on a bench beside the door as the images above us kept spinning. "Do you know what you must do?"

"Agbala told us that your sister, Princess Amina, stole the gods' gifts from you, and the only way to bring you back to power and to close the barrier is to stop her and to retrieve your gifts. But I don't understand why you didn't keep fighting. It's the reason Amina became angry with you."

She gazed at me. "I've grieved for centuries for what happened to our people during the slave trade. My mother and father did everything they could to fight, losing their own lives in the process. Sometimes, I regret calling on the gods after my parents rejected their bargain. But, Cameron, you must believe me. At that time, there was just so much death and destruction that I felt I had no choice but to deal with the gods."

She riffled through her robes and took out two plums from a sack, offering me one. "I don't regret all of it. Because of my decision, our people were saved from a fate worse than death. But I do regret giving up our people to the gods, giving up our concept of time. I saved their lives but also changed the nature of them entirely. Amina was never able to forgive me for what I'd done."

"And that's why you've been alive for centuries," I said.

She nodded. "Chidani lives outside of time. Anyone who was older than seventeen when the barrier was created is the same age now. Days or years here are mere minutes in your world.

"I became so caught up in this world that I forgot about yours," she continued. "But Amina never forgot the decision I made. She bided her time for years, and then she acted. She stole the three gifts."

Queen Ramala's eyes bored into mine, and she squeezed my hand—hard. "But she goes about it the wrong way. She wants to unleash demons on both worlds. She doesn't think I deserve to be queen. And that's not the answer, either."

"But I don't understand. Why would she want to control both worlds?" I asked.

"Amina thinks that if she can break the barrier and rule both worlds, the descendants of our people wouldn't have to live under oppression ever again."

"I can understand a little bit of what she means," I whispered. "The legacy of slavery exists still in my world."

"It's a noble plan, but it's foolhardy. So many people will lose their lives. The mmo will destroy everything. Think about your grandmother and your friends."

"What is her ultimate plan?" I asked. "I don't really get it."

Ramala's eyes turned distant. "To rebuild anew. To *kill* anyone who is not Igbo, man, woman, and child. Almost everyone on this earth will die. And she will rule over what's left."

A steely determination gripped me as I thought about Zion, Aliyah, and their families. That meant they would die, too. Many innocent people would die. "I will try to help you," I said. "But we don't know where to find the three gifts."

Ramala stood, and she led me to the revolving image of Onitsha. "We have gained intelligence from the Onitsha clan to my crown's whereabouts. It is as I feared. Amina has aligned herself with Ekwensu, the Igbo death god. He controls the mmo. I didn't think it could be true, but this is the reason she has been able to use the mmo to fight you and . . . kill your parents. The crown was spotted on the Isle of Onitsha. That's where you must go. You may take Halifa, Bakari, and Makai with you."

"But why is it there?" I asked. "If the crown is far away from her, doesn't that mean she will die, too?"

The queen shook her head. "As the rightful queen, only I bear that consequence. Not her. If I die, then she will become queen and the same will apply to her."

"Will you go with me?"

She shook her head, her eyes leaving mine for the first time. "No, I am weakened by Amina's treachery. The little magic I have left is here. If I leave, I will die. I . . . I . . . Agbala says I only have three moons left to live. And if I die, Amina will earn, by inheritance, my throne and the three gifts."

"Aliyah and Zion won't let me go alone."

She nodded. "They can go if you wish."

She grasped my hands again. "Be careful, little one."

We left the swirling map and walked back to the Palacia, arm in arm. My thoughts swirled as well, but I didn't dare ask any more questions. Ramala seemed so confident I was up to this task, ready for my destiny as Descendant.

I only had three moons to prove myself worthy of her trust.

CHAPTER SIXTEEN

Zion, Aliyah, and I spent the next month practicing Dambe; flying our gryphons; eating too much food; collecting cuts, gashes, and bruises; and being healed by the aziza. I grew more frustrated by the day. One month of training and I was still not succeeding.

One of those days, Aliyah had made Bakari completely surrender. He had sent a punch toward her, fast and true. She grabbed it so quickly that it seemed like she was in one spot, and in another second, she was in another. The only evidence that she had moved was a small shift in the air as the heat rose from the ground. He grunted as his fist struck her hand, but she disappeared again. *Crack!*

Bakari yelped as she appeared behind him, pulling his arm so far back that his bones snapped. "That's enough!" he screamed. She wrapped her hand around his neck and pulled him down. "I said that's enough!"

Bakari ended up limping back inside the Palacia to be healed, a grimace lining his face.

"Now *that's* how you take a man down!" Zion had screamed, doing an impromptu dance as Bakari shoved past him. I tried that same move with Makai, but I was rewarded with a mouthful of sand. Again.

Another morning, Halifa was determined to show no mercy to Zion, a response to him mocking Bakari. She got a surprise that day, though. She swiped a sharp sword at his chest, but he was much too quick for her. He disappeared in a hush of air, reappearing just a few feet away, catching her off guard. He waved at her, a smirk brightening his face. She swirled around him like a cyclone, trying to confuse him, but he matched her every stride. With a yell, he kicked at her sword, making it fall to the sand. In another swipe, the sword was now in his hand. With a determined cry, he flipped the sword and jammed its butt into her stomach, right through her armor.

She gasped, bowling over. He caught her in his arms and pushed her upward. "Ow," she said, clutching her abdominal muscles. "That really hurt, Zion."

"I know," he said. "I meant to make it hurt. Just like you meant to make lunch meat out of me with your sword." She grunted in assent and limped inside the Palacia.

I know I can do that, too. Though, when I tried that move with Makai, I was the one who ended up bowled, another day with a mouthful of sand. I stalked off once again after he helped me to my feet. I refused to train with Makai after that.

"That's never going to happen again," I complained to Agbala as she healed me afterward. "Keep him away from me!"

Agbala sighed. "You must continue, Cameron. He only means to help you. He's not treating you any differently than anyone else. You will get this. I promise."

"I meant what I said. Keep him away from me."

A week later, Zion and I were practicing Dambe for fun, me wearing my red Chucks to see if that would make a difference in my luck. It was a way for me to relieve some tension after refusing to keep training with Makai. Makai had no qualms with continuing to point out my weaknesses, but he kept his distance like I asked.

Practicing with Zion, though, kept my mind off the fact that we didn't have long before we set off to find the crown, that we didn't have long before Ramala would succumb to her illness. And then Amina would win. I couldn't have that, but I couldn't shake the fact that I wasn't doing well. All the faith everyone had in me, I didn't see it in myself.

I rolled to the sand as Zion's foot connected with my stomach. I grunted and fell over. He moved so fast that he was swirling shadows and sand. I narrowed my eyes and jumped quickly to the side. Time slowed, and I saw him scatter to my left. I brought my arm up, slamming it in his chest. He grunted as he almost fell to the ground, but not before I bent low and tripped him up just because I could.

I laughed at him sprawled out like that. His hair, armor, and clothes were full of sand. He coughed out some. I reached and helped him to his feet. He took my hand, squeezed it hard, and a slight grin appeared on his face. That was my mistake. I didn't have enough time to call for Dambe before he twisted my arm and threw me over his head. I flipped in midair and dropped to my feet, but I wouldn't give him the satisfaction of falling to the ground again. This time, I was ready for him. The sand shifted again, and I could see him running across the pit and then doubling back toward me, trying to confuse me.

It worked. He moved so quickly that I didn't know where he was coming from. Sand whipped around me in a blur. I gritted my teeth with frustration. *Why can't I beat Zion?*

I tried to push away those negative thoughts and refocus. The air vibrated near me again, making me take the sword off my waist and use its pummel to slash to the side. When the flesh gave way, I knew I had made the perfect contact. Zion wheezed as I attached the sword back to my waist. I turned and disappeared, this time making sure he didn't see me. Air and sand *whooshed* as I moved.

I ran up a nearby sand hill, hoping to confuse him, but he was much too fast. We crashed against each other at the top of the hill. Time slowed as we both went into Dambe. I saw his face, dripping with sweat and fierce with determination. He threw his sword to the ground, and we continued in hand-to-hand combat. He threw a punch my way, and I parried it. I pushed against his chest with a flat hand, like Makai had taught me. *A punch is effective but requires more force. Save your strength for when you most need it.*

"Oof," Zion said. He grabbed my hand, twisted it, and I cried out in pain. He twisted it harder and sent a kick to my stomach again. I flew off the hill and landed on my back. I closed my eyes, momentarily blinded by flying sand.

"Ahh!" Zion said. I opened my eyes to see him jumping, soaring in my direction. His body connected with mine, knocking the breath out of me. I expected him to continue the beating, but he didn't. He tickled my stomach instead.

"Stop, Zion!" I giggled. "We're supposed to be fighting, not playing around."

"We *are* fighting," he said, pinning me down to the sand so I couldn't move. "Surrender and I'll stop tickling you."

"Never!"

"Wrong answer," he said. He proceeded to tickle my stomach *and* my armpits.

"Surrender and admit that I won!"

"Okay, okay," I said, laughing so hard that I was beginning to cough. "I surrender!"

"Finally," he said. He stood and reached out his hand to me again. "Now, let's go inside and get something to eat. I'm hungry after all this fighting."

"You're always hungry," I said, taking his hand. We continued to laugh and talk as we walked toward the dungeon doors. The conversation kept me from thinking about the fact that I had lost again. I had lost to Aliyah yesterday, and I thought Zion would be an easier opponent, but that wasn't true. If I couldn't fight, all of this would be for nothing. Even Zion's constant joking didn't stop him from being better than me.

"I see this is funny to you." We were so engrossed in our conversation that we didn't notice the lumbering shadow in front of us, barring our way to the Palacia. We stopped when we finally saw Makai. He shook his head in disgust before speaking again.

"I'm disappointed," he spat. He turned accusatory eyes on Zion. "You're supposed to be teaching Cameron, not making him laugh. This is serious!"

"Man, whatever," I said. "I'm not a fighter, okay? I can't be good at everything." I was beginning to stalk away when something stopped me. "Wait!" I said. "Zion was supposed to be teaching me? Zion?"

Zion grimaced when I turned to him.

"That's not a response. I don't speak Neanderthal."

"I told him to help you," Makai barked. "You're not taking any of this seriously. We are teaching you Dambe because you'll need it for the trouble ahead."

I rolled my eyes and sidestepped Makai to make my way back inside. "Seems ridiculous to prepare for a trouble that my own family didn't prepare me for." Of course, I knew I needed to learn everything I could to face Amina, but it was easier to act like a child than admit I still had so far to go.

Anger burned inside me. Everyone else had parents, or people who loved them and were waiting for them to succeed. Me? My parents had died before I even got the chance to really know them, and Grandma had taken it upon herself to keep my lineage away from me. It was unfair.

I turned and marched back to my chambers. I didn't need any of this.

"I'm obviously not good at this. Let Zion and Aliyah be the heroes you need me to be."

CHAPTER SEVENTEEN

"Listen, I know how you feel. You've been overwhelm—" Zion said as we returned to the sitting area outside of our bedrooms.

"Leave me alone," I interrupted. "You could've told me that Makai asked you to help me. And you *don't* know how I feel. You've been succeeding since day one." Aliyah came out of her room at the noise and crossed her arms when she heard us arguing.

"No," Zion said, spinning me around to face him. "Aliyah, help me out here."

"He's right," Aliyah said calmly. "We only wanted to help you."

I sat on one of the large couches and folded my arms. "You guys just don't understand. I lost everything, everyone. I feel like I'm failing them, failing my parents. And now you have to help me? You could've told me! You're my best friends!"

Zion stood in front of me. "I know, and I'm sorry. And I hate to say this . . ." His voice trailed off as he looked to Aliyah for help.

"The entire world will be hurt if you're not ready," Aliyah continued, her voice wavering. "If *we're* not ready," she corrected. "Our families will be hurt. We don't want you to lose anyone else."

"My parents are gone," I said, wiping angry tears away. "And I can't even live up to their legacy, live up to Mama's legacy."

"You will," Zion said, sitting next to me. "Just let us help. You will learn this."

"We'll make sure of it," Aliyah said.

"Whatever," I said, shame showering over me but determined for them not to see it. "I need to eat."

Makai came inside our chambers later as we ate and threw three wool riding packs on the ground. "I have an idea."

"Is this about me practicing Dambe again?" I said while eating a piece of venison. "Not interested."

"You don't have a choice," Makai grunted. "We need to move on to the last part of your training. Halifa and Bakari say that you are too young for this, but I disagree."

"Now? It's nighttime!" Aliyah said.

"Yes, the last part of your training begins now. What better way to learn than to be thrust into a new adventure?" He smiled at us. I was wary of that smile; there was nothing good behind it. Especially since he hadn't done so for the entire month I'd known him.

"Everything you'll need is inside your packs. Eat the rest of your dinner and then we will go."

We finished eating in silence as Makai stood at the door. I deliberately ignored Aliyah when she came to refill my goblet with freshly squeezed fruit juice. When we were done, I put on my pack, grunting at the heaviness of it. We followed him down flights of stairs, into the great hall, and then outside into one of the royal courtyards. We waited until a carriage came for us. Soldiers helped us inside, and we made our way past the Royal Court.

Everything looked different at night. Although the sky was dark, the air was filled with fireflies and winged beetles illuminating the path the carriage took past the Palacia. The noble dwellings were lit with torchlight, giving the lake an emerald glow. The mondao swam through its depths, their tails brightened and showing deep shades of ruby, cobalt, and tangerine. I knew where we were heading as soon as the carriage climbed up the rocky path to the bridge that connected the Royal Court to the Animal Court.

I shivered, but I refused to ask Zion or Aliyah what they thought was going to happen. The gate to the Animal Court opened, and we passed through. This time, our carriage was surrounded by thunderous rain and lightning strikes. Zion scooted over to me and buried his curly head under my arm. I didn't push him away.

"Really?" Aliyah asked.

"What?" Zion said, the sound muffled by my dashiki. "You know I hate storms."

We sat in silence as the sky thundered, so loud that even if we did talk, we wouldn't be able to hear one another.

"All this rain reminds me of the storms back in Atlanta," Zion said. I took a peek outside and could see only darkness and rain, almost as if the night was swirling with mmo smoke.

The carriages halted, and nobody seemed to know what to do next. After about five minutes, the downpour stopped and Makai appeared.

"Bring your packs," he said as we stepped outside in the inky blackness. Without another word, he jumped back inside the carriage pulled by the snorting battle horses and began to move away.

"What are you doing?" I said to him, speaking for the first time. "You can't just leave us out here!"

"I can and I will," Makai said. His words and face were stony as the carriage pulled him into the darkness. I started to run after him, but as soon as I did, he disappeared. When I turned around, I could barely make out Zion's and Aliyah's silhouettes. I waited for my eyes to adjust before walking back to them.

"Anyone know what's supposed to happen now?" Zion asked.

No one responded. An unnatural chill snaked through me. I hugged myself as the darkness drifted away. We stood in a sparsely wooded area, surrounded by trees, sand, and haphazardly growing underbrush and vines. Light streamed through the trees, leading to a cave at the base of a mountain. I wasn't sure if it was part of the Igbo mountain range or how far we had traveled.

We waited in silence for a while.

"We might as well go toward that light," I said, tightening my grip around my pack and trudging forward. I gripped my sword, just in case this was some sort of test. Makai had said it was the last part of our training, but I hadn't a clue what that meant.

"I wonder what this all means?" Aliyah asked, putting words to my thoughts.

"Guess we gotta find out," Zion responded. As they spoke, I couldn't help but let my anger at them subside. It wasn't their fault I wasn't progressing the way I needed to—it was mine. To be honest, I knew I could do it, but there was fear there. Maybe I faltered because I wanted the safety of the Palacia, because I didn't want to face what my parents had to go through when they were last in Chidani.

A figure walked out of the cave, its body covered in an ocean-blue kaftan. It was Kali, holding the same knife he'd held when we rode the gryphons.

"Looks like it's safe," I said, walking faster.

His face was grim when we stopped in front of him. "Welcome to the Cave of Shadows."

"The cave of . . . what?" I asked. I racked my brain for any mention of it in the *Book*, but there was none.

"Shadows," Kali responded. "The last part of your training. Once you walk through the opening, you will not return until you defeat your enemy."

He looked directly at me. "Fear is holding you back. It's time to look it in the face and confront it for what it is. You can't fight unless you do. That goes for all three of you."

"Did Mama and Daddy go through this?" I whispered.

He nodded and touched his knife to the opening of the cave. Flames appeared around its perimeter. "What's inside won't physically harm you, but you must pass the test to be a warrior. Step forward."

"Yeah, that's not happening," Zion said.

"Pssh," Aliyah said, stepping forward. "I'll go first. Let's get this over with." She went across the cave's threshold and disappeared.

Zion grabbed my hand. "I'm scared."

"C'mon," I said. "If we do this, we do it together," I added, using our shared refrain. He nodded and we both followed her.

"Okay, now what—" I said, turning around. There was no opening, and Kali had disappeared. It was like we had traveled deep within the mountain just by taking three steps inside. We now stood in a low, circular cave without any visible opening to walk through and no way to escape. Although the inside was cool, a fire had been started in the middle. While Zion went to inspect the flames, I trudged over to the walls and rubbed my hands on the rock.

"Who knows how long this cave has been here," Aliyah said, joining me. We both looked for cracks in the rock, trying to find a way out.

"Kali said we won't be able to get out until we fight our fears," I whispered. I bent low and rubbed my hands along the bottom of the wall where the sand met it, but I could find nothing that would help us escape. There was no crack, no line that seemed out of place, or a lever of some sort to pull. I went over to the roaring fire while Aliyah continued her search.

"There's *always* a way out," she was whispering to herself.

"Found anything?" I asked Zion.

"Just food," Zion said. "I don't think we're meant to leave, at least not tonight."

I looked at the flames. "There is no food. What are you talking about?" I touched a hand to his forehead. "Are you hallucinating?"

"No!" He pointed at the flames. "Look."

I looked again, and Zion was right. Shadows swirled all around the flames, and an animal, a dead goat, appeared there, roasting on a spit. I stood back as it magically started to rotate slowly.

"How did you know that was here?"

He shrugged. "I just wished for food, then smelled it first before it appeared."

"This . . . this is weird."

By now, Aliyah had joined us. "There's no way out."

"Told you," I said.

Zion took his sword and cut himself a huge piece of juicy meat. "Nothing we can do but wait. Might as well eat."

After we ate to our hearts' content, the rest of the meat disappeared in shadows, leaving nothing but the smell to tell us it had been real. My eyes began to lower as soon as I finished eating. I wiped the grease on my pants and walked over to the nearest cave wall, just close enough to feel the fire's warmth.

I sat my heavy pack against the wall, lay down on it, crossed my legs, put my hands behind my head, and closed my eyes. Someone shuffled near me right when I thought I was falling asleep.

"We only did as Makai asked," Aliyah said.

"I know. I'm not mad anymore."

"Good."

"Where's Zion?"

"Already asleep."

"Good. Good night. Or good morning. I don't know what time it is in here."

"Yeah."

I thought about what Aliyah and Zion had said, about

how they wanted to protect their families, too. I had Grandma. But I had them, too. And friends could be as good as family. I knew I needed them if I was going to fight Amina and save the world. We would do it together.

CHAPTER EIGHTEEN

I opened my eyes; the cave wall in front of me had disappeared. Cool air rushed in. I shivered and looked for the fire; it had been snuffed out.

"Zion? Aliyah?" I groaned as I rubbed my eyes. There was no response.

I heard water rushing and wings fluttering. "You guys? Stop playing around!" There was still no response from either of them. They were gone.

My heart raced as I sat up. The rushing water became loud when I stood. I put on my pack and gripped my sword, then laced up my Chucks, closing my eyes, taking deep breaths to center myself. I walked slowly out of the cave. As soon as my shoes touched the ground, the cave disappeared behind me, leaving me a small stretch of sand to stand on.

A lake surrounded me, large and all-encompassing. If I moved an inch, I would fall in. It was the color of the night sky. Small droplets rained down onto my skin, and fog lowered around me. I closed my eyes, willing my heart to still. *This is just a test, Cameron. This is not real.*

But when I opened my eyes, this place was very much real. And cold. And menacing.

Something spoke to me.

It was a soft but powerful sound, as if it could break me on command. *You must look at me.*

The words were quiet, but they commanded me to look, like a knife digging through my mind, fishing in my memories, seeking my deepest secrets. I clamped down on the feeling, but I knew I was too late. Everything was laid bare before I was able to push the speaker out of my thoughts.

I knew who it was before I lifted my eyes to the floating figure in the center of the deep, dark lake. The pages of the *Book* flipped in my mind. It was Nsi, the god of divination and prophecy, the one who could read minds. I stared at the god, covered in white light. When he moved over the water, I didn't feel the penetrating impact of his power anymore. It all made sense now; the Cave of Shadows was his domain, the place where all secrets were relinquished.

Welcome to my temple, Nsi said. His mouth didn't move, but I could hear him in my thoughts. He wore a long, flowing ivory kaftan, embroidered with rubies. Gold bangles covered his arms, and his hair rolled down his back in waves of green, red, and brown. His dark skin was smooth, in sharp contrast to the flowing water beneath him.

"Thank you," I responded. What else do you say to a god? Do you bow? Do you tremble?

Nsi laughed, but not aloud. His voice rolled through me like a storm, almost like Daddy's. *Everyone is on equal footing here. You came to my domain for a reason. I do not know what that reason is, but I've read your mind. I know there are things that trouble you.*

I snorted. "Understatement of the year."

Nsi floated closer to me, so close that the light from his eyes almost blinded me. He pointed toward the lake, and it began to churn and swirl below him until a whirlpool formed. I sniffed the air and could smell Grandma's peppermints. I took a step back, but I knew there was nowhere to go but forward.

Pass the test, Nsi said. He floated upward as the water churned and swirled faster. I took a tentative step forward. The lake contracted and split into two with a thunderous clap. My clothes fluttered as the wind whirled around me. Rickety wooden steps appeared in the separation and led down into a black void. My heart began to beat so hard, I thought my chest would explode.

Face your fear, I repeated to myself. I took another cautious step forward, then stopped. I glanced at the flying Nsi. "Where are Zion and Aliyah? Can they come with me? Please?"

Nsi refused to answer. He just continued to float above the lake.

I glared at him. "Some help you are."

I clenched my pack tighter, stepped on the stairs, and began to climb down. The water roared on either side of me as I continued down the steps into the black void. I chanced a glance to my rear, but the water obscured my view.

"Here goes nothing," I muttered as I jumped off the steps, the water falling back into place behind me.

CHAPTER NINETEEN

I thought the water would smash into me, but when I opened my eyes, I stood in a white room. Well, "room" wasn't exactly what I would call it. It was more a space where nothing existed except me. I wasn't even standing on a floor; it felt like I was walking on air.

My feet were bare, my pack was gone, and I was wearing a billowy emerald kaftan. *How am I supposed to learn if I have no weapons?* I rolled my eyes. I was going to seriously hurt Makai when I left this place.

I stepped forward because that was the only thing I knew to do, but there was nothing except whiteness, a blank canvas. I kept walking until my feet began to tire. As soon as my mind registered the pain in my legs, it was gone, the exhaustion replaced with renewed energy. Was this some type of endless void? Was this supposed to teach me patience? Or was this a punishment that only I had to go through?

Give me something. I stopped in my tracks as a shadow moved to my left. I thought it was a trick of the eye, but then it moved again. I heard distant sounds, like an object was crashing onto hard ground. I turned to my left to see a scene, blurry at first and then expanding as it came into focus. It was almost like a picture hanging on a wall, a picture of a wooded area and clearing. My stomach seized as I recognized the place.

I didn't want to go there.

You don't have a choice, Nsi said to me. *Everyone must see.*

I closed my eyes and willed the scene in front of me to leave, but the crashing and grunting sounds only grew louder. I took a deep breath, opened my eyes, and stepped up to the animated painting-like structure.

I gripped the edge of the image and pulled myself up with all my strength, then crawled into it and plopped down on the ground, my kaftan covered in dirt. I stood shakily and walked forward through the maze of trees to where I heard the noise growing. I came to the clearing but hid behind a jackalberry tree.

The sound of a gurgling stream drew my attention past the clearing. A figure was draped on the ground, one of its boots on the grass while the other sank into the water.

I began to walk toward the figure when something hit the tree I was standing behind. Whoever it was stood and picked up a sword. I walked around the tree to get a better look and gasped. It was Mama; she hadn't changed at all. It was uncanny how much we looked alike—we had the same dark skin, dark eyes, and the set mouth that always seemed to be determinedly fixed in a straight line. Her hair was braided, growing past her shoulders in the time since she had left me.

The expression on her face was serious; this woman was a warrior.

"Mama?" I managed to say before I felt the tears stream down my face. *What is this? Is someone playing a trick?* This wasn't like the visions the *Book* had given me.

She was *real.*

She didn't respond to my question. I said it again. She looked at me and tore her sword from her side, then threw it right at me, and I gasped. The sword flew through me like a blast of air, and I felt nothing. I looked down in shock but was brought back when Mama ran in my direction. She ran so fast that I didn't have a chance to move. She rushed through me as if I were a shadow.

Shouts came from behind me. I jumped behind the tree again, understanding that I was looking at the past, looking at my mama fighting in Chidani. Terror grew in my chest at what I knew was coming, but I couldn't tear my eyes away. The clearing swarmed with mmo, some of them materializing from smoke and some of them falling from the trees. I glanced at my side. *Where is my sword?* I needed to help Mama, to keep her alive. If I could do that now, maybe she would come home.

Mama picked up her sword and began to move, so fast that I could barely see her. She was an amazing fighter, much better than I was. The mmo crowded around her, and she destroyed them as if they were mere nuisances. She twirled her sword like an extension of herself, as if it belonged to her, then cut them down in complicated arcs, so quickly that they died as soon as they materialized.

One of them kicked her from behind, and I started forward. I picked up a fallen branch and tried to jump into the fight to help her, but every time I struck out, my makeshift weapon turned to black smoke. I stumbled back and continued to watch. I felt helpless, unable to do anything to affect the past.

"No, I can't see this," I mumbled as I turned to flee. An invisible barrier stopped me from leaving the clearing. I was forced to look at the fight. Two of the mmo tripped Mama up, and she fell to the ground, crying out. They climbed on top of her, beating and scratching her with long nails. One of them wrenched her sword from her hand and threw it to the dirt.

"Mama!" I yelled, but to no avail. She couldn't hear me; she never would again.

Mama rolled to the side, kicking as she did. She moved again and struggled to her feet. She used her fists now as her weapon, moving so fast that wind kicked up in the clearing. By the time she had grabbed her sword again, they had all died. Two more materialized in shadow, and she fought them. I heard a noise behind me, pulling my attention away from the fight.

An explosion sounded, like something had ripped open the sky. A red light almost blinded me as I looked upward.

Someone, shrouded in shadows, was descending from the sky. The figure dropped to the ground, its boots digging in the dry dirt. It unsheathed a long sword and calmly walked toward Mama, who had cut down the last mmo.

Mama stared at the figure with pure hatred. "Amina, you won't *ever* get the *Book*!"

I gasped, and my heart raced faster as Amina took off the hood of her agbada. She looked just like Ramala, but where the queen's eyes were kind, Amina's were full of hatred. She walked tall and sure, as if she had all the time in the world. Her hair flowed down her back, corded into a long braid, like a striking snake.

A sly smile bloomed across her face. "I'm stronger than you. I'll have the *Book*. And then I'll take over *both* worlds."

"Never," Mama spat.

They began to fight, clashing against each other. The dirt moved so fast that I could barely see.

"Help me," someone said. I jerked my eyes to the creek past Amina and Mama, to the figure lying on the grass. The voice was familiar; it was like rain on a dry plain.

"Daddy?" I croaked. I ignored Mama and Amina's fight as I walked over to the creek, trying my hardest not to turn around and run again. I had to face this; I had to see this. There he was, almost fully submerged in the water. His hands clutched at the wound in his chest, right where his heart was. His sword lay on the wet sand in front of him.

I reached out to touch his face, praying that I would be

able to. But my hands passed through him. I couldn't even touch or hug my parents one last time. Anger built in me. The light in Daddy's eyes began to dim, and I tried to force myself to look away, but I couldn't. A large object fell next to me. The sounds of the fighting faded until I could hear nothing but boots sloshing through the mud. I looked down.

It was the *Book*, shining in golden light. I didn't even turn around. I knew what had happened. Mama was no longer alive, the *Book* no longer a part of her. I stilled my breathing and felt the anger leaching from me, replaced by determination. My heartbeat returned to normal, as did my breathing. I felt for the music of the air, just as Makai had taught me. It was a haunting music, as if even nature knew that evil lived here.

"As I said, I will have the *Book*."

When I thrust my hand forward, it was immediately swirled in shadows. My sword appeared there; I wasn't even surprised. My kaftan drifted away in the wind to be replaced by my soldier's clothes. I stood and, with all my strength, thrust the sword at the approaching Amina.

The image shattered as my sword connected with her chest. I could see nothing but shards, as if the vision in front of me were a mirror. I stumbled forward as the shards pierced me, although I felt no pain. The shards turned to shadows, swirling around me in a vortex, blowing against me so hard that I thought I would fly away.

A figure kneeled in front of me, shaking violently.

It was Zion; his shoulders shook from the force of his cries.

I stood and faced him, wiping his tears away. He refused to look at me as the tears continued to fall.

"It's over now," I said, helping him to his feet and wrapping him in my arms as the winds blew around us.

I hoped I was right.

Aliyah was waiting for us when we returned. After the swirling shadows dissipated, we stood at the opening to the cave, the lake flowing behind us. I didn't know what to say. I stumbled over to my corner and turned my back to them. I couldn't stop the tears from falling. There was relief there, too; at least I had been able to see my parents one last time. I wondered if Mama had even known that the mmo had killed Daddy before she ultimately lost her life, too.

I guess it didn't matter; wherever they were, they had each other.

I wished my sword could have killed Amina for what she had done, but I knew it was just a vision to teach me that the past was the past, the future my destiny. And I couldn't meet my destiny if I was weak, if I was holding back from what I needed to do. Someone sat next to me as the tears continued to fall.

"What did you see?" Aliyah asked.

"Nsi," I said, although I knew she wasn't referring to just him. "There was a lake and rickety stairs. And then there was a vision."

She handed me cloth from her pack. "Use this."

I wiped my eyes. As the tears dried, so did the confused emotions.

"You don't have to tell me what you saw," she said. "It must have been . . . powerful."

"Did you pass the test?" I whispered.

She nodded. "I . . . I don't think I liked this one, though."

We joined Zion at the roaring fire. The three of us ate in silence and watched the now placid lake. Zion seemed to be trying his hardest not to look at me, but he had passed his test, too.

After we had eaten our fill, I went to the lake. I pictured my daddy at the creek, submerged in water as the light drifted from his eyes. I was glad that I hadn't seen him or Mama actually die; I had seen them doing their duty to protect the world.

After washing, I rested on my heavy pack along the edge of the lake. I closed my eyes, forcing myself to find sleep.

When we woke up the next morning, the cave had unsealed, and Kali waited outside for us. His gaze was somber.

"Your training is over," he announced.

CHAPTER TWENTY

When we returned from the Cave of Shadows, Agbala brought us small flasks of the iridescent light from the aziza. It was all that was left after they returned to the Crystal City. She said they would heal us if we were hurt on our journey to find the gifts.

"You're also the Descendant of the *Book*, Cameron. You have a connection with the other gods and me. If you need me, you can always call me. My brother Ekwensu is a powerful god; his strength comes from the souls of the dead. But death is also his weakness. He cannot come into the land of the living because of the punishment my father gave him centuries ago. That is why he needs Amina to help him control the world."

The night before our trip to the Isle of Onitsha to search for Ramala's crown, Zion stumbled into the spacious bed we shared after his bath. "I don't think I'll ever be able to get used to the spells of the pool."

"New world, new rules," I said, but by the time the words had left my mouth, Zion was asleep. I picked up a pillow and hit him in the face with it, but I knew nothing could wake up Zion. As he slept, one of his hands reached out and curled around mine. I tensed at the feeling before gently letting his hand go.

I wrapped one of the sheets around my body before opening the door to our suite. I tiptoed across our sitting room and knocked on Aliyah's door. "Hey, it's me."

After a short while, she appeared, still in her clothes from our final training day in the sandpits. She sat down in a chair close to her window and looked outside.

"Are you thinking about home?" I asked.

She shook her head. "No. I don't want to go home. Not yet. I'm scared, but we've learned how to protect ourselves, something I could never do where we come from."

I sat on the satin sheets of her bed. I didn't say anything.

"Zion will be okay," Aliyah said.

"What does he have to do with anything?"

She turned from the window to stare at me, not saying anything at first. "You want to protect him. He took a couple of hits, but he learned Dambe. He's awkward and sleepy and argumentative and combative and scary, but he's just as sweet, caring, and courageous as you are."

"Do you think anything will change when we return home?" I asked.

"Between you and him? Or just in general?"

"Just in general," I lied.

"I think Zion loves you and always has," Aliyah said, catching on to my lie. "I love you, too, but what you guys share is something deep. Zion filled the void of your parents dying. He means something to you that I'll never mean. I think things may change, but not for the bad."

"I just don't want to lose him. I'd never forgive myself if something bad happened."

"Zion is strong. Nothing will happen to him. You've seen him fight—he's a master."

"But I—"

"Cam," Aliyah said, looking at me intently. "You'll *never* lose Zion."

"I wonder if anything else will change. Like, will we be able to fight when we go back home? Will we still be able to use Dambe?" I asked, changing the subject.

"I don't know," Aliyah said.

I didn't know, either. A part of me wanted to go home and find out, but my parents' sacrifice stilled me. It had been important to them to save the world; that meant their legacy was now mine, and I was comfortable with that.

"Halifa and Bakari will be traveling with us tomorrow," I said.

She turned from me and peered out her window. She opened its latch and stuck out her head. I came over, and we both saw our gryphons fly past. "They'll be coming with us, too," I said.

"Good, I'm glad. It seems like we'll need them."

CHAPTER TWENTY-ONE

The Igbo mountain range spread around us on both sides as we traveled away from Asaba on the backs of our gryphons.

Flying Ugo was like a dream, especially since he had belonged to Mama. His wingspan almost matched the width of Grandma's house. Every time I wanted Ugo to go faster, or slow down, or veer to the right or left, all it took was a single thought. I couldn't do that with the gryphons who had saved us our first day in Chidani. No, *claiming* a gryphon felt totally different.

Every time I touched Ugo, light flowed from my hands, connecting with him in ways that seemed alien to me. Makai had reminded us of what Kali said—after I had forgiven him, of course—that the relationship between a gryphon and its rider was the closest thing anyone could have.

Connecting with Ugo almost felt like . . . love. The magic in me attached to Ugo's, and Mama appeared in my mind, granting me access to her own relationship with the gryphon. It was even more of an emotional feeling, too, because the *Book* gave me visions, even when I wasn't expecting it. I began to recognize the warm sensation that washed over me, right before an image came to my mind.

"Lonnie, don't get too close to the rocks!" The scene in front of me disappeared as I repeated Mama's words. I could see them both, Mama and Daddy, flying close to the Palacia. She swooped low on Ugo's back, and edged him closer to Daddy's gryphon. Either he ignored Mama or he hadn't heard her, but he tried to do a complicated trick with the gryphon, flipping backward in the sky over and over. With a screech, his gryphon threw him off. Daddy screamed as he tumbled toward the ground.

"Lonnie!" Mama called, her eyes a blaze of fury as she urged Ugo downward, following as Daddy fell from an impossible height. Ugo caught him with his large talons, destroying his armor. Mama reached out, leaning over so far that I thought she would fall, too. But her feet caught on Ugo's straps as she leaned.

"Grab my hands!" she screamed. Daddy climbed Ugo's talons, jumped with all his strength, and grasped Mama's hands. She pulled him up, grunting the entire time. When he was safely secured behind her, she gently pushed him.

"I told you...no tricks!" she yelled.

"I had to," Daddy said, a smile brightening his face,

although fear glinted in his eyes. "It's not every day you get to own a gryphon."

The vision disappeared, leaving me wishing for more. It was great to see them together, living out the same life I was now living. They truly were living through me now, because of the *Book* and Ugo. I wondered if Agbala even knew all the magic she had given the *Book*.

For a time, we continued to fly high above the Noble Road. On one side, a huge expanse of water stretched as far as I could see. Where the water and sky met was darkness. I had a suspicion that I was staring at the Atlantic Ocean, the body of water that had led the captured slaves to America so long ago. On the other side was a line of trees. I shivered at the thought of the Supernatural Forest, but I remembered that the forest sat to the south of Asaba, far away from where we were now.

Bonding with a gryphon also allowed its rider to communicate telepathically with those traveling together, which came in handy as we soared through the sky at top speed. *Reports came in from our scouts that the crown passed through Onitsha not too long ago*, Halifa was saying from her gryphon at least a mile ahead of us. *We don't know how reputable those reports are, but villagers have said they've gotten glimpses of it in the waters of the Isle of Onitsha. A child lost her life trying to dive for it. They don't know Ramala is weakened, but everyone knows what the crown looks like.*

Makai, flying below Halifa, veered to the right, and we

followed. *We will travel through Sanaga Forest until night comes. Then we will rest. After that, we will continue on to Onitsha.*

The sun was still shining in the sky, its light filtering through the green leaves of the trees. Ugo screeched as we flew over the forest, and I reached out to pat the side of his head, realizing that I *had* changed. I was becoming part of this place. My armor fit me in ways my regular clothes never had, my arms were strong and slowly becoming corded with small muscles, and my senses were keener. Mama and Daddy had learned how to save an entire world, and now I was stepping into their place.

Although I was proud, I also wished my parents could've taught me all this. I wished my grandma hadn't been so broken after they died.

By the time darkness came, I was so tired that I thought I would fall from Ugo. Likely sensing me sway in my saddle, Makai found a clearing and halted us all with a whistle, and we alighted on the forest floor. I gave Ugo a small pat on the side of his face; he gurgled in pleasure, closing his eyes. After a while of scratching, Ugo lifted up into the air and flew away with the others, looking for food.

Makai and Halifa pitched a few tents on the forest floor, securing them with nearby stones. When we went inside ours, Zion fell asleep almost immediately. I placed our packs on the floor so that we could have somewhere to rest our heads. By the time I was done, I smelled fire. I was just about to wake Zion, but overhearing Makai speaking, I stopped.

"I keep forgetting how young they are. Are they *too* young to handle this mission? Do you think Nsi helped them?"

The deep timbre of Bakari's voice reached me now. "Nsi doesn't let anyone go until they learn their lesson. And by 'they' you really mean Cameron. He's ready, Makai. The Cave of Shadows saw to that."

I heard grunts as something heavy was moved across the forest floor. There were more sounds, and then the smell of roasting meat tickled my nose.

"I'm not so sure."

"Didn't Zion and Aliyah do well during Dambe practice? I think you are giving them less credit than they deserve. Cameron is of my bloodline; I knew he would eventually get it. I say they are ready. And if they aren't, they will be ready by the time they face Amina. Well, by the time Cameron faces her."

I watched Zion sleep for a bit longer. Makai was right; we were just kids. My parents had died here, but I'd never forgive myself if I didn't at least try. However, I had dragged Zion and Aliyah with me. They didn't deserve this responsibility.

Reaching out, I shook Zion—not too hard but hard enough. "Wake up. It's time for dinner."

He turned over and ignored me. I hit him a bit harder, and he yelped.

"Next time, I'll punch you," I said.

He held up his hands. "Okay, okay, I'm coming."

I helped him to his feet as we walked outside to where

Makai and Bakari stood in front of a blazing fire. A deer was being roasted on a spit. Halifa reached out and turned the handle.

"We eat first; then we rest," Halifa said.

When the deer was done, the fire and the azizan light emanating from our packs provided the only illumination.

Bakari passed plates around while Makai cut the dripping meat from the firepit and gave each of us a large piece. Halifa pulled out raw cucumbers, cut them up with a knife, added salt, and passed them. After everyone had been served, we all scooted closer to the fire and began to eat. The mosquitoes and flies had come out, but the fire's smoke drove them away.

The meat was well cooked, juicy, and filling. Makai disappeared after a while and then appeared with flasks filled with water.

"There's a freshwater stream just a few feet away. Here," he said, passing out the flasks.

After he sat down, I drank. "What does Onitsha look like?" I asked, but the pages of the *Book* began to rustle in my mind as I spoke. They answered my question—but I wanted Zion and Aliyah to hear, too.

Halifa's eyes took on a bit of wonder as she remembered. "I went to Asaba when I was eleven years old, so I don't know how much has changed, but when I was there, it was like the beauty of summer had blessed the place eternally."

We all inched closer as she spoke.

"The Onitsha are the ocean clan, so we pray to Idemmili,

the Igbo goddess of waters, Agbala's sister. It wasn't until Amina took the three gifts that Idemmili appeared to the people who prayed to her. Some say she rushes across the water close to shore, and some say they can feel her hands guide them through the water as they swim. I am the only child born to my father, Chake, the Onitsha chief. I was supposed to take over his role when he died, so I spent my time learning Dambe, hunting in the woods with the boys, and eating. Too much eating.

"In Onitsha, the mangoes are sweet, the water is constantly warm, and the markets are crowded with trade. Merchants travel through bustling cities and treacherous forests to visit the simplicity of Onitsha. We never had much, but the fruit grown in our village is flavorful, the air is clean, and the wagons overflow with produce. When the children are done helping with harvesting and trading, they run toward the ocean and build makeshift boats to fish in its depths and boards to surf through its waves. Then they send a prayer to Idemmili and return home. At night, we used to eat plates of goat and deer meat, jollof rice, beans and gravy, with juicy fruit for dessert, all in front of roaring fires while Ramala's azizan gifts settled in the trees. Even as we ate, the wind would carry the sweet scent of grass. Papa would open the partitions on our windows so that the smell could spread through the room and cool us down after long days. Then we would send one more prayer to the ocean goddess and prepare for bed, to repeat our activities the next day."

Her eyes closed as she remembered. I felt the pages flip in my mind as the images materialized there, embellished in gold.

"Sometimes," Halifa continued, "soldiers would come to our small village. One such visitor was from Asaba. He spoke to my father when he entered his hut. Chake yelled at me to go away as the man spoke, but I hid in my bedroom and listened to everything the man said. He claimed that he was a soldier sent on a mission to gather up other young boys to serve the queen. My father scoffed and told him that I was the one he really wanted, that the boys in my village were nothing compared to me."

She opened her eyes and smiled. "And he was right. I had been preparing to succeed Papa as chief, so the boys could never beat me in a footrace. I learned Dambe quicker than they did, like a gazelle jumping so fast that the only thing they could see was dust gathering around my skirts. By the time the man had reached the door, I had gathered my meager possessions. I came straight to Asaba, and that's how I became a soldier. That man was Makai."

"Chake was right. Halifa is my best warrior."

We all sat marveling at Halifa's words. Zion and I had seen pictures of Onitsha in the *Book*, but now we would really see it.

After we finished eating, I stood close to the fire as Aliyah whispered with Halifa near the edge of the clearing. Halifa was pointing to different places. "When I became a solider and trained across the country, Makai taught me that it was best to always bury provisions. So I did. You never know when you'll need help or get separated from your regiment. I also use this marking to find them again . . ."

A hand pressed against my shoulder, interrupting my eavesdropping. "You can use the stream to freshen up."

Makai led Zion and me to the stream. Bending down, we washed our plates and refilled our flasks with water. I pulled off my dashiki and waded until my feet no longer touched the bottom. After a while, all sound drifted away.

"How does it feel? You know, being the Descendant?" Zion asked, swimming toward me and flipping to his back.

"Right now, it feels . . . like I'm just a young boy filled with words, information, and pictures. When Agbala pushed the *Book* into my chest, it was a pain I had never felt before. But now it's a part of me. I would think separating from it would be even more painful. But even though I feel as if I *know* everything, what if I can't actually *use* this knowledge to defeat Amina?"

"But you can use that knowledge. I know you can."

A sense of peace settled in my heart. He and Aliyah had always believed in me, to the point that I had no choice but to believe in myself.

We floated for a little while longer before Zion spoke again. "We've come a long way from Grandma Ana's house, huh?"

"You know, I didn't think you would take all this so seriously."

He reached out in the space between us, grabbed my hand, and squeezed, just like last night. "I was there with you when your parents died. Of course I'd take it seriously, Cameron."

Thinking of how he had been there for me through everything made me smile.

I squeezed and released his hand, swam back to the shore, and waited for my body to dry off in the hot air. Even though it was night, the temperature hadn't dropped much. Just like the summers in Atlanta. At least this part of the journey reminded me of home.

By the time I dried off and put my clothes back on, Zion had swum back to shore. "I'll see you in the tent," he said. But I didn't want to return just yet. I stayed along the shores of the small creek.

At first, I wanted to call to him, to beg him to stay, but I didn't know what I would say to him if he came back. I couldn't explain what was going on inside me.

"Mama loves you," a voice said.

I stood, turned around, and walked past the trees shrouding the creek. "Mama?" I called.

But there was nothing. I went back to the creek and sat down again. "Mama loves you." I heard it again.

Okay, now I knew I wasn't imagining things. It was my mama's voice, bright and clear. Where was it coming from? At my wordless question, a sharp pain shot through my chest, and I saw a sliver of gold light. I shook my head to clear it. The pain in my chest pounded again, but it was lighter this time, not as agonizing.

"Mama loves you." The voice was louder and much more insistent. As the pain shot through me one final time, I released myself to it, wanting to feel everything. I knew in my bones that it was a memory, something the *Book* was giving me.

As I surrendered to the golden light, it surrounded my body, making me close my eyes. When I opened them, there was nothing but brightness at first, but then I was on the couch at Grandma's house, when I was much younger. Music was playing on the CD player in the living room, and Mama and Grandma were in the kitchen cooking. Like always, they talked in hushed voices, but I was much too young to care what they were saying.

One of the picture books Mama had just bought was on the couch with me, and I was staring at the drawings, smart enough to read the small sentences. One second, I was reading the book, and the next, I was swept off the couch. It was my daddy, gathering me up in his arms, holding my hand in his big calloused one, and circling me around the room. Both of my feet left the floor.

He laughed as I smiled back at him, not understanding what was going on; I was smiling because he was smiling. "Come on, Cameron, dance with me!" he said in that deep voice of his. He released me to the floor, held both my hands, and glided me around the living room, making sure I didn't fall. I followed his movement.

Mama came into the living room, her face flushed from the hot air in the kitchen, a dishrag stuck in the side of her pants, her mouth breaking into a smile.

She watched us for a second before her eyes filled with tears.

"Nina?" my daddy said, gently placing me on the ground, then going to Mama. When he let me go, I cried so loudly that both of them ran to me.

Mama scooped me up into her arms while Daddy turned the music off. "Mama loves you," she said, staring into my eyes. "You know that, right?"

"I do."

She pulled me closer. Then she moved across the room, mimicking the movement of my daddy, even though there was no music playing. In that moment, it was just us, and I felt closer to her than I had ever felt to anyone.

The golden light of my memory disappeared, and the pain in my chest was fierce. I missed my mama and daddy more than anything.

But I also felt ready.

Ready to do what I needed to do to save the world.

CHAPTER TWENTY-TWO

Did Mama know what was going to happen to her and Daddy? Did she know that they would have to leave me?

These were the questions burning in my mind as we soared over Sanaga the next day. I was quiet on Ugo, thinking about the memory the *Book* had shown me. I thought about calling for Agbala, but I stopped short. Did I want anyone to have access to the memories of my mama and daddy?

Zion, flying behind me, must have been able to tell that something was bothering me. *I stayed up a little bit after I left you*, he said telepathically. *You didn't come back until late. Did something happen? Does it have anything to do with what we saw in the Cave of Shadows?*

"I'm fine," I said.

He didn't pester me anymore.

I was sorry for speaking to him that way, but I couldn't put into words what I'd felt last night.

My thoughts were broken when Aliyah spoke to me. *I think we're close to Onitsha*, she said.

Yes, very close. I can feel the djembe drums beating in my blood already, Halifa said. *That's how you know you are in Onitsha. We play the drums once a month as we worship Idemmili. Tonight is one of those nights.*

Straining my ears, I listened for the djembe drums. I could hear them, too, pounding deep in my chest.

Makai signaled and we flew to the ground, in front of a village. He pulled back the cover of trees with his sword and beckoned us forward. We alighted, and the gryphons flew away. We found ourselves on a dirt road leading to a wooden gate.

As we walked closer, the music grew louder, waking me up from my deep thoughts.

Zion whispered in my ear. "Look, there are soldiers."

As if he could hear Zion's hushed tones, Makai pulled out his sword, too, and Halifa followed. Bakari whispered, "We don't know if these soldiers are loyal to Ramala or to her sister. We've heard reports of guards joining Amina."

Waving his arm behind us to stop, Makai traveled the rest of the distance alone. We waited behind him, and my hand went to my sword, but Zion stopped me with a soft pat. "Not yet. They might be good."

After a short while talking to the soldiers guarding the gate, Makai came back to us as the wooden gate was pushed open. I sighed in relief. We followed Makai through Onitsha's entrance, the music inviting us in.

We could see nothing at first besides a barn standing to the right. I rolled my shoulders to ease the tightness in my muscles as Makai continued to speak with the soldiers.

A burst of color moved toward us through the darkness. "Halifa!" the figure said.

"Papa!" she cried.

"What are you doing here? I got the message that soldiers would be traveling through, but I hadn't a clue you would be with them. My gods, look at you—a true soldier."

Tears fell from Halifa's face as she looked at the old man, the chief of Onitsha, Chake. He looked as the *Book* had rendered him: tall, majestic, lined with wrinkles, gray hair peppering the crown of his head and his beard.

"I would never miss a trip to Onitsha, even in these perilous times," she responded.

Chake, draped in a long, flowing white agbada with gold bracelets and tattoos adorning his arms, looked us over. His smile was replaced with a frown as his eyes flitted to me. "Yes, these *are* perilous times. We must talk in private."

We followed him past the barn, through another set of trees, until we came to a series of huts built into a circle. We passed by them until we arrived at a center dwelling built higher than the others. Here, the music was louder, and I caught a glimpse of fire, but Chake ushered us inside his home before closing the flap behind him. Bakari stood outside as a lookout.

We sat around a small table, and Chake produced goblets. His eyes flashed cerulean as he prayed to Idemmili. "Thank you, goddess, for always being there in our time of need." Once he was done, his fingers glowed blue, and water appeared in our cups.

"The current chief of Onitsha gains a portion of Idemmili's powers whenever the previous one dies," Halifa whispered to us.

Chake waited until we all took sips of our water before speaking. "If you're here, that means the rumors are true— that all three gifts were stolen from Ramala."

"She never thought Amina would steal from her," Makai responded.

The chief drew back. "Amina did this? Are you sure?"

"We are sure, Chake," I said, not certain if I had broken protocol by speaking. I gestured to Zion and Aliyah, who both looked terrified. "When my friends and I came here, the mmo attacked us. Ramala told me that Amina is able to control them because of her association with the death god, Ekwensu."

Chake let out a cry as he stood and paced the room.

"Wait," he said, turning to me again. "You say you 'came here'?"

"He means that we came through the barrier," Aliyah responded.

He closed his eyes and sat down again. "Then you need the gifts back to fight her. I have caught glimpses of the crown in the waters. Because Idemmili can't directly interfere in human matters, Amina was smart enough to place it in the ocean. If so, there are powerful dark forms of magic surrounding it. There's no way you can get to it if she has aligned herself with Ekwensu."

"We can now that we have the Descendant of the *Book* with us," Makai said.

"Ahh." Chake's eyes found mine once again. "I knew I could sense magic when I saw you come through the gate."

Leaning forward, he grasped my chin and inspected my face. "You may dive into the ocean to find the crown, but it will be dangerous. First, though, we must pray to our goddess."

We were able to see where the drumbeats were coming from as we approached the shoreline of Onitsha. We passed through many circles of huts before we reached the worship celebration on the beach.

At the sight of the chief, the people of Onitsha, who were sitting in multiple circles around a huge bonfire, whooped and yelled into the sky. Chake raised his arms, and the wind picked up. The moon's light was even brighter out here, and it shone on the villagers' faces. The circle closest to the bonfire was smaller, but it became larger as more people joined in. We found a spot in the middle, where we grasped hands with other villagers.

Teenage boys and girls stood in the center of the concentric circles and beat the djembe drums faster and faster as Chake stood tall right before the bonfire, facing the people. Other villagers stood by the drums, swaying and dancing to the beat of the djembe, stamping their feet on the ground, kicking up sand, and moving their arms as they marched. Their braided hair flew through the wind as it roared.

"There's magic here," Aliyah whispered as she gripped my hand even tighter.

"Yes, there is." I could feel the magic become heavy around the fire. I rocked back and forth, left and right, alongside the other villagers. My eyes drifted downward and closed, but I forced them open. Zion, with eyes wide open, swayed in the wind just like the rest of us. I gazed at him, noticing how his bright eyes shone emerald in the moonlight and how the wind rippled his clothes.

"We are gathered to celebrate Idemmili, whose waters provide us with sustenance," Chake said, his voice carrying to where we were sitting.

The villagers yelled again as he finished his words. "Idemmili! Idemmili!" they cried.

I waited to hear from him again, but that was the last time he spoke. He turned around, his kaftan flying in the wind, and we swayed again as the magic became heavier and the wind blew against our backs. As Chake turned and turned, a blue light shone above his head, causing everyone in the crowd to gasp.

Our eyes followed while the light shifted and turned to match Chake's moves before circling around the villagers' heads and flying toward us.

"Idemmili?" Zion gasped. The circle of light grew larger until a woman stepped forward, covered in cobalt illumination. Her iro swept the ground as she walked. She reminded me of Agbala, but in different ways. Her dress bared one shoulder. She was even taller than her sister, and her crown stretched to the sky. As she walked around the circles, she stopped at certain village people and grasped their faces. Her body dripped water droplets that shone like crystals.

By the time she reached us, some of the villagers had fainted to the ground, while others had started crying. Chake continued to spin around in a circle, faster and faster. When Idemmili reached us, the air was so heavy, I thought I would faint. She stood in front of Zion, caressing his face. He released a squeak of fear.

"No need to be scared, little one," she said, stroking his cheek with her long, dark fingers. It was the first time she had stopped to talk to anyone. Even though she spoke softly, her words were powerful. "You've seen me before, haven't you?"

He nodded, looking too scared to say anything.

"I could see you marveling at my drawings in the *Book* even in your own world. There's a brave warrior inside you.

You will help to usher in an era of new freedom to Chidani. Help me do that and you will be rewarded."

He opened his mouth, and another squeak came forth.

She turned her gaze to me but kept her hands on Zion's face. "The *Book* has returned. Finally." Lines appeared around her mouth as she frowned. "I will see you again soon."

She swept her hand in Chake's direction. The blue light flew from him and enveloped her body again. Then she disappeared.

When she was gone, everyone was quiet. I sat in the sand, humbled by her presence but confused by her final words. Chake spun one last time, and when he was done, the heaviness lifted from my chest.

We said nothing as Chake stood perfectly still in front of the roaring fire. I chanced a glance at Zion, hoping he had something to say, but he was speechless. I reached out and gripped his hand, but he did not grip mine back. He was far, far away.

I waited for Chake to say something, but he didn't. Halifa took her father by the arms as he slumped forward with exhaustion and led him back to the tall hut we had just come from.

Once he was gone, the drums sounded again. The villagers stood up and began to dance and sway around the fire, holding one another's hands as they moved. I pulled Aliyah and Zion back under the cover of some trees close to a small hut.

"Tell me you saw that!" Zion said, his voice rising, words coming out of his mouth like lava, spilling over the area faster and faster.

"Of course we saw that. We both were there. Right, Cam?"

My gaze had fallen to my chest, right where Agbala had pushed the *Book*. Even now, I felt information squirming inside me. "Yes," I said, raising my head to Zion and Aliyah. "I had no idea being around a god could be that beautiful. Why . . . why did she say that to me?"

"No clue," Aliyah said. "Also, why is she not like her sister? Agbala seems . . . human—at least sometimes she does. Idemmili doesn't."

"Well, the *Book* says it's because she's spent most of her life in the ocean," Zion pointed out. "The human world would look different to us than it would to her. Agbala appears as a human because she is around the queen and the other nobles more than she is not. Right?"

"Yes," I said, remembering now.

"Hmm, I don't know," Aliyah said. "I think there's another explanation. We might need to ask Agbala."

"What about the crown?" Zion asked. "Why couldn't she do anything about it? Why couldn't she bring the crown back to Ramala herself? Or her sister?"

"She can't directly interfere," I said. "Remember what Agbala said."

"That sounds like a good explanation," Makai said, walking up to us with a plate of food in his hands. "I was wondering where you three had gone. Let's eat. After, we will take a boat to the Isle of Onitsha."

We walked behind him now, our conversation cut short. I couldn't wait to get them alone again. Once we got back to the circles, plates of food were given to us, filled with many different types of foods. There was jollof rice seasoned with palm oil and shrimp and fried yams and beans. There was roasted deer, antelope, and chicken and goblets of fresh water.

We ate silently, sitting on the sand, enjoying our first meal since the forest the day before. Aliyah whispered to us as the villagers danced and ate around us. "So back to the crown. How are we supposed to find it once we get to the isle?"

"Don't know," Zion said, his mouth full of meat.

"Close your mouth when you eat," I said, making gagging noises. "You know I hate when you do that."

He kept chewing with his mouth open. "Like I said, I don't know. Maybe it will just . . . appear to us?"

"I doubt that," I said.

Aliyah put her wooden spoon down on her plate and took a sip of water. "What about Cameron? If you're the Descendant, you should be able to sense it some way, right?"

"Maybe," I said. "But Idemmili spoke to Zion!"

Zion pointed a drumstick my way. "But Agbala spoke to you first."

I put my plate on the ground and made my way back to the line of huts, annoyed with it all. I felt this new power, but without any real understanding of how I was supposed to actually *accomplish* any of this. I was growing tired of these gods' riddles.

I again doubted myself, doubted the idea that I could save everyone. The entire fate of both worlds felt like it was on my shoulders.

That's because it is. The Book *belongs to you. Not them.*

I knew who the voice belonged to the moment it came. "Agbala, why does it have to be me? Why can't they help me?"

Cameron, if they weren't meant to help you, do you think the Book *would have brought them to Chidani? If I thought they couldn't help you, I would never have allowed them to practice Dambe. You need your friends. But ultimately it is you who will save the people.*

I sat on the ground right outside an empty hut and slammed my fist into the sand. "But how can they help me if they have no power? You say I have magic because of the *Book*, but all I get are visions."

The goddess's voice did not come for a while, as if she was thinking about my question. *I made the* Book, *which means you have a sliver of my own power. It comes differently to each Descendant, and I do not yet know what yours is. But it will come to you.*

When she was done speaking, her consciousness left mine, and I found myself feeling lonely. I pushed against her leaving, urging her to stay and talk to me, to show me what it was I needed to do, but she was gone. Just like how Mama and Daddy left me, much too early and too fast.

I settled on the sand and tried not to let the tears fall, but they came anyway. This entire time, I had been hoping I could keep it all together, but not now, when so many people depended on me to save them. According to Agbala, Aliyah and Zion were supposed to be here to help me. But what could they do? What if they died in the pursuit of a mission that was supposed to be about me?

Someone walked through the sand and sat down next to me. I hurried to dry my eyes.

"It's okay. We are encouraged to show our emotions here. Is that not how it is in your world?" Bakari said.

"Absolutely not," I said, still hiding my tears but snorting a bit from laughter. I bet I looked terrible at this point, snorting and crying at the same time, and that made me even more embarrassed.

Bakari lifted my chin. "I've always wondered what it would be like to live in the outside world. I've known the terror and pain of slavery. I've seen family members and friends caught and pushed into the ocean to never be seen again. Is your world still like that, even all these years later?"

I wiped my tears away and looked at Bakari. It was still uncanny how similar we looked. He couldn't have been much older than I was.

"In some ways. But no, chattel slavery was done away with almost two hundred years ago. I can't believe you haven't aged at all since then."

"Like Makai said, time moves differently here. To me, I'm

just a seventeen-year-old boy, who left his family to help the queen fight against the slavers. Once the barrier was made, I stayed in her service."

"How did you get that scar?"

He ran one of his hands over it. "That's the reason I obtained permission from my family to join the army. Slavers almost captured me while on a hunt in the woods with friends. They found us after we downed a deer. My friends were captured and dragged away, but I fought back. The man who captured me died at my hands, but another one whipped me until I fell down. After he hit me in the face with his whip, I found strength I never knew. I broke his neck and was able to flee. But I never saw my friends again. Soon after, everyone in my family, except my mama, was captured, too. I just hope they found some peace. And looking at you, the child I am related to, shows me that they might have."

I hadn't the heart to tell him that millions of the enslaved didn't even make it to the New World, and maybe that was a blessing. I didn't tell him that, once in my world, they were treated with such brutality that many of them wished they had died on the way.

Bakari brushed the sand off his pants and helped me to my feet. Villagers had started to walk back to their huts after the celebration, and the night had taken on the pinkish hue of the morning. "Come," he said. "I *will* protect you as my family. It's time to find the crown. You are ready, Cameron Battle."

CHAPTER TWENTY-THREE

We pushed off in a small boat that carried us toward the Isle of Onitsha. As the night drifted away, the sun began to peek out of the clouds, but it didn't look as it did in our world. It was cut in half from top to bottom, with one side of it shining bright light and warm heat, while the other side was gone, hidden by darkness.

Bakari and Halifa pushed us with heavy oars while I shaded my eyes until a sliver of land could be seen. If I squinted a little bit more, I could see a structure growing from the sand.

"The temple to Idemmili," I whispered. "The villagers believe she had a hand in creating the barrier. So to this day, the only thing on the island is the temple. The villagers travel to it to worship her at times."

"I'm never going to get used to you doing that," Zion said.

It wasn't until midday that we reached the shores of the isle, but we didn't leave the boat. Makai came to stand next to me. "Do you feel anything yet? Is the crown here?"

"I don't feel anything," I said, my face burning.

"Maybe close your eyes?" he said. "Seek what is down in the water."

I did as asked. I didn't expect anything to happen—until it did.

My head started to ache, but it was a dull pounding at first. My mind pushed back against the pain building in my head. Though I could feel my feet on the boat's wooden bottom, my consciousness was no longer there. In front of me, there was the dark blue of the ocean. Black lines appeared next, going back and forth in my vision. They turned to smoke, familiar and haunting to me. I pushed deeper into the image until I saw something glistening and rotating.

The item circled around in the black smoke until it took shape. There was the crown, covered in diamonds, rubies, and emeralds, each point of it stretching upward. It looked as if it weighed a ton. Once the smoke settled, I saw it lying on the floor of a cave. I opened my eyes to everyone staring at me.

I started to take off my dashiki. "I know where it is."

"We have to go with you!" Makai said, pulling at my arms.

"No," I said. "I don't think you can." I dropped my dashiki on the floor and unbuttoned my pants until I stood in my swimming shorts. I placed my sword in the hilt along the side of them. "Dark magic surrounds the crown."

"Amina," Makai whispered and stood back. "I still don't think we can let you go by yourself."

"It's too late for that!" I yelled. "Listen," I said, lowering my voice. "I have to do this alone."

"No, you don't," Zion said, taking off his dashiki as well. "I'm going with you."

"No—" I managed to say before Aliyah shimmied out of her clothes, too, wearing a tight black shirt and shorts.

"Can't make us do anything, Cam. You're not our parent," Aliyah said, smiling at me, but I noticed that nervousness flitted through her eyes.

"No, I'm going alone. I'm not going to say it again."

"Too late," Zion said, grabbing Aliyah's and my hands, hard and fierce. Before I could open my mouth, he toppled over into the deep water, and Aliyah and I crashed after him.

My chest began to glow as soon as we entered the water, and I felt a surge of power. The *Book* stirred inside me, and I let out a howl of pain, but no water entered my mouth to drown me. Red light spread from my chest and into the arms and bodies of Aliyah and Zion on my right and left. It felt as if my chest was going to burst open, like a weight was dragging us through the water at lightning speed, deeper and deeper into the ocean. I closed my eyes against the excruciating pain.

By the time I opened them, our hands had broken apart. We were floating in the water, breathing the water's essence, and very much alive. I narrowed my eyes at Zion but couldn't say anything because I was too busy marveling at the idea of breathing underwater. *How did this happen?*

A vision passed across my mind again. It was Mama! I saw her jumping into the ocean with Daddy and knew exactly what the *Book* was showing me. I smiled at the short memory.

I hate you, Zion, I thought as the vision disappeared.

Zion smiled at me. *And I love you, too. I . . . I didn't think we would travel this far.*

Wait, you can hear me speaking? I thought.

They both nodded.

Looking upward, I expected to see the bottom of the boat, but only water surrounded us.

Aliyah swam closer to me. *Are you sensing the crown?*

I swam around in the blue water, trying to orient myself, but nothing came to me. My only inclination was to dive deeper until something became clear.

Pointing downward, I began to move. We swam for a while, and the water got darker, but I could still see some of the sun's light above us.

I bet Makai is mad right now, I said.

Zion chuckled, but I glared at him, causing him to laugh even harder. *I'm not apologizing.*

Will both of you shut up? Aliyah said. As she spoke, energy built in my chest as something nudged me deep within my soul. I narrowed my eyes against the pain. I almost opened my mouth to groan, but I kept it in, clutching at my chest. I stopped swimming, and Aliyah and Zion treaded next to me. I was now able to put the mysterious pain into words. It was evil, and it was directly below us.

I—I think it's the crown, I stuttered as red light spread around my chest and shoulders. *I-it's right below us.*

Before they could respond, I dove even deeper into the ocean. We swam for what seemed like forever until the water around us was a deep blue, almost black.

A rock formation peppered with a series of underground caves appeared. Holes bored into the rock, making the oblong shape of dwellings. I shuddered at the thought of what could be inside them, but my attention was drawn to a white light shining from one right in the middle.

We swam closer to it as panic built in my chest. I stopped swimming, and Zion and Aliyah did, too. I looked around to see if any evil creatures lingered around the rock formation, but there was nothing. The memory of the black smoke surrounding the gift gave me pause.

Y'all, I'm scared, I admitted.

So am I, Zion said. *But we're here with you. You won't go it alone.*

Using his words as encouragement, I set off toward the rock formation. One side of the structure shot up through the water, but the other side was black and seemed to disappear.

Ow! Aliyah said. She had reached out to the black side of the mountain, then pulled her fingers back. *It's hot, Cameron!*

I think the barrier is here, I said. *Don't touch it again.*

Swimming closer to the cave openings, I found the one with white light shining from it.

So . . . we're supposed to go into the cave? And . . . nothing bad will happen to us? Zion said.

I grunted as pain shot through my chest. *I know the crown is inside.*

None of us moved. After a few minutes, Zion pushed his hand through the light and kept it there. *See, nothing happen—*

His words were cut off as the light grabbed him and he disappeared. For a second, I floated in the water and looked around for him.

Zion, are you playing a joke?

When he didn't appear, I looked to Aliyah, whose eyes were full of terror.

Holding out my hand to Aliyah, I spoke. *We have to go after him.*

She grabbed my hand and closed her eyes. I moved one foot into the light at the opening of the cave. Almost immediately, I tumbled forward, too, pulling Aliyah right along with me. We flipped through the brightness until we crashed onto a hard surface.

We sat in the cave, completely dry. My chest still ached, but now the sharp pain had become dull. I stumbled to my feet and let out harsh breaths while I stood on the wall to the left of the cave opening. Most of the cave was covered in slick rock, but a small part of it was shrouded in black.

"Are y'all okay?" I asked.

"I'm fine," Aliyah said.

"I'm a bit banged up," Zion said.

The only way forward was into the blackness of the cave. "Since you were the one who went into the opening first, shouldn't you lead us?" I said to Zion.

"Nice try," Zion said, cradling the underside of his left arm but pushing me to the front with his right.

I crept forward while Aliyah and Zion followed. As we walked, it seemed the darkness deepened. I stuck out my arms and could feel the rock walls on both sides of us. I felt more in control now that I had something to hold on to.

The white light began to shine again, right in front of us. Even though I was scared, I started to walk faster toward it, sure that the crown was just ahead. I could feel the *Book* inside me stretching to it, as if it were a living, breathing thing. It wanted to be one with the gift. The gods wanted their gift back. *I* wanted the gift back.

We came into another cavern built into the cave. Its ceiling reminded me of the grand rooms in the Palacia.

I stepped forward into a small stream of black liquid that led from the opening of the cavern to a raised dais in the middle of the room.

"Look, Cameron," Aliyah said, pointing toward the platform.

It was made of old, rotten wood, and on top of it was the crown, turning in a circle.

"Queen Ramala's crown," I said. After that, the darkness of the cavern lifted, bringing everything into clear focus. I walked forward with Aliyah and Zion holding on to me. As I did, the pain turned from dull to excruciating. I stumbled, but my friends helped me up.

"It h-hurts," I stammered, trying to gain my footing.

"We can't go back now," Zion whispered. I shook my head and stood straighter, showing that I didn't need to go back. I wanted to run away from the crown, but I knew I had to stay.

Pushing them away, I walked toward the dais, trying to ignore the pain. By now it felt like my skull was cracking in two. But I still continued. I placed both my hands on the dais and grasped the crown. The pain ceased as soon as I touched it.

Screams filled my ears. Black smoke lifted off the dark stream of water. The skin on my arms felt as if it was burning. The crown began to release more black smoke into the cavern.

With a yelp, I dropped the crown, and it went spinning in the darkness. The smoke took form, encircling us. "Mmo!" I screamed as I pulled out my sword and prepared for them to materialize. Once they did, I ran, my mind focused only on the safety of my friends. By the time I crossed the cavern, they both had pulled out their swords. A creature appeared right in front of them, and I arced my sword down in a deadly swipe, killing it instantly.

I stood right next to them, and we all turned to face the rest of the creatures appearing around us. "Dambe," Aliyah whispered, and a second later, she was gone. Zion looked just as scared as I was. My sword shook in my hand, but I managed to grab his arm before the creatures ran toward us.

"Go! Remember your training!" I said, and in a flash, he was gone, too. Three mmo came for me. I fell to the ground and managed to scuttle to the right as one of them bared down on me, its eyes red and its teeth sharp. Trembling, I reached up, but the mmo pushed the sword out of my hand, and it clattered across the floor. All three of them jumped me, slashing at my arms and legs. I pushed out with my elbow into the face of the one closest to my head.

I was able to pull myself up just in time to see the one slashing at my legs disappear in a cloud of smoke. Aliyah stood in its place.

"Concentrate!" she yelled before disappearing again. And I did. Although I hated to close my eyes, I listened for the sound of the water.

This sound was different; it felt deeper and heavier than wind, but it allowed me to move at a breathless pace as Dambe caught me. I opened my eyes and grabbed my sword from the ground, ignoring the pain that racked my body from the slash of mmo nails.

The scene around me slowed as Dambe took over. I could make out at least ten other creatures stalking us inside the cavern, but I could also see the crown glistening on a wall behind the dais. I moved forward and started to slash, bringing down mmo. I turned to see Zion battling four creatures at once.

Three more rushed at me. I fell to the floor and slid underneath their feet, slashing as I went. The mmo fell to the ground. I ran forward again and leaped into the air, feeling as if I were flying. I slammed my legs into their chests; we all tumbled to the ground. Before they could move, I brought my sword down and slashed at their faces; their bodies turned to smoke.

Fingers sliced at my arms as I stood, thrusting me back into real time. A mmo spirit grabbed me by the throat. It lifted me off the floor as I struggled to breathe. With my free hand, I reached around and punched the creature in its back, over and over again, but to no avail.

"Let . . . me . . . go," I said through clenched teeth, but it only squeezed harder until I was no longer able to speak. I looked down and saw the rows of sharp teeth, the red eyes, the slanted nose, the gray skin, and the bald head. In a swift movement, as if the mmo had learned Dambe, it launched me through the air. I flew across the open area and slammed into the opposite wall.

When I stood, the creature disappeared and appeared right in front of me before I could run. Its arm reached up to strike, but my sword blocked the movement. I gritted my teeth as the hand solidified and my weapon glanced off it. I pushed with all my strength against the arm and then kicked its chest, sending it flying to the floor. I stood over the creature as it disappeared again.

Frustrated, I closed my eyes, and when I opened them, I was floating in the air. I stayed there for a bit, then saw the mmo climb the wall and launch itself at me as if in slow motion. I slammed into the ground as the spirit came toward me. Using the magic of Dambe, I thrust my weapon into the air and pushed it into the mmo's chest.

I stumbled forward after killing the last one. The pain reached me now from the scratches and gashes on my body. I looked past the dais and could just make out the crown behind it. I walked to it, too hurt to run. By the time I reached it, Zion and Aliyah had joined me. But I didn't touch it just yet.

"There might be more dark magic," I managed to say.

"I don't know, Cam," Zion responded.

I snapped my fingers, thinking aloud. "But doesn't it seem too easy?"

"No one said the mmo are smart creatures. Most of them *want* to die."

"Hmm, maybe," I said.

"It should be you," Aliyah said. "You should be the one to grab it. And then we can get out of here."

I reached out to the crown but stopped, shaking my head. "No, we all came down here. We all should take it."

Aliyah pushed me forward. "No, no deal."

I reached out to the crown again and grabbed it from the floor. I was turning around to say, "Let's go," when their jubilant faces disappeared. Darkness fell across my vision, and I reeled and stumbled forward, hitting the ground and losing consciousness.

CHAPTER TWENTY-FOUR

"Are you sure about your choice?"

I fell into darkness, monstrous shadows tumbling around me. As my vision cleared, my clothes rippled in the breeze. My feet touched the ground, crunching against gravel and dirt. Harsh, cold wind attacked me, causing me to grip my dashiki close to my chest. I was standing upon a rock outcrop of a large mountain. The moon shone in the sky, so close that it almost scared me.

A throne made of bone appeared in front of me, a shadowy figure seated upon it. Another figure knelt on their knees, their head bowed, a cloak shrouding their face. I looked around the space, hoping to find a door, an opening, a rip in the air, *something* that would lead me back to Aliyah and Zion, but I could find nothing. When I walked backward, my feet shifted through the rock like a ghost. The voice brought my attention back to the shadowy figure on the throne.

"This choice cannot be taken back, Princess Amina." That voice struck a chord in me, an evil that reached to the *Book* inside me, causing me to stir. I grunted as pain struck me across the chest. It was a grating sound, like teeth grinding together.

"I understand the decision I am making, Ekwensu." She lifted her cloak, glanced backward, then turned back to Ekwensu.

He leaned forward, his face falling into the moonlight. Although I had read about him with Mama, nothing compared to seeing him in the flesh. Or lack thereof.

He was a living skeleton, fire replacing his eyes, broken teeth filling his mouth. His voice was like slithering snakes. "Stand up, my new daughter."

Amina stood, dropping her agbada to the floor, the moonlight shining over her sleek black armor. She shivered when Ekwensu touched her arms, and I had a feeling it was not because of the cold.

"Why are you scared? You sought me out here in Shukti." His voice turned bitter. "Here in my prison."

"I have a bargain for you," Amina said. Her voice turned dark. "Grant me a sliver of your power and I will share . . . my kingdom with you. Here in Chidani and beyond the barrier. We can rule together."

"Hmm, interesting," Ekwensu said. "So you know my story, then? That Ala banished me here centuries ago?"

"Yes." Amina nodded. "You're not like your brothers and sisters. I know that because the citizens of Chidani never age, your power wanes. With no dead souls to replenish you in Shukti, your power is limited. I can help you if you join me."

"The Descendant is dead? That's the only way you can become queen."

Amina grunted. "Yes. Dead by my own hand. Her and the husband."

She's talking about Mama and Daddy. I moved forward, pulling my sword from my side and slicing toward Amina. It passed through her like smoke. Realization washed over me like heavy rain. The *Book* was showing me a memory, a memory stored in the crown that had released when I touched it. I moved to the side to hear more.

"That means the barrier will break down. What about Ramala's gifts?" Ekwensu asked.

"Safe in my sacred places, places she wouldn't dare to look," Amina responded.

"If this means what I think it means . . ."

"It means that soon she will die, and *I* will be queen."

"And once that happens . . ."

"*I* will have control over Chidani and will invade both worlds and bring my people to full supremacy. My people, those sold as slaves and taken from my land, who Ramala forgot about. I will need your souls, the mmo, to aid me in my goal."

"And you want the dark prince, the death god, to help you?" Ekwensu asked, rising from his throne and walking— no floating—around Amina, regarding her with suspicion. "I have been in Shukti for centuries beyond centuries.

Weaklings have tried to make deals with me, but they never want to agree to the terms. If you agree to my terms, little one, you can have my souls."

Taking a deep breath, Amina thrust both her arms upward. "I accept your terms."

Ekwensu descended to the ground and peered at her, his long tongue slicking out of his mouth and licking his lips. "You understand that I will need *your* soul in exchange. My magic does not come cheap."

She nodded. He pulled back the sleeves of his kaftan and snapped his skeletal fingers. A long blade appeared in his right hand, the hilt of it made from shards of bone. With a swift movement, he swiped down both her arms, leaving blood to fall to the rock. I cringed as the blood began to boil, releasing a noxious smell as Amina moaned in pain.

Ignoring her agony, Ekwensu thrust forward, slicing Amina in the chest, right in her heart. She screamed as she fell to her knees. I wanted to run, but my feet were rooted to the ground. *Whoosh.* A substance extracted from her wound, something milky white. Thunder sounded in the sky as the essence turned into a creature, falling to the ground and yelping as it did. It slithered along the gravel, releasing small cries. It had the shape of a lizard, but it had a striking resemblance to Amina. She fell down to the floor, prostrate, shaking violently.

Ekwensu eyed the creature. "Ahh, your soul ... So ... *scrumptious.*"

He snapped his fingers again, and Amina's wispy soul

flew into his hands. He curled it, caressed it lovingly, and coaxed it into the sharp edge of the blade. When he moved his hands this time, Amina rose from the ground, floating in the air. Her eyes were open, seeing nothing.

"I left a small piece of your soul inside your body, as part of our bargain. Keep your end of the deal and release me from Shukti, and I will return your soul. If not, I will kill you where you stand. Understood?"

"Yes, Ekwensu. I am in your debt."

The scene disappeared, covered in shrouds of inky black. I turned around multiple times but couldn't see in front of me, behind me, or to the side. My heart beat faster and faster against my chest as I realized that I was lost, that I might never get back home.

"Who dares to disturb my memories?" someone said. A figure stepped through the darkness. A flowing tangerine kaftan drifted from her shoulders while a ruby circlet crowned her braided hair. Kohl lined her eyes while her arms dripped with diamonds.

"Amina," I managed to say. She tensed as I called her name. Recognition bloomed in her eyes, and her breath seemed to catch in her throat.

"No, it can't be. If you're here . . ."

I narrowed my eyes. "Yes."

"The Descendant is alive."

"And I have the crown." To my surprise, Amina walked closer to me. The *Book* stirred within me and gave me an emotion. *Sadness.* She felt sadness. It passed through her like wind before it was replaced with darkness. I moved forward; she sliced her arm in the sky, and I froze mid-step. I pushed against her power, but it was like a solid rock in my way.

"You killed my parents!" I screamed.

She stroked the side of my face and lifted my chin. Flames erupted all over me at her touch. "I did. I have no qualms about that, though. I had to do what Ramala wouldn't, to take the throne away from her. She *promised* she would one day open the barrier for good, but she did not. All lies. I must do what I can to defeat her so that I can usher my people into prosperity after four hundred years."

Neither Ramala nor Agbala had told me that part. I gritted my teeth as the tears began to fall.

I struggled against her grip, but I was still rooted in place. "It's been four hundred years, Amina. Four hundred years. Why now? Why my mama?"

"Silly boy," she said, a ferocious glint crossing her eyes. "So young. So *ignorant.* It's not about time. It's about what is right. They never told you the entire story, did they?"

Her tone turned steely. "Agbala and her stories, her way of turning the wrong into right. She was the one who counseled me, who told me everything would be fine with Ramala ruling. She even used her magic on me, using it to heal my mind, to show me that Ramala had taken the right course of action."

"And you believed her for a time," I said. "Maybe Agbala knew you might go against your sister, so she did what was best for you." I thought of Mama and Daddy, how they had done what they thought was right for me, to protect me and the entire world.

"Like I said, so *ignorant*," Amina said, grabbing my dashiki and pulling me closer, so close that I could feel her breath. "It was with sheer willpower that I was able to resist Agbala after so long. In my anger, I left the Palacia and settled in my late father's palace, a military fortress in the desert. There, I cultivated my anger, planning. I realized that if Ramala made a bargain with the gods, I could, too."

"And that's when Ekwensu stepped in."

She nodded, that same sadness returning. "This is the memory you see. He gave me the mmo in exchange for my soul and helped me see that Ramala doesn't care about our people; she only cares about power. With his help, I *will* get my sister's throne and avenge my people."

"*No.* I will defeat you first. I have the crown. And I will have the rest of the gifts to give back to the queen. You act like you're so noble. You're not. You're not doing anything good."

"I'm doing this for my people. *Your* people."

"No!" I screamed. "No, you're not! You're trying to open the barrier, flood both worlds with the mmo, and kill everyone who isn't Igbo. That means almost everyone dies. My friends die! There's got to be a better way!"

"True, but that means I can remake both worlds and control them." She continued to stroke my cheek. "You look like both of them, your mother and father. But you really favor your mother. I guess I should've known she might have had a child somewhere." She sighed. "You may have the crown, but not for long. I will end you before you find the other two gifts. With Ekwensu on my side, I am invincible."

"And I will stop you! And then I will kill you like you killed them!"

She grasped my head, hard, and I screamed. "You viewed my memories. It's only fair that I view yours." She riffled through my thoughts, causing me more pain. "Yes, you do have my crown." Her eyes flashed. "Ahh . . . and Makai helped you get here. You flew on gryphons."

The *Book* stirred in my chest again, and Amina's figure blurred. There it was, that piece of her soul that Ekwensu had let her keep, humming along in her chest. It was a small portion of her humanity, fighting against the darkness that encompassed her entire being.

"I will stop you," I vowed again.

A smile spread from left to right along her face as her eyes grew cold. "Let's see if Makai, his soldiers, and the gryphons can help you when you're far away. I'll send you back to Sanaga, hundreds of miles from them. You won't find my gifts without the help of him or Ramala."

"I *will* stop you," I repeated.

"So be it."

CHAPTER TWENTY-FIVE

I struggled to catch my breath, feeling as if I were drowning. At first, there was the sensation of cold air, and then someone settled my body on a rough surface. But I was unable to open my eyes no matter how I struggled. A hard pressure settled on my shoulders, causing me to gasp aloud, like something was trying to move me from one spot to another. *Amina's magic.*

Zion shook me. "He won't wake up, Aliyah."

Shuffling and guttural sounds grew louder and louder.

"Help me carry him!" Aliyah said.

They lifted me as I forced my eyes open.

I was being dragged through the water, crown in hand, sandwiched between them.

"Go faster!" I screamed as clouds of smoke followed us. They were much too close. We couldn't outrun the mmo.

The smoke materialized into gray creatures swimming through the water. They struck at us with long fingernails.

I reached out and grabbed Aliyah's and Zion's hands as I felt Amina's magic finally take over and the pressure become unbearable.

We tumbled through darkness at first until a blue light appeared. "Hold on!" I said, gripping their hands.

The light and water disappeared, giving way to a night sky. Zion screamed as we fell to the sparse grass far below. Then our bodies stopped in midair before falling to the ground; the pain was dull and short-lived.

Aliyah stood, looking around the clearing, her face registering where we were. I felt the wounds I had sustained in the battle; the agony was so great that I turned over and vomited in the grass. A consequence of using Dambe while hurt, just like Makai had said.

"Cam?" Aliyah called out, her voice soft and low. She reached to me. My eyes rolled just as I saw Zion staggering toward a tree trunk and resting his head on it, breathing in and out over and over again.

I rested my face on the cool dirt beneath me.

Aliyah shook me. "Listen..."

"What?" I croaked.

She shook her head. "I know how to help you! I need to find our packs!" That was when I remembered what I had overheard Halifa and Aliyah talking about earlier. It all seemed so long ago now. I forced my eyes open, strength returning to me.

"Halifa was telling me that as a soldier, she buried things

across the country to help her if she ever needed it. I helped her bury supplies when we were here the first time. We can use them to heal. She used azizan light to mark her hiding spots. Now I just need to remember where . . ."

I followed Aliyah around the clearing, pawing through the dirt as she started digging, our hands moving faster and faster. The pain was great, but the desire to be healed was greater.

"Come on, come on," Aliyah kept saying as we continued to look. To cover more ground, I switched to the other side of the clearing, digging through the dirt to no avail.

Even though all seemed lost, I started to dig another hole, and this time a pearl of bright light blinded my eyes. "I found the hiding spot!" I yelled to Aliyah.

"Yes!" Aliyah said. She helped me finish digging, and we pulled out three packs from inside the hole.

"Here," she said, unscrewing the cap off the flask of azizan light. I opened my mouth while she poured liquid inside. As soon as I swallowed, the pain began to draw away from me. I looked down at my body. The gashes were healing, my entire body suffused with light. The magic felt like the warmth of Agbala, like the embrace of my parents.

"Halifa is such a genius," I said.

Aliyah nodded. "According to her, 'a warrior is always prepared.'"

She poured some in her mouth before moving to Zion. She forced his mouth open and made sure he swallowed the light. By the time she placed the top back on the flask, I was fully healed. After, she put the three flasks into the three separate bags and closed the clasps on them.

"How did we end up back here?" Aliyah said.

Zion walked over and sat down with us. "Where did you go? As soon as you grabbed the crown, you disappeared."

"Shukti."

His eyes widened. "Wait, you went . . . there?"

"The Underworld, yes. I saw and spoke with Amina. Agbala was right; the queen's sister is working with Ekwensu. Amina sent me here—she said she would place me far away from Makai's help so that I would be alone, so that I wouldn't find the rest of the gifts. I grabbed your hands just in time! How are we supposed to locate the last two gifts if she has a powerful god on her side?"

Zion took the crown from me. "Well, we have the first one. She can't open the barrier without all three, right? Apparently Ekwensu isn't as powerful as she thinks he is."

"You don't understand," I said. "They are working together to hide the last two gifts. I don't know where to find the scepter of lightning or the ring of immortality. We . . . don't have much to go on."

"Well, what else *do* you know?" Aliyah asked. "Maybe we can help you out."

I concentrated hard, telling them what I had seen and heard.

"Amina knows I'm here. She controls the mmo with

Ekwensu's permission, bargaining her soul in return. She mentioned Mama and Daddy. And that she killed them . . ."

"Oh my . . . Cam, I'm so sorry." Zion wrapped one of his arms around my shoulders.

"Well, we already knew my mama and daddy died . . . but, oh God, y'all, what if she turned them into one of those *demons*?"

"No, you can't think like that," Aliyah said. "Now, let's put our heads together. Where would the scepter or the ring be?"

"I don't know," I said, closing my eyes. "I just don't know."

When I opened my eyes again, Aliyah and Zion were trying to set up a tent that they'd pulled out from one of the packs. They went off into the woods to collect branches. When they returned, they found rocks to beat the sticks into the ground. I went over to help, and in another fifteen minutes, we had pitched the tent. We were able to find the creek once again; there, we washed our bodies and changed into clean, fresh clothes. We managed to start a fire to keep the mosquitoes away.

My stomach gurgled as Aliyah pulled out plums, peaches, and some sugar. It wasn't exactly filling, but none of us wanted to venture out into the forest to hunt anything. I was such a fool; I couldn't even lead my friends into battle without remembering that we needed to eat to survive.

"Wait. That's it!" I said so loudly that Zion jumped, his head brushing the ceiling of our tent.

"How could I have been so ridiculous?" I stood up and paced the tent, trying to make sure my words wouldn't tumble out of my mouth without making any sense. "We read about the gifts in the *Book*, right? Well, we may have all the information we need right at our fingertips. We just need to call the *Book* forward somehow. Maybe there's a clue there."

"Whoa, calm down," Zion said, his mouth full of fruit. "We don't have the *Book*, remember? It's inside you."

"Right," I said, sitting down. "It's inside me to protect it from Amina. But who says I can't somehow pull it out?"

I closed my eyes and concentrated hard, shutting myself into darkness. I called the *Book*. The pages flipped around in my head, and I searched every inch of it, but every time I got to the section about Ramala's gifts, dark shadows obscured the words. I wasn't calm. I was too frustrated to think clearly, to really see the pages.

"I can't do this!" I said. I took the crown, walked out of the tent into the clearing, and started pacing again. I heard and felt the hard thuds of boots hitting dirt behind me, but I didn't turn around. "Give me some space!" I yelled at Zion or Aliyah—whoever it was who had followed me.

They left me alone. I fumed and closed my eyes again. I didn't mean to be so irritated, but I couldn't help it. It was all too much. And now I couldn't even use the *Book* when it mattered most.

I took a deep breath and tried again. I felt the energy of the *Book*; I mentally flipped the pages until I got to the section where the gifts were. My body warmed with sweat at the effort. Still, the pages were blurred; I couldn't see what I needed to see. In frustration, I sat down at the roots of the nearest tree.

Agbala! I screamed. *You need to help me. I cannot help my friends or keep them safe on this mission anymore. I never asked for this. Help me!*

I waited for her words. It felt like someone or something was tugging at my insides. I slipped from my body and floated above the tree line, looking down to see my body slumped against the tree trunk. I could just make out Zion peering from the tent flaps, watching me.

A golden opening appeared in the sky, growing bigger and bigger. I felt no fear, just reached up and slipped through the light, hoping that Agbala was on the other side of it.

"You called?" Agbala said when I saw her. "I heard you, so I pulled you to me."

She was standing in front of me in a river of flowing water. It encircled her feet, her arms, and her head.

At the sight of the goddess, my anger was replaced with deep sadness. "Yes, I called you," I managed to say.

She stepped forward, but I took two steps back.

"No, stay away from me. I don't want to be touched." If she hugged me, I would feel Mama. She stopped walking at my request.

"We found the crown," I said, swallowing hard, handing it to her. "But we were all hurt in the process. And Amina separated us from Makai, Halifa, and Bakari. She put dark magic around it. She's working with Ekwensu, like you said."

"I knew you would find it. You're so brave, Cameron. The queen will be grateful to hear of this news. I will take it to her."

"I'm scared. If it took this much effort just to get one of the gifts, how are we going to survive finding the other ones, too? How are we going to survive Ekwensu?"

"You should come back to the Palacia," the goddess responded, the ivory hue returning to her form. "I don't know where the other two gifts are, either. The queen will be happy with the crown for now."

I shut my eyes. I still needed answers. "How do I access the entire *Book*? If it's mine and it's inside me, then why can't I see the pages I need to see? It might help us learn where the other two are before we come back."

Even though I had told her not to, she reached out and stroked my cheek. In a second, I was crying again as I opened my eyes, missing my mama. "My dear boy, if it's inside you, you have the power to retrieve it. But you must be calm. You are just now coming to understand the magic that surges within you. If you grow frustrated in any way, the *Book* will remain beyond your grasp. You need to be fully in control."

The tears continued to flow. "What about my mama and daddy? Amina said . . ."

As soon as her hand left my cheek, the tears stopped. Her

eyes hardened. "She's working with my brother, a vile creature. You can't trust what she says."

"My mama and daddy . . ."

Sighing, she reached out to me again, but I stepped back. "You must trust me, Cameron. You mustn't think on such things. Remember the work before you—it is your duty. Your mother left it for you."

The tears fell down my face again. She wrapped me in her arms. I hated myself for crying, but I couldn't help it.

"I know you want to see them again," she whispered in my ear. "But right now, your hope must rest in your friends. They are here for a reason. And they are counting on you. You must finish what your mother and father started."

She rocked me back and forth for a long while, until the tears were gone. "Now, you must return to your friends. I can hear them calling. Remember, you have the *Book*, which means you have power. Use it. And then come home."

CHAPTER TWENTY-SIX

I barely registered two pairs of hands shaking me when I returned to Sanaga. A hand slapped my face. I quickly rolled away. "I'm awake! I'm awake! What's the problem?"

"We thought you were dead! You've been out for hours!" Zion said.

I rubbed my face. "Ow! Look, I went to see Agbala. I gave her the crown."

Aliyah punched me in my shoulder.

"That hurt, too!"

"If you would have told us that instead of just disappearing, you wouldn't be in pain!" Aliyah screamed.

I braced my hands over my head to stop any forthcoming blows. "I know how to find the second gift, the scepter. And if you stop hitting me, I can tell you!"

"How?" Aliyah said flatly.

"Let's go back inside the tent. Agbala said something that made a lot of sense to me."

Zion narrowed his eyes, but they followed me.

"Okay, I'm going to need some space. Go to the other side of the tent and let me calm down. Agbala said that I've been so wired that my magic isn't working, just as I thought."

I didn't really trust myself with this, but I had to try. I closed my eyes and searched my soul. I'd let out all my frustration, anger, and tears with Agbala, so now my head felt clear. I was ready to release the *Book*.

I concentrated on it. It was like a big rock had been squeezed inside me and was now returning to the surface. It hurt something fierce, but I kept going, feeling the magic build within me. When I opened my eyes this time, a little girl stared at me, no more than eight years old, her smile like sunbeams. I recognize her instantly: the first Descendant Agbala had raised in the vision she had given me, when the *Book* was fused with my soul. Braids spilled down her back, their ends tied with cowrie beads.

She giggled as she gazed at me, her eyes the color of deep night.

"Hey, I know you," I said.

"You do," she said.

"Nneka, the first Descendant. You've gotta be, like . . . centuries old."

"I am," she said. "I've come to help you." She gestured toward my chest. "Looks like you are having problems." She grabbed my hand, curling her fingers around mine, and led me through sand to a small river that gurgled and coursed to the left as far as the eye could see.

She pulled me to the ground.

"I don't understand all the magic of the *Book*. I've been surprised each time. It has given me images of you, my ancestors, of . . . my mama and daddy. It makes me speak facts that I did not know before. It makes me speak the words my mama spoke, too."

Nneka giggled again. "I don't even think Agbala understood the magic she gave the *Book*. I had those moments, too."

"I figured she didn't. Can you help me? I'm trying to pull the *Book* from inside me. To access it, to read it."

She caressed the still water with her fingers. At her touch, small ripples of waves flowed, soaking my bare feet. "In those moments when I felt overwhelmed, I had to calm myself. You can't imagine the fear and frustration of being enslaved." Eager eyes peered at me. "But looking at you now, I can tell that the world hasn't changed much since we became free."

"Not much," I agreed.

"Then you must learn the way I learned." She picked up a lump of sand; it had formed to the size of a rock. "When you realize that nothing much matters but the happiness of yourself and your family, your magic will flow. The *Book* makes your senses and emotions heightened. You must learn to control them."

"But it's hard," I whined.

"How hard do you think it was for my people?"

Those words shut my mouth before I could complain again. She closed her palm, and the lump of sand crumbled. A soft wind carried its essence in the air, where it disappeared.

"Understand?"

I nodded. "I do understand now."

She pressed a hand to my heart, feeling my heartbeat. "Remember—calm yourself. You're no good when your ego grows. When you're inside yourself, when your mission becomes obscured by your own feelings, you lose track."

"How do you know so much?" I whispered. "I'm older than you!"

She laughed again. "I promise, I'm *much* older than you." She placed a kiss on my cheek. "I'm glad to help. Until we meet again, Cameron Battle."

Just like the rock, Nneka lifted into the air, swirls of sand encircling her, carrying her away from me, farther and farther. Her laughter filtered through my mind.

I know what to do. The love of my friends and family compelled me to act. With another mental thrust, I closed my eyes and flung the *Book* forward and out of me. When I heard Zion and Aliyah gasp, I opened my eyes and there was the *Book*, shining and revolving right over my head. I reached out, and my hands went through its pages. It was transparent, like a ghost.

I pointed toward the center of the tent, and the *Book* soared through the air.

"Go to the scepter," I commanded it, and the pages flipped. My voice was low and in control.

When the *Book* settled, Aliyah looked down at the picture of the wooden staff before reading.

"Amadioha, the thunder god, gave Ramala his scepter in exchange for her prayers. Agwu, the trickster god, wanted it for himself, though. At first, Agwu demanded the scepter from his brother. He was told no.

"Angered at his brother's denial, Agwu used his magic to trick Queen Ramala and took on Amadioha's face. He told her, 'I have decided to give the scepter to Agwu with your permission, Ramala.'

"Ramala used a spell, the power of the Igbo word 'ikposa,' which allowed her to dispel the trickster god's magic to reveal his true nature and motives. Once Agwu was revealed, she laughed at him, used the scepter against him, and banished him with lightning from her kingdom to the island of Okeniyi. The scepter remains in the queen's hands."

We all looked at one another as the page turned, but the other side was blank. The *Book* continued to revolve above us as it closed.

"So . . . what does that tell us?" Zion asked.

I thought long and hard before responding. "If Agwu, the trickster god, wanted the scepter but wasn't able to gain it from Amadioha . . . we still don't know where it would be."

"Can't you see?" Aliyah said. "Read between the lines. If Agwu wanted the scepter and failed to get it, he might know where it is now, or he *might* even have it. Listen, *I* didn't read this book before coming here, but even I can use my common sense in this situation."

I shook my head. "What are you getting at?"

She sighed. "This is just a hunch, but if Agwu wanted the scepter, Amina could have hidden it with him, right? I mean, he would have been happy about that."

"Okay . . . what else you got? That's it?" Zion asked.

"No, that's not it," she snapped, glaring at him. "I think we should go to Okeniyi. If Agwu wanted the scepter so badly, it totally makes sense that Amina would have hidden it there."

I finally understood. "Yes . . . Amina said that all the gifts were hidden in places the queen would never think to look . . ."

"And if she banished Agwu to Okeniyi, then she probably wouldn't think to look there!" Zion finished my sentence for me.

"Okay," I said. I closed my eyes and tugged at the *Book*, bringing it back inside me. This time, it didn't hurt. When I opened my eyes, Aliyah began to pack our bags.

"If we want the scepter, we should leave now. Amina may try to move it since we have the crown."

"Um . . . how are we going to get there?" Zion asked as

we followed Aliyah outside into the clearing. She snuffed out the fire; then, we helped her pack the tent in one of the bags.

"Hmm," I said, thinking. "I have an idea. Amina may have sent us back here without Makai and without the gryphons, but . . ." A slow smile spread across my face. "We have a connection with them. As Kali said, 'the relationship between a gryphon and its rider is the closest thing anyone could have.'"

We stood in the middle of the clearing. The link to Ugo was like magic, a string that I could tug on. It was like a *pull* and a *push*, me pulling for him to appear and him pushing to get to me. I sank to my knees as the feeling overpowered me. The sound of wings filled my ears as Ugo responded to my call. The ground reverberated as tendrils of dirt and leaves rose in the air. I hadn't a clue how long I sat there, waiting, pulling for Ugo.

Suddenly, strong lion feet thumped on the ground, knocking down saplings and trees. Three gryphons stood in front of us, their wingspans making thunderous noises. Ugo stepped toward me, his wings the color of ice. When I scratched the side of his face, gossamer strands of energy radiated through my body, causing me to gasp. A low grumble rose from his throat as he bent low to me. I stepped on the leather straps and hoisted myself up, tying myself down to his side.

"I don't think I'll ever get used to this," Zion said as he got on his.

I smiled. "I'm thinking the same thing, brother."

Aliyah jumped on hers, too. "Nice to see you again, my friend. Let's do this," she said, her eyes glinting with happiness.

I pointed at the sky. "To Okeniyi!"

The gryphons lifted us from the ground, and we shot toward the night sky.

CHAPTER TWENTY-SEVEN

I hadn't a clue how far Okeniyi was from Sanaga, and I didn't even want to look through the *Book* to find out. I was too tired. I needed sleep.

When I woke up, the darkness had turned to the bright blue of the morning. We were traveling over a body of water, not the Atlantic Ocean but a sea that jutted to the west. When a small strip of land appeared, I whistled. Zion and Aliyah woke up. I pointed forward.

"I think we're coming up on Okeniyi." As we moved close to it, the gryphons began to screech. The island was very small and full of dense trees.

We dove toward the shoreline and fell to the sand with a thump. "I'll be back," I reassured Ugo. "Fly over the island until I call for you. Stay hidden so that the trickster god can't see you." Ugo took off, and the other two gryphons followed him.

I gazed at the line of trees. "Nothing to do but walk until we get a glimpse of Agwu. Remember, he can take any form."

We started to traipse through the trees, cutting down branches and stems with our swords. It was clear that no one had visited this place in years, decades even, because everything was tangled together, and the vines grew with reckless abandon. Once we got through the thickets, we found the inside of the small forest to be cool and a great protection from the sun.

We walked in silence as we moved deeper through the forest. I hoped that we would hear something soon, but nothing but darkness and more trees greeted us. By the time afternoon came, I was covered in mosquito bites and was beginning to get cranky and hungry.

"Whose idea was this again?" Zion asked, his face full of sweat. "What if Agwu isn't even here?"

"I doubt that," Aliyah said, pulling fruit from her bag and passing it to us. "The *Book* hasn't been wrong yet, has it?"

I couldn't disagree with that, so we kept moving. Finally, we reached slivers of sunlight filtering through the trees. I moved the branches aside with my sword, and we walked into a bright, oval-shaped clearing, complete with deep green grass that held the scent of home. The sun shone down on the flower-filled ground, the sight a welcome respite. Through the trees, a small home sat, smoke billowing from its chimney. The smoke smelled of roasted meat.

Although the house was small, it reminded me of the

warm presence of my grandma's home. "Is anyone else hungry?" I asked.

"I am," Zion responded. "The peaches and plums didn't really do much for my stomach."

"We need to be careful," Aliyah said, her brow furrowed in concern.

"Come on, Aliyah, don't you smell that?" Zion said. "A smell like that can't mean anything evil."

Aliyah stepped back into the cover of the trees, shivering a bit. "No, I don't think so. I've felt this feeling before. Once when we got the crown. And now here. I have to pay attention to that feeling. And I think y'all should, too."

"Aliyah, just listen—" I pleaded, but she had already backed far into the woods.

"Come on, Zion." I sighed. "We can't do this without her help." We found Aliyah standing near an old tree, a hollow carved out in its middle. A frustrated look crossed her face when we joined her. She interrupted me as soon as I was about to call her name again.

"No," she whispered. "Open the *Book*, Cameron. I don't like this feeling."

I closed my eyes and brought it forward again. It swirled around the clearing, zipping from tree to tree, shining with a ruby light. It stopped in front of me.

"Didn't we already read it?" Zion whined. "I'm *hunnngrry*."

"Aliyah is right," I said, even though my stomach gurgled. "We can't walk into this without a plan."

Aliyah reached up and grabbed the *Book* with both hands; it turned solid at her touch. She raced furiously through it until she got to the passage about Ramala's scepter. "We need to read it again," she murmured to herself. "There *has* to be something in here about how to fight him. He's a trickster god who tried to steal from the queen. There can't be anything good about him." She read the passage aloud again.

Zion's forehead crinkled. "I think 'good' is a term that doesn't really apply to a trickster god, right? Like, I don't think Agwu would be good or bad. He's a trickster by nature, not because he wants to be."

"Shh," Aliyah said as she continued to read aloud. It was a short passage, not much connected to it at all. "There," she said, pointing at the end of the section. "It says that Ramala used a spell, 'ikposa,' to unravel Agwu's magic to overpower him. It's probably the only word you can use to defeat him."

"Did she really defeat a god, though?" I asked. "Or does the spell only work for a time?"

"It has to be just for a time," Aliyah said, handing the *Book* back to me. "Which is why she put a barrier around this island, right? A human being can't really kill a god, I don't think."

"So what's the plan?" Zion said, shifting from foot to foot.

"Ramala was strong when she used that spell," I pointed out. "The gifts gave her the power of the gods. She was no mere human. Only a godlike person could take out a god in that way, even if it was just for a short time."

"We need to use it against him if he doesn't help us," Aliyah said. "It's the only way."

"No," I said. "Believe me, we are nowhere near as powerful as Ramala was when she used that spell. We could get hurt if we used it."

"I don't know," Aliyah said, beginning to pace back and forth. "I just don't know about this."

"Well, Cam and I can go," Zion offered. "That way, if something happens, at least you can fly back to the Palacia if you need to."

"I agree," I said. I took her hands, which had begun to tremble. "I have the *Book*. Nothing will happen to me. I'll protect Zion as well."

She nodded and gave me a hug. "Be careful, okay? I'll be right out here."

"If we don't come back in thirty minutes, get help. Fly quickly."

"But we don't have watches and if we did, they probably won't work here," Zion said.

"I'll count down in my head," Aliyah said.

"Okay," I said. I took Zion's hand and used our catchphrase. "We do this together." He nodded in response as I yanked the *Book* back inside me. We walked past the cover of the trees again and into the clearing where Agwu's house sat.

The wooden door opened, and a figure stepped out. My hand tightened on my sword. "Agwu," I said. The figure walked into the light. He didn't have the tall stature of a god;

he wasn't much taller than us, actually. Unlike the other gods I had seen, he looked human, with brown eyes, brown skin, and hair cut close to his head. He wore a long kaftan and sandals. No weapons appeared on his body, and no scepter was in his hands.

"Children," Agwu said, his voice deep, reminding me of my daddy's. "You must be hungry. Come inside. No one has visited Okeniyi in decades."

The god gestured us forward, and we walked closer to him.

"I must admit that I may have lost some of my human attributes since being put here, so excuse me. I will leave the door open for you. If you would like food and shelter, please come in. If not, you may leave. I won't harm you." He walked inside.

"He's a trickster," I said.

"Maybe he's changed!" Zion said. "If he's been banished here for decades, I'm sure he's had a lot of time to think about his actions, right? And anyway, like I said, I'm hungry."

"Same."

"Also," Zion said, "we're smart. We can play tricks of our own. And we have Aliyah."

"True. Okay, let's do this."

Zion followed right behind me.

The home was fashioned and furnished for a god. Large brass spears were positioned in each corner, their spikes so heavy and big that they held up the mud-woven ceiling. Igbo ceremonial face masks etched in the shapes of lions, elephants, leopards, and tigers were fastened to the earthen walls, made with beads and strung together. Djembe drums, covered in fabric and shells, were set haphazardly around the room, drumsticks made of hard animal bone resting on the floor near them. Mallets, swords, and hammers were pinned to walls, shining with a silvery glint. Plush ruby rugs sat on the floor, spreading from the entrance to the home, to the common areas, and to an enclosed back area that I could not see.

In the middle of the common room sat a throne, its center furnished with large pillows, its back made from metal that soared to the sky.

A roaring fire crackled in the hearth; large multicolored cushions, the size of big animals, spread around it, thrown on the rugs with reckless abandon. Agwu's place felt . . . peaceful. A sense of warmth settled upon my shoulders as I took in the sight.

We sat at a wooden table in the middle of the room. Agwu was nowhere in sight. There was a closed door to the left of the cabin.

A few minutes later, he came through that door and placed warm goblets of tea in front of us. "We shouldn't," I said as Zion reached for them. The god left and returned with trays full of honey cakes, spring rolls, spiced venison, jollof rice, and fresh greens. After setting the trays down, he produced eating utensils and placed them in front of us.

He sat and waited for us to eat. When we didn't touch the

food, he reached out for some meat and took a bite. "The food isn't poisoned. Like I said, I don't have many visitors."

How did he prepare food so fast and have it waiting for us? Did he know we were coming?

Zion shrugged and began to eat.

"I don't think this is going to work," I said, standing up, about to pull Zion with me. Agwu grabbed my hand and inclined his head to the side; an immediate sense of peace flowed through me.

"I shall do you no harm."

"Yes . . . no harm," I repeated, sitting back down.

"We have a specific question to ask you," I said, stuffing my face with the much-needed food.

"Oh?" Agwu said, taking another sip of his tea. The right side of his mouth lifted.

"We are looking for a specific artifact, something Amadioha made. Do you happen to know anything about that?" I asked.

"Hmm, very curious," the god responded. "No, I do not."

I kept going. "Well, the *Book* told us that you wanted Amadioha's scepter. So we thought you might know something about it."

"Ah, the scepter. *That's* what you're talking about? Well, while I did want it, I wasn't able to convince my brother to give it to me. I haven't seen the scepter for years, my boy."

"According to the *Book*, you tried to trick the queen.

However, she banished you here to this island. It makes sense to me that you would want it back."

The air around me vibrated a bit, almost like heat was rising in the cottage. I shook my head to clear it.

"How would you know such a thing? Who are you?" he asked.

I leaned forward. "Let's just say that I know more than you think I do."

"Then you would know that I don't have it. The queen used her magic to send me here, and I haven't been able to leave this place, although I've tried."

"Well then, do you at least know where we can find it?"

"Do you know how I can leave this island?" The god smiled sweetly at me, but there was danger in his eyes. There was something else, too, but I couldn't place it. It was as if someone or *something* was trying to warn me.

"No, I don't know how to get you off this island," I said.

"But if you are here, and you want the scepter . . . does that mean it is now lost?"

I shook my head. "Maybe? What if I'm not here on the queen's behalf? What if I'm here just to ask about the scepter? What if I want it for myself?"

"Then you would be a fool. No one goes against the queen and survives."

I lifted my goblet to toast to him. "But you did."

He laughed so loudly that the house shook. Zion looked confused, and then went back to eating.

"You *are* a smart one, aren't you?"

I shrugged. "Maybe. Maybe I'm smarter here than I am back . . ."

My words made him perk up a bit, and he raised his eyebrows. "Smarter here than . . . where?"

Returning my attention to my food, I began to eat again. "Back in my home . . . in Asaba."

His eyebrows lowered. "Oh."

He turned to the open window. "It's grown dark. Maybe you want to sleep, and we can continue this conversation tomorrow? Maybe you can help me and in return, I will help you find the scepter?"

"Wait, we've been here that long? We just arrived!" Zion said.

"Well, he is the trickster god, right?" I said.

The god smiled and waved his arms around the living area. "I assure you that this is no trick. You must sleep. You are tired. It must have been forever since you last ate anything of substance. *You are certainly tired and sleepy after all that food . . .*"

Before I could say anything else, he disappeared in a ball of light.

The serving trays and cups disappeared from the table, too. I couldn't help but pat my stomach in satisfaction. The sound of a chair scraping the floor brought my attention back to the present. Zion stood, stretched his arms over his head, and proceeded to one of the large cushions in front of the fire. He got underneath the covers, laid his head on the pillow, and closed his eyes. A distinct memory of Aliyah floated through my mind, but it disappeared quickly.

"Good night," he said.

"Was he telling the truth?" I asked him.

"I don't know, Cameron. I'm tired. We can discuss tomorrow."

At his words, I felt drowsy, too, but I kept myself awake. Everything seemed confusing and disorienting. Something told me that I should also go to sleep. I looked around, and the images in front of me blurred. There was something behind the images, something gray and sickening, but I couldn't quite figure it out.

Shaking my head, I grabbed a blanket and a pillow and curled up on an area rug. I placed my sword right beside me.

"Zion?"

I heard him snore.

"Zion?" I called again.

"Cam, I'm trying to sleep."

"Do you believe Agwu?"

"Hmm . . . yesnoyesno, Mama and Daddy," was his response before he was snoring again.

I rolled over, another memory of Aliyah coming to my mind, but it disappeared once again. I reasoned that whatever I wanted to say could wait until tomorrow . . . or the next day . . . or centuries from now . . .

CHAPTER TWENTY-EIGHT

A deep and biting pain in my chest woke me. This wasn't a good sign. I grabbed my sword.

I looked around the living room. Something was wrong. The space was no longer warm and inviting. Although the fire still roared in the grate, the room was cold, as if I'd stepped out of summer and straight into winter. When I turned my head, I saw that the cushions Zion and I were lying on were not new. They were dark, dirty, ripped in places, and smelled of mildew.

I sniffed again and noticed the walls were leaking water, dirt was caked around the baseboards, and small bugs streamed up and down the walls. The table we'd dined on was broken. The chairs were rickety. Something inside me said, *You need to leave this place.*

The clasps on the packs we'd brought with us had been broken, as if someone had been rummaging inside them.

I shook Zion awake. When he opened his eyes, I placed my index finger over my lips and then pointed at the room. He looked around and scrunched his nose in disgust.

"I'm gonna find out what Agwu knows," I whispered.

"We have to leave!"

I shook my head. "No. You leave. I'll be back."

"I'm not leaving you."

He reached out to clutch my hand as my eyes closed. I stilled my heart, releasing all emotions, and brought Dambe to the surface. One second I was right beside him, and the next, we became part of the air.

The music inside the house was haunting, deep, and evil, almost like what I had felt in Shukti, but not quite. We moved as quietly as a breath across the room, sensing the god nearby.

I heard a scurrying in the darkness. I slashed my sword. Agwu grasped it and stopped its momentum.

"Ikposa!" Aliyah yelled. I turned to see her standing in the open doorway, her eyes ablaze.

My heart almost stopped. "Aliyah, no!"

Zion screamed.

The images changed in front of me like a whirlwind, air rushing through every opening like a cyclone. I looked down to see Agwu morphing into a small being hanging on to my sword, small, ugly, with mottled skin.

The sword moved, and the creature raised its arms.

"Aliyah, Zion, *run*!" I yelled.

"Ikposa!" Aliyah screamed again.

The home exploded in flames, and the blast sent Zion and me flying through the open doorway, causing me to lose consciousness.

The smell of ash forced my eyes open. A mixture of flames, wood, and rock surrounded me as I stood, my ears ringing. I couldn't hear much, but I could see.

The god held two blades in his hands. I turned and saw Zion and Aliyah, covered in soot and coughing. Agwu soared over our heads, holding his blades, looking nothing like the warm figure we had seen when we were under his spell. His red eyes bulged from his dark head, which was bigger than his overall body. His stomach was rotund and spilled from underneath his filthy dashiki. He reminded me of an oversize baby having a fit because they didn't get what they wanted.

Aliyah and Zion pulled me to my feet. I crushed myself against them. "Aliyah, you shouldn't have used the spell!"

She shook her head. "You were gone too long. You said wait half an hour. Fifteen minutes was enough for me. I was *not* gonna leave you on this island alone." She stared at her hands. "I was strong enough to use the spell. I knew I was."

My eyes widened. *Fifteen minutes? How? We had eaten and slept! It had felt like hours!* Zion pointed to the sky. "Incoming!"

As the god flew above us, the blades he held crackled with energy, with lightning.

"Move!" I screamed, throwing my full weight against Aliyah's and Zion's bodies as two bolts of lightning hit the ground.

"Where's the holder of the *Book*? I can *sense* him," the god screamed, raising his blades above his body. His voice wasn't the voice of a child's. It was deep, rich, and powerful; it cut through me like a knife.

We scrambled out of the way as another blast lit the grass around us. It was dead; even the trees surrounding us were nothing more than dried-out, dead things.

"Go, run, hide, do something," I said to Zion and Aliyah. "I'll try to get the scepter from him."

In a split second, they disappeared, the magic of Dambe taking over. I cowered behind a boulder as another bolt of lightning hit the ground. I held up my hands in surrender as a plan began to form in my mind.

"I can't help you if you kill me!" I said.

The ugly god looked down at me with his red eyes before lowering the blades. "Where is the holder of the *Book*?" he asked again.

Raising my hand in the air, I called, *Ugo!* The air vibrated with the force of his wings.

To Agwu, I said, "What do you want with the *Book*?" Even though I was fearful, I tried to keep my voice calm.

"I want release from Okeniyi! Only the queen or the holder of the *Book* has that power. The princess promised me that I would get it if I kept the scepter a secret until the right time. *This* is the right time. Did she send you?"

At his words, I felt a pain in my chest. I kneeled on the ground. Something in me reached for the god and the lightning radiating through his body. His eyes followed me as I sank to the dead grass.

"Hmm, what do we have here?" A devilish grin appeared on his face. "I *knew* you were the one with the *Book*. The power of the gods swirls within you, boy. Let me out of this prison."

"I will free you," I lied, gasping the words out because of the pain. "Give me the scepter first. The princess wants it back."

He raised his hand in the air as he floated downward just a bit. "Give me the *Book*, and I'll give you the scepter. You can't argue with a god, boy."

"Why not? You're not much of a god if you've been trapped here for decades," I said.

He whipped his blades in the air and sent another bolt of lightning toward me. Thunderstorm clouds gathered in the sky, and rain began to fall. I wiped my forehead and stood again.

"You don't know how powerful the queen was," Agwu said. "She might as well have been a goddess based on the magic she was gifted. When I lost against her, I was driven back here, ripped of my will. I wanted to die, but I could not."

His voice turned deep and bitter. "No human should be able to wield such powers. Those belong to us."

He glared at me. "And look at you, with more power than you should have," he spat. "I knew you were human as soon as you stepped on my island. I slowed your journey through the forest to my home just because I could. We are gods. We have existed for thousands of years. Being a prisoner here is *beneath* the dignity of a god."

"Are you going to give me the scepter?" I asked.

"Are you going to give me the *Book*?"

When I shook my head, both his hands went into the air. "Then you will die like everyone else who has dared to come here!"

"I don't think so," I said, moving into Dambe. Lightning struck the ground where I'd been standing.

I bumped right into Zion. "What are you doing? Get outta here! Call Ike, your gryphon!"

"No, I'm staying!" he said. Our conversation was cut short by identical bolts of lightning that came our way. Agwu had descended from the sky, his face leveled with ours.

"We have to fight," I said, clutching my sword.

"What about the scepter?" Zion asked.

"I know *exactly* where the scepter is." At least I thought I knew. From the pain building in my chest, it had to be close by. I disappeared in the wind again and climbed the nearest rotten tree. My feet caught on one of the hard branches, and I used that momentum to launch myself toward the god with my sword outstretched.

Agwu saw me coming. He reached out and punched me in the face. I fell to the ground and felt a sharp pain in my shoulder and from where Agwu had hit me. I rubbed my face and rolled as another lightning bolt crashed into the ground.

I moved away again as the god swooped toward me. Zion appeared, let out a bloodcurdling scream, and tackled Agwu from the sky.

Agwu tumbled to the ground, his body forming a small depression on the island floor. Zion's face scrunched as he struggled with the god. With one swipe of Zion's hands, Agwu's blades fell to the ground. In another swift movement, Zion held the god's arms behind his back, sweat dripping from his face.

"If you have a plan, do it now!" he yelled at me.

The god lifted himself into the air and carried Zion with him. Zion held fast. Something stirred beside me, and Aliyah appeared.

"Let's get the scepter," she said.

"I think it's inside him, just like the *Book* is inside me. We need to get it out of him somehow. Call your gryphon, Odum—once we find the scepter, we need to hurry out of here."

I ran to a tree on one side of the clearing, and Aliyah ran to the other side, following my lead. We both hit the trees at the same time, our bodies making a sound like Agwu's lightning bolts hitting the ground. We launched ourselves into the sky, careening toward the struggling god. We crashed into Agwu, and the momentum sent Zion screaming to the ground. His body smashed into a boulder, and I heard a sickening *crack*. Aliyah took Zion's place as I grabbed the god by his filthy shirt.

"The scepter is mine," I said as the most horrible pain radiated through me. Before I lost my nerve and my grip on the screaming god, I punched through Agwu's body, the magic of Dambe aiding me.

The god stopped screaming, as if my fist hadn't actually harmed him. I could hear wings around me as I gripped the long staff inside Agwu's body. I pulled on the scepter, and the pain in my chest went away. In one movement, Agwu expelled it from his body and sent me falling toward the ground.

Ugo caught me as the staff began to vibrate in my hand. Aliyah fell, but her gryphon caught her, too. Zion was trying his best to keep his screams at bay as he gripped one of his legs. Ike was pawing at him with its beak.

In a swift movement, Ugo landed, and I was by Aliyah's side, helping Zion onto the saddle of his gryphon as Agwu languished in the sky, dazed and confused.

"Time to go!" I yelled.

Agwu screamed and followed us.

CHAPTER TWENTY-NINE

"Give it back to me! Give it back!" Agwu screamed as he chased us. We flew to the top of the tree line and shot in the direction of the sea.

The god soared over us. Ugo reared upward, screeched, and scratched Agwu across the face with its talons. He screamed and fell.

By the time we reached the sea, he was coming after us again. As soon as we flew across the water, I glanced backward. Agwu flew forward, then hit an invisible barrier. His small, dirty hands beat against the barrier as he raised his blades, but we were too far away.

Aliyah flew closer to me. "Cutting it close?"

"I had to make sure he had the scepter," I said. Zion was moaning, lying awkwardly on his saddle.

"It's going to be okay," I said. "We're going back to Sanaga."

He moaned again in response. One of his legs was

positioned at an unnatural angle. I sucked my teeth at the damage.

"We were only inside fifteen minutes? It seemed like we were in there all night!"

"The spell undid the magic," Aliyah said. "Just like when Ramala banished Agwu." She scoffed at the island as we flew away. "For good reason, apparently."

"Do we have some more of that azizan magic?" I asked.

"Yeah, we do back in the forest," Aliyah said. "I buried the rest of it before we left."

"Good."

I felt a twinge of guilt at leaving Agwu behind, but I didn't have a choice. Anyway, he'd tried to kill us. I couldn't feel too sorry for a god who had gotten Zion hurt.

By the time we reached Sanaga, it was dark. Gently, we picked up Zion. He woke with a jolt and started screaming again.

"Sorry to do this, Zion, but you'll be fine in a minute," I said. Aliyah went toward a group of trees and pawed her way through the ground. She removed a flask of azizan light and came over to us.

I did my best to keep Zion on his back, but the pain was too great. He kept trying to sit up. In defeat, he finally just lay on the ground, half sitting, sweat running down his face.

"This should work," Aliyah said, sprinkling the magic on Zion's ruined leg. Nothing happened.

"Cam . . . it's not working," she said.

Zion had lost consciousness again. The light surrounded him, but I couldn't see it doing anything, just hovering in the air. "Why isn't it working?"

"I don't know. I don't know." Aliyah stood and started pacing.

I walked over and grabbed her shoulders. "Listen, I can't lose you, too. You need to help me think. Why wouldn't the magic work?"

Tears were streaming down her face. "Cameron, I really don't know. I can't think straight right now."

I let her go and paced around the clearing, emptying my mind of emotion and letting logic take over, just like Nneka had told me. I turned back to Aliyah.

"Wait. A god injured him, right?"

"Yes."

"Maybe the azizan magic isn't working because only a god can heal him?"

"That makes sense. But who can we call to get him healed?"

"Agbala."

She looked at me as if I had lost all sense. "Why would she come?"

"Well, I saw her before we left for Okeniyi. You weren't there . . . It was different. She really does care about us."

Her expression turned dark. "I don't think she cares about us at all."

"But, Aliyah—" I said.

"No," she interrupted. "Look at Zion! He's really hurt. They sent a bunch of kids to do their dirty work!"

I turned my back on her, using my shirt to wipe Zion's forehead.

"Agbala does care," I said, my voice faltering as the truth settled on my shoulders. "I'll call her—you'll see." I stood and walked to one of the trees surrounding the clearing, closing my eyes. I mentally called for her, *screamed*, even. Nothing happened.

Aliyah folded her arms when I came back. "I told you."

Anger burned like flames inside me. I walked back and forth, trying to shake the emotion, but I couldn't. I walked away from Aliyah, turning my back so she couldn't see my burning eyes. "We're out here, alone and afraid. I'm tired, Aliyah. Tired."

Aliyah wrapped her arms around me. "It's okay, Cameron. I'm so sorry."

"We should've gone back to Asaba like she asked," I said. "I need to call her again."

"I'll be here."

I hated this feeling, that my friend's healing depended on me in such a real way. There was also something else, too. What if we really were just being pawns? Panic rose in my chest, threatening to cut off my air supply, as I extricated myself from her arms. But I had to try.

I closed my eyes and called for her. *Agbala, if you're out there, we really need your help.*

Nothing happened. I called for her a second time, but nothing came. I looked into the sky, remembering how I had floated from my body. I willed for it to happen again; still nothing changed.

"Cam, what's going on?"

I went back over to her. Aliyah had torn a piece of her dashiki and was wiping Zion's face.

"She's not responding."

"He's sweating and shivering! What are we going to do? Aren't you the Descendant? Do something!"

"I don't know what to do!" I screamed. I walked away from Aliyah. But her words made me think. "I'll be right back," I said. "I'm going to the creek. When I get back, I'll have Agbala." *She needs me. If I put myself in danger, she will come.*

By the time I got to the creek, I was losing it. But just like Nneka said, if I wasn't calm, I couldn't call for my magic in the regular way. I would need to take a chance.

I waded into the creek until my feet left the ground. I turned on my back and floated there for a second, looking at the night sky littered with bright stars. That was something I'd always remember about this place. The stars here were clear, and they seemed more real.

Although it was dangerous, I'd never felt more at home than I did in Chidani. I dipped my head underneath the water and waited. I almost struggled to the surface, but I kept my face under to help Zion, willing myself to be calm. By the time stars danced across my vision and darkness came, a light shone in my mind.

When I came to, I was still in the creek, but a river of gold surrounded me. Agbala paced on the bank.

"Why did you put yourself in danger?" she asked.

I told her the entire story of what happened.

"I always believed you could do it, Cameron! We must get it back to Asaba immediately."

She began to walk away. "Hold up!" I yelled.

She turned to me, her eyes full of surprise. "What do you mean?"

"I just said that Agwu almost *killed* us! We can't keep fighting if we don't have any help! Zion is hurt, and he needs you! I'm not doing anything until you help him."

Her eyes narrowed. "Well, I *did* tell you to come back to Asaba."

"And then we wouldn't have the scepter," I responded, trying to sound bold. But she was right. I felt a twinge of guilt for not listening to her. "We almost *died* in the process."

Agbala's face contorted in a mixture of sadness and anger, the first time I had seen her this way. "You're not the only one who has lost something. I almost died creating the *Book* and protecting the humans. I've lost something, too . . . There were consequences for my actions . . ."

"What consequences?" I asked.

"Never mind that," Agbala said, her face returning to its normal impassiveness. "Lead me to Zion."

I kept my emotions at bay and led the goddess back to Zion. Aliyah was still sitting next to him and wiping his face. She turned to us when she heard our footsteps.

"Good, you came," she said.

"Cam?" Zion said in a low voice. His eyes were closed.

I sat next to him. "I'm here, Zion." I signaled to Agbala, and she stood over him. She touched the light around her head and blew it toward Zion's leg.

He tensed as the magic poured into his body.

"It's shattered. Hold him down or he will hurt himself," she said.

Aliyah grabbed his arms, and I held his chest down. It took both of us to keep him still; it was like Zion had grown stronger than all of us put together. He shifted on the ground and moaned even louder as the bones stitched back together in a sickening *crunch*. Then suddenly, it was over. I watched his breath come back. I looked down at his leg again and saw that it was healed. Aliyah let his arms go and sat back in the dirt, seeming exhausted. I kept my hands on his chest.

I didn't cry. But I wasn't happy, either. The emotion I felt was deeper than that. Zion lifted himself off the ground and pulled me into a hug. "Thank you, thank you, thank you."

"You're welcome," I whispered.

I was so relieved that I almost forgot what I needed to say to Agbala. I went inside the tent, grabbed the scepter, and walked back outside. I threw it at the goddess's feet. Zion and Aliyah gasped.

"Here. This is what you wanted. This is what we almost died for. I'm done. We are finished with this dangerous mission. These . . . *gifts* are tainted. I'm not doing your dirty work anymore—do it yourself. Send us back home."

Even as I said the words, I knew I didn't want to go home. I wanted to stay. I knew that maybe it was our fault for not going back to Asaba when she had asked us to. But I also knew that it wasn't worth my friends' lives, that I at least wanted *them* to go home.

The goddess tilted her head to the side. "You don't mean anything you say."

I clenched my fists. "I mean *everything* I say. We won't fight for you anymore."

Agbala picked up the scepter. Spreading her arms, she lifted herself from the forest floor and floated over our heads. "The queen and I will be waiting for you back in Asaba. If you decide to join us, you will be taken care of, and we can talk about all of this. If not, you have the power to go home—you always have. It is up to you. But please, think about what is at stake if you do."

When she finished, she soared through the trees and disappeared in a shower of white light.

Zion made his way over to me. "What was that all about?"

My face burned, and I turned my eyes from him to Aliyah. "You know I'm right. Even if I can't leave, I want you two to be safe. I can do this alone."

"No, you were telling *your* truth, not mine. *We* decided to go to Okeniyi. We knew the risks."

"Don't y'all see? We're risking our lives for these people. And for what? For Agwu to seriously hurt Zion?" I said.

"I don't know. It doesn't seem like we have a choice, do we?" Zion said. "Plus, I'm pretty much healed."

"No, we don't. If we leave Amina with the last gift, she will find the other two again and open the barrier. I don't want my mother, father, or brother to be killed by demons," Aliyah said.

"Y'all just don't understand," I said, turning from them. "If I hadn't touched the *Book*, y'all would never have come here. I would've come alone. Let me finish this on my own."

"But you can't change what happened, and you can't change who you were born to be," Zion said. "And you can't change us being here."

Zion took my hand. I gazed at him.

"I vote for finding that ring," Aliyah said. "After we do that, then we go home."

Zion raised his hand. "I'm down for that."

Aliyah smiled. "Majority rules."

"Dang it," I whispered. "I just want you to be safe. Let me handle the rest."

"And we will be safe," Zion said. "But we have to find that ring first. And we won't leave you here by yourself."

I shook my head, seeing no way out of this, and I walked to the tent alone.

CHAPTER THIRTY

I slept for so long that it was afternoon when I woke up. I was still alone. My heart beat fast. *Did they leave me because of my outburst? Did they go for the ring on their own?* I walked outside and saw Zion and Aliyah packing up our bags. I breathed a sigh of relief.

"Good, you're up," Aliyah said, swinging her bag around her saddle.

I tried one last time. "Have you changed your minds?"

They both shook their heads. I sighed and joined them on the gryphons. We kicked off from the ground and flew in Asaba's direction. I didn't speak to either of them, but I really wasn't mad. I just blamed myself for everything.

Once we flew past the Palacia walls and touched down into one of the sprawling courtyards, Makai, Halifa, and Bakari ran in our direction through the throngs of soldiers standing outside. Makai grasped each of our shoulders and squeezed, hard. "You all look terrible."

They didn't look so good, either. Large scratches marred Halifa's forehead, Bakari was cradling his left arm, and Makai was almost stumbling as he walked.

Zion and Aliyah laughed. I forced a smile.

We walked to the doors of the Palacia. "What happened to you?" I asked.

"When you disappeared from Onitsha, we thought you had died in pursuit of the crown," Makai was saying as we strolled through the Palacia, past the Throne Room doors, and upstairs to our royal chambers. "We waited for hours, but once it was clear you weren't going to resurface, we sent a message to Asaba. Agbala told us that if you had died, Ala would have felt it, so we trusted that you would return to us when you could. But that wasn't all. As we tried to return to Onitsha, mmo spirits surrounded our boat. They attacked us, and we fought back. Bakari almost drowned, but we were able to kill them all, except not before suffering our own injuries."

By now, we stood in front of the doors to our chambers. Aliyah pulled out the flasks of azizan light. "You need to heal." They took them gratefully.

"I'm just happy you are well. Rest now and we can talk later," Halifa said before they all walked away. Bakari gave me a warm hug.

My heart sank as we opened the doors to the sitting room

in front of our bedrooms. Dabir, Amir, and Moro, Aliyah's servant, stood there staring at us disapprovingly.

"Lord Cameron," Amir said, moving across the room and gripping my shoulders. "My gods, you need to be cleaned. The queen will not be pleased if she sees you in this condition."

Although the magic of the bathing room was disconcerting a bit, a sense of peace settled upon my shoulders. As the dirt and grime washed away, so did the trauma from earlier. I thought about Grandma, how she had made me feel warm and safe after Mama and Daddy died. How, even through the grief, she had been there to make me feel good, just like this bath. For the first time in a while, I was being taken care of like Grandma used to . . . like Mama used to. It made me want to be the Descendant even more. Even though Mama and Grandma had a legacy to live up to, they still had found the time to take care of me, too, to keep me safe.

After, I wrapped a towel around me and stepped back into the bedroom. Zion was sitting on the cushions right in front of the bed, clothed in a big towel, too. My face grew hot as I walked across the room and dressed in some nightclothes that were inside our armoire. Then I slithered underneath the covers and rested my head on my pillow.

"I don't think I'll ever get used to being cleaned with magic," Zion said.

He put on his nightclothes and got underneath the covers. We both lay there for a while. Everything I had been feeling for days, months, *years* was finally coming to the surface now that we were safe. We had done so much good in just a short time, but I still wished my parents were alive, that they could see me grow into a hero.

Zion spoke first. "Cam?"

"Yeah?" I sniffled.

"Are you okay?"

"Don't worry about it," I said. "I'll be just fine."

I felt the covers move and one of his hands reach out for mine. It was warm from his hot bath. "You don't have to pretend with me. I'm your best friend. No, I'm your brother, man."

I turned to him so he could see the feelings that I knew were plain on my face. "It's just so hard, Zion. So hard to be here where death is so close at our doors. Mama and Daddy are gone, and all I have left are you, Aliyah, and Grandma. And I almost lost you. All it takes is one sword jab, one fall, one injury, and you're gone. I'm so scared."

We both looked at each other for a long time. I swiped my thumb across his palm. He didn't let go of my hand.

"I'm not going to die, Cam," Zion whispered. "I love you, and I'm not going away. You're my family now. Listen, you protect me with all your strength, and I'll protect you. Deal?"

"Deal."

"Good. Now wipe your tears. It's going to be fine."

After about five minutes, he got up, grabbed another pillow, and turned over. He closed his eyes.

"Are you really about to go to sleep already?" I asked.

"Mm-hmm," he said. He started snoring softly. As tired as I was, I couldn't fall asleep.

I stayed up, wondering what would happen to us when we returned to the real world. More than anything, I hoped our friendship would endure when all of this was over. For the first time, I felt like we had finally accepted each other, and I didn't want that to change, no matter what the future held.

After tossing and turning for a while longer, I slept for the remainder of the night and well into the next day.

When I woke up, I saw the sun directly overhead. Zion was gone. I dressed and walked out into the sitting room. Aliyah and Zion were eating plates of fruit, breakfast porridge, and steaming fresh-baked bread sprinkled with cinnamon.

I grabbed a plate and joined them. Apparently, they had also just woken up.

"Agbala left a note," Zion said, pointing toward one of the end tables. I ate a few pieces of fruit, then walked over to the table. On it was the scepter, the crown, and a hastily scribbled note.

I read it aloud:

"'I think it important that you are the ones who present the gifts to the queen. Once you have finished eating, please come to the Throne Room. —A.'"

When we finished eating, we placed our empty plates on the table and walked to the Throne Room. Makai led the way.

He whispered to the soldier guarding the door to the Throne Room. The guard left for a second and then came back to get us. The soldier announced our presence.

"Queen Ramala, the three heroes want to present you with a gift."

As we walked through the Throne Room, the onlookers grew silent. We marched down the marble floor and stood right in front of the steps leading up to the throne. The queen looked even older than she did the last time we'd seen her. Agbala stood at her side. I couldn't read much from her expression.

Makai gave a slight push on our shoulders, and we all kneeled. I reached out the scepter, and Aliyah presented the crown.

"No need for formalities. Not today," the queen said. "Rise. Stand, heroes, and approach. The gifts have returned."

We stood and climbed the steps. Agbala's face had brightened. She lifted her right hand high in the air, and music from harps and flutes began. Behind us was the swish of dresses sweeping the floor as the nobles began to celebrate the gifts returning to Asaba.

The queen took the scepter from me with shaking hands. We watched, and she inhaled sharply as the scepter sparkled with electric energy. The lightning traveled from the scepter to her hands and then to her face. She sat up straighter, the lines in her face reduced, and she returned to full color.

Aliyah passed her the crown. Ramala gently placed it on her head, inhaling again and sitting up even straighter. As she did, applause rang from behind us. Her hair was still gray, but she looked years younger and much healthier.

"I thank you so much for returning the gods' gifts to me. Now we must devote our energies to finding the ring. We can't have Amina ruling both worlds," Ramala said.

"Have you decided if you will stay in Asaba to fight for the ring?" Agbala asked.

"We have decided," Zion said.

"We are staying," Aliyah finished.

"Oh? I was led to believe that you had changed your minds," Agbala said.

"We did. Well, *I* did," I said, gritting my teeth. The ice in my heart was melting, even though I was trying to keep my anger on the surface. "But I realized that I can't make my friends' decisions for them." Even after I spoke, I thought of Mama and how Daddy had helped her fight. I was a child, but I had Aliyah and Zion to stand with me. We could do this. I knew we could.

Agbala clapped her hands. "Marvelous decision!"

"We must discuss the ring's whereabouts," the queen whispered. "You may do what you want today: rest, explore the grounds, swim in the rivers, go to the spa if you would like. Let me know when you are ready."

We proceeded down the steps, through the milling crowd of onlookers, and out into the hall in front of the Throne Room.

"Do you have any clue how to find the ring?" Aliyah whispered.

I shook my head. "No, I really don't."

CHAPTER THIRTY-ONE

We decided to devote our time to research. After ditching Makai, we walked outside the castle, past multiple court-yards, until we got to the library. We went in and found a cozy nook with a small table. Torchlight illuminated the darkness.

"Any ideas?" Zion asked, as we sat.

"I think we need to consult the *Book* again," I said. I closed my eyes and called for the magic within. When I opened my eyes, a shower of red light burst above us, and the *Book* appeared, swirling and turning in the light.

"I'm never gonna get used to *that* happening, either," Zion said.

"Show me the ring," I said.

The *Book* flipped open and fell to the table, solid. We all peered over as Zion read.

"The ring of immortality was created by Chukwu, the creator of all things. He gave his favorite son, Anyanwu, dominion over the sun and gave him the Sun Kingdom to rule. For millennia, Anyanwu rose in the sky and settled into darkness at night. For his faithfulness, Chukwu decided to give Anyanwu the ring of immortality.

"Anyanwu appeared at night with the other two gods when Ramala prayed to them for help. After she struck the bargain with them, Anyanwu gave her the last gift, his ring."

And that was it. We all sat back in our seats. The *Book* lifted itself off the table and continued to swirl around overhead. It turned back translucent.

"So . . . we're supposed to go to the sun . . . the actual *sun* to get information about the ring?" Zion asked. "Okay, it looks like I need to be the one to say it: *please* tell me no one is even *thinking* about doing this?"

I laughed. "No, we shouldn't go to the Sun Kingdom. But then again . . ."

"We were able to swim and breathe underwater . . . ," Aliyah pointed out.

"Right," I said. "But how are we supposed to get up there?"

"The gryphons?" Zion asked.

I sighed. "Maybe?"

We didn't say anything for a long while. I looked at the torchlight, trying to think of anything we might have missed. I directed my frustration toward the *Book* to force it to move, to show me something, anything. But it only revolved around my head as if my frustration didn't matter.

"Wait!" Aliyah said, so loud that Zion and I jumped in our seats.

She reached up, grabbed the *Book*, and slammed it down on the table. When she touched it, it turned solid again. She began to flip through the pages, faster and faster. "I *know* I remember seeing something . . .

"Ahh," she said when she reached her desired page. She pointed at an image. "Here it is."

Zion and I scooted closer to Aliyah and watched as the words translated to English. This page showed a coronation ceremony and an image of the queen and a tall man I assumed was Anyanwu—he looked human enough, but he was taller than anyone in the scene, and his body was covered in flames.

"Ooh, I remember the story now!" Zion exclaimed. "After the barrier was created, Anyanwu wanted to marry Ramala, but the queen was offended by his gesture."

"So . . . Anyanwu wanted to marry the queen, but she was angry about it? Why?" I asked.

"Look here," Zion said, pointing at a paragraph. "Because he didn't really love her. He wanted to bring his kingdom and Ramala's together as one."

"Right," Aliyah added. "And it says here that she had come

to love Anyanwu, almost from the time she met him. But the crown she wore gave her wisdom and knowledge. She realized that he had ulterior motives, that he was trying to use her."

"But how does that help us?" Zion asked.

"We know that the crown was in Onitsha," Aliyah said, running her hands through her hair.

"We know that Agwu was jealous of Amadioha for having the scepter and wanted it from Ramala after it was hers," I said.

"We also know that Amina eventually gave it to him. She saw the island of Okeniyi as protection for it," Aliyah said.

"But we were able to steal it from him." I smirked.

"So . . . that leads us nowhere." Zion groaned and plopped his head down on the table.

"Well, that leads us back to Anyanwu, the sun god," I said. "He would be the only one who might know where to find the ring. Just like Agwu was the key to the scepter."

"And that leads us back to the queen," Aliyah said. "You think she might know anything?"

"Pssh," Zion said. "She didn't even know where her sister took her gifts. Some queen she is; she can't even keep track of her stuff!"

"Well, the conversation isn't about how this woman rules her country or watches over her things," Aliyah said. "It's about returning *stolen* property."

Zion sat up and narrowed his eyes at her. "Look, I'm not trying to criticize her; I'm just saying—"

"Oh, I think we *both* know what you're trying to say." Aliyah huffed. "You're blaming the victim." She turned to me. "So what do we do?"

"There's only one thing we *can* do," I said. "We talk to the queen."

We asked Makai to take us to the queen. He led us to a grassy courtyard.

Ramala was sitting outside, surrounded by ladies-in-waiting. They were fanning her with palm leaves while she rested on a settee. Soldiers guarded the courtyard. She drank from a goblet, overlaid with gold and rubies.

"Queen Ramala, the heroes would like to speak with you," Makai announced.

She gave her goblet to a servant and shooed everyone away. "I will let you know when you may come back."

We sat across from her on soft, plush cushions on the ground. "We need to talk about Anyanwu," I said.

One of her eyebrows arched. "What about him?"

I tilted my head to the side and frowned. "Well, we were reading in the *Book*—"

Ramala's entire disposition changed. "What did you read?" she asked. What was once light was now dark. What was warm was now cold. Her mouth drew into a straight line as she glared at us.

"The *Book* mentioned Anyanwu gave you the ring of immortal—" Aliyah picked up.

"He didn't *give* me anything." Queen Ramala sat up straight. "I earned it with my prayers."

"Um . . . I don't think we meant to imply that you—" Aliyah started.

"Then what are you saying?"

We all fell into an awkward silence, none of us knowing exactly what to say. I wasn't a genius in the love category, but there was clearly something behind the queen's anger.

"We're asking because we need to know where the ring is," Zion finally said, cutting the tension. "Since you were the last one to have it—well, before your sister took it—then it's important if you know where she could possibly have hidden it."

"I mean, if you're going to have a bunch of twelve-year-olds find your ring, you'd better give them some information to go on," Aliyah said, annoyance clear in her voice. "We could be at home enjoying the pool, lazing around. It's summer. We're supposed to be on vacation, but instead, we're risking our lives. You're not."

The queen sighed. "You're right."

Ramala's eyes took on a reflective tone as she remembered. "I must admit that at one point, I was in love with Anyanwu. He was my sun, always shining eternally. But I knew I could never marry him. He didn't belong in my world. I told him I couldn't be with him, and he was angry about it. Yes, it is true that Anyanwu gave me his ring, granting me eternal life. But he did not love me back."

Ramala grew silent now as she seemed to be remembering her younger days as queen.

"What else?" I asked.

"That's about it. He asked to marry me, to merge our kingdoms together, but I said no. The bargain I'd made with the gods was the only bargain I was interested in." She then confirmed what we had found out in the *Book*.

"Men." Aliyah snorted, glaring at Zion.

"What?" Zion said.

"Yes, men," Ramala said, chuckling a bit. "The crown gave me wisdom and knowledge. I would not place my kingdom at risk anymore."

"Do you think Amina may have left the ring with him?" Zion asked.

She shook her head. "I do not think so. I haven't seen him in his human form or heard from Anyanwu in centuries. There's no reason to believe that Amina would use him to hide the ring."

"There was no reason to believe that Amina would use Agwu to hide the scepter, either," I pointed out.

Ramala leaned back on her settee. "That could be true, but I highly doubt it. Amina never knew about his marriage proposal. At least . . . I don't think she did."

Zion, Aliyah, and I all looked at one another.

"So . . . we don't have any clue as to where Amina may have taken the ring?" Aliyah asked.

"No, we don't," the queen said in a tone of voice that told us the conversation was over.

CHAPTER THIRTY-TWO

We returned to our chambers after our talk with Ramala. The sky was getting dark. The table in our suite was piled high with different varieties of food. Zion made himself a plate and started chowing down.

I was resting in a reclining chair, thinking about Ramala's words, when a sharp pain glanced across my chest. It felt much like it did when we had retrieved the gifts.

"Ow!" I said.

"What's wrong?" Aliyah said.

My vision began to blur. I tried to force my eyes to stay open, but I could feel myself losing consciousness. Zion shook my shoulders to wake me up. "Cam, what's wrong?"

I leaned forward but met only the crushing weight on my chest again. I shook my head, leaned back in my seat, closed my eyes, and succumbed to the pain.

For some reason, the *Book* sent me back to Shukti. I could

tell because of the deep darkness. I marched over the rock outcrop to the jumbled voices I heard, then stopped before Ekwensu's throne; a mass of mmo, speaking to one another in their own garbled tongue, stood behind him.

The death god bellowed, "Silence!"

They slunk away to the shadows, leaving a figure prostrate on the ground, covered by a long cape.

"You said you had protected the scepter. You said Ramala would *never* guess that it was hidden on Okeniyi," Ekwensu said, his voice low and icy, still reminding me of snakes slithering on the ground. He sat on his throne staring down at what I thought was Amina.

When Ekwensu raised his skeletal hand, Amina's body floated off the ground a few feet before she slammed right back onto the floor. She screamed, but the death god compelled her to stand up. He raised his hand, and her body flew upright, with her toes only barely touching the ground.

"Answer me, my darling princess," Ekwensu said, his voice still calm and low.

"I thought I had taken all the precautions," Amina struggled to say. "But the *Book* has returned."

"You said you had taken care of it!"

Ekwensu closed his hand into a loose fist, and I could hear Amina gasping for air as her breath was restricted. "I did . . . take . . . care of . . . the . . . *Book*," she managed to say.

He opened his hand. "So how is it here again?"

She rose in the air a couple more feet. She gasped again. "I talked with Agwu after the scepter was taken. He said three children stole it from him."

"Children?" Ekwensu said, his eyes burning with fire. "What does Ramala need with children?"

"One of the children who took the scepter is the Descendant. The last one had . . . a child. I . . . I am sorry I did not tell you when I found out."

With another flick of his hand, Ekwensu sent Amina down toward the ground again. She groaned as she hit the floor.

"Then you know what needs to be done. You must get the crown, the scepter, and *kill* the *Book* once and for all! My patience grows thin with you, Amina. If you fail, I will be forced to enter this fight."

"I promise I will not fail," Amina groaned. "I will storm the Palacia and kill the Descendant."

"Ensure that you do not," Ekwensu said. "For if you do, I'll destroy you and take over both worlds *without* your help."

I woke up. My chest was hurting so badly that I knew instantly this was not a dream or an illusion.

Zion and Aliyah shook me violently.

"I'm back," I said, breathing hard. "I'm back."

As their faces went from shock to overall concern for me, I stood and walked toward the door. "Where's Makai?" I asked.

"What's going on, Cam?" Zion asked.

"We need Makai. The soldiers must surround the Palacia and every courtyard. Amina is on her way to kill me."

"Wait, what? What do you mean?"

But I wasn't paying attention to them. I opened the door, stormed down the steps, and warned the guards there. Then I climbed back up the steps, two at a time, and ran toward the bedroom. I flung the door open with such force that it slammed against the opposite wall. I grabbed my armor.

Zion was right behind me. He said nothing at first, just followed my lead and started to prepare himself for battle.

"I saw Amina again," I said, pulling on my boots. "Ekwensu was torturing her. She convinced him that I stole the crown and scepter. She is amassing her mmo army right now and is about to storm the castle."

"I believe you," he said, putting on his armor.

By the time we got back to the sitting room, Aliyah was ready to fight, her sword tied to her waist. I told her what I had seen. Then we marched to the hall leading to the Throne Room, just as Makai barreled through the crowds of soldiers.

He grabbed my shoulders. "Cameron, are you sure of this information?" he asked.

The pain in my chest was still there, evidence to me that what I had experienced and heard was real. "I'm telling the truth."

The Throne Room door opened, and Ramala appeared,

holding her scepter and wearing her crown, dressed for battle.

"My queen, you must go inside," Makai said. "I will set soldiers around your rooms to protect you. You must not be seen with the gifts in front of Amina. She comes for them and to kill the Descendant."

She brushed him away with a wave of her hand. "Nonsense. Chidani is *my* country. The Palacia is *my* home. The reign is mine. I will not allow Amina to take my throne or destroy the Descendant. I am ill, but with the gifts that have already been returned to me, I am now well enough to fight. I will stand for the Igbo people, with or without the ring to aid me."

Makai took her hand and led her to the courtyard. We followed behind them and watched the skies. Soldiers spilled into the other courtyards and gates, securing the perimeters of the Palacia. I gazed at the stone wall surrounding us. I had a feeling it wouldn't hold against the mmo.

The queen beckoned me forward. "You must go inside, Descendant. If Amina spots you, she will attack with the full might of her power. We must protect you; only you can find the ring."

I shook my head. "Absolutely not. I will fight with my friends, for my friends."

She signaled to one of her Queensguard. "Lock him down until the fight is over."

A noise stopped us all in our tracks. The sky darkened,

and a sound like trumpets blaring met our ears. The ground shook.

"What's going on?" Zion asked, but no one answered him.

We all heard a ripping sound as we watched the skies. In the middle of a cloud, a deep white line appeared, so bright that it almost burned my eyes. The rip opened farther and farther until a figure, riding on the back of a fearsome gryphon—much bigger than the ones we had ridden— appeared. I could barely see the figure, but I knew exactly who it was.

"Sister," Amina called out from her perch. "It's been some time since we last saw each other. Hand over the *Book* and no harm shall befall you or the people you are protecting." Although she was far away, we all heard her voice. Scores of mmo appeared through the rip and surrounded Amina.

We waited to hear what the queen would say, but nothing came. Ramala only put her fist in the air, the symbol to hold. I could just make out the sounds of soldiers' boots running on the castle walls, getting into position from everywhere inside the Palacia.

"This is your last chance," Amina called. "I don't want bloodshed, but you shall have it if you do not deliver the Descendant."

Again, the queen said nothing.

"So be it," the princess said. "I *will* have the *Book*, even if blood runs down the streets of Asaba." She released the reins of the gryphon and stood.

The queen opened her hand. At the top of the Palacia, the archers raised their arrows.

With a flick of her hand, the princess soared toward the Palacia. A red light appeared around her body as she descended, and the *Book* within my chest stirred. As I gritted my teeth, the sky exploded as the mmo unleashed themselves through the light and tumbled toward the ground.

Ramala brought her hand down and raised her scepter. "Attack!"

CHAPTER THIRTY-THREE

I unstrapped the sword as the mmo traveled to the courtyard grounds. Someone grabbed me by the shoulder and pulled me upward a bit.

"The queen gave an order," Makai said. I tried to squirm away from him, but his strength was considerable. He placed my feet back on the ground and began to walk me toward the Palacia doors. "If Princess Amina is able to capture you, then everything we have fought for is for nothing."

He tightened his hold on my shoulder as we went through the doors. I turned to see Zion and Aliyah following us, Halifa and Bakari leading them. I tried to squirm away again.

"Makai, she's going to destroy everything! I need to fight! It's my duty as the Descendant!"

"No, your duty is to stay safe," he said as he led me up the spiraling staircase to our rooms. "This isn't your fight.

Not yet." He opened the double doors and gently pushed me inside. Zion and Aliyah joined me, along with Halifa and Bakari. Makai started to close the door in my face as I marched toward him.

"Wait!" I said. I balled my fist in anger and resisted the urge to stomp my feet. They were already treating us like children; I didn't want to give them any more opportunities to speak to us as if we were inferior. "If this isn't my fight, then what is? Because *we* found the crown and the scepter. *We* trained and successfully fought a god. Let us protect the barrier! I didn't go through the Cave of Shadows for nothin'!"

"A true soldier listens to their superiors," Makai said before shutting the door.

"This is outrageous!" I said, pacing back and forth in front of the oak door. I pushed against it, but it wouldn't budge.

"Listen to what the queen is saying, Cameron," Halifa said. "We would rather fight as well . . ."

"But you're much too important," Bakari finished. "If you die, everything fails. And then what? Makai is right: all we have fought for would have been for nothing."

I heard footsteps behind me. "Cam—" Aliyah said.

I shrugged her off and walked to our windows overlooking the Palacia grounds. I groaned. There was nothing but gray sky in front of me. I heard muffled sounds of a distant battle, but that was it. The *Book* twitched in my chest, and I expected to feel pain, but there was none.

"Well, I guess there's nothing to do but to wait here," Zion said, walking to the table, grabbing a plate of food, and pouring himself a cup of water.

I rolled my eyes. "Is there anything else you can think about besides your stomach?"

Zion was unfazed. "Listen, there's nothing we can do now."

Aliyah came to stand beside me as I returned my gaze to the window. I heard a flapping of wings as black shadows pierced through the skies. I strained to hear the battle below us. My heart began to beat faster and faster. I clutched at my chest.

"Breathe, Cameron," she said.

I shook my head. "Something's wrong."

"Do you see something?"

I shook my head again. Fear built inside me. The scene in front of me vanished, and I found myself falling toward the ground, my body covered in shadows and smoke. I saw myself and Aliyah looking out the window. There was a realization now, a rushed feeling of exhilaration. I had found them.

I opened my eyes and stumbled back. Aliyah grabbed my shoulders while Zion dropped his plate.

"I saw them," I said, taking deep breaths. "They know where we are."

"Wait, what do you mean—" Halifa managed to say before a sickening crunch stopped us all in our tracks. We immediately removed our swords from their sheaths.

"It's coming from the ceiling," Bakari said.

We all looked above us. A crack appeared in the ceiling. Another crunch sounded in the room, and everyone took a step back. Plaster fell to the floor, and the fissure opened wider. By the time we realized what was happening, it was much too late. An explosion rocked the room, sending us all falling. Zion and I stumbled backward toward the entrance to our chambers.

I tried to stand, but a piece of the ceiling slammed into me. I heard a groan as I was pinned to the floor. Zion was knocked out beside me, curled up near one of the floor cushions next to our chamber doors. I pushed on the stones, but they wouldn't move. There was another explosion; then all sound ceased. A shadowy figure stepped to the side of me, obscuring my view of Zion. I tried to grab at my sword, but I couldn't move.

A snakelike voice spoke, sending chills coursing through my body.

"Akwukwo, akwukwo, akwukwo," it said. It was a haunting sound, almost like the way Ekwensu spoke. And it was chanting the Igbo word for "book." The mmo in the room were looking for the *Book*, and they had found me.

"Aliyah! Halifa! Bakari!" I managed to choke out. The shadowy figure beside me solidified into hard gray skin and walked toward me. With one swipe, the piece of the heavy ceiling pinning me down crashed against a wall, shattering apart.

The dead spirit repeated its refrain as it stared down at

me. "Akwukwo, akwukwo, akwukwo—book, book, book." Its voice was strained. Hollow. Tortured. It towered above me, weaponless. Its mouth was twisted in a harsh smile, its nose sloping downward, and its head shorn except for a few patches of hair. Corded with muscles, it wore no clothes except for a dirty loincloth around its waist. Repeating the same word over and over again, it took another step toward me. I struggled to move, but the pain was much too great.

It reached to grab me.

"No!" I screamed as dust swirled around us. There was another explosion, and the door behind me blasted open. A shocked expression crawled across the mmo's face. A sword tip had pierced its neck. Bile and black blood rolled down to the carpet. The mmo stumbled and turned to dust as it fell. Zion was standing behind it, trembling with his sword in his hand. Halifa was right behind him, covered in dust. They ran over to me as the slithering sounds increased.

"Get up—we have to go," Zion said.

I coughed and tried to stand, but agony constrained me. "I can't," I managed to say.

Halifa removed a flask from her pocket and kneeled down to me. "Hurry. Drink this."

Shadows dropped from the ceiling and into our destroyed chambers, so many that I could barely count them. Smoke filled the room as they materialized.

Halifa picked me up from the floor as I was unscrewing the cap of the flask and swallowing the azizan light. The icy liquid fell down my throat as time shifted until everything slowed down. I felt my injuries heal as Halifa carried me through the blasted door, down the staircase, and toward the Throne Room. I could just make out Zion traveling behind her, concern for me drawn all over his face.

By the time Halifa placed me on my feet, I had healed. She stepped out of Dambe and looked around. Crowds of soldiers were standing around the Palacia doors near the Throne Room. I shivered when I saw the smashed marble in the middle of the floor, bearing a hole that burrowed deep into the dungeons.

"Where are Aliyah and Bakari?" I asked through clenched teeth.

"Don't know," Zion said.

"One minute we were in your chambers, and the next . . . ," Halifa said.

"They broke through the ceiling," I said, almost wanting to curse. "The one that was standing over me . . . it . . . it knew I was the *Book*, that I had it."

"They are coming for Cam," Zion said, fear plain in his voice.

Someone barreled down the hallway we had just come from. Everyone turned. It was Bakari, his face dripping with blood. Fear gripped me as I ran to him. *Please, please, don't be hurt.* He stumbled to me, breathing hard, crushing me to him.

"I tried to stop them . . . I tried . . . I wasn't fast enough . . . ," he said.

"Where's Aliyah?" I asked.

He shook his head. "We were fighting together at first. But when the dust cleared, she was gone. I'm sorry. I thought she was beside me the entire time."

"We need to find her," I said. "Halifa, heal him." She handed him a flask of azizan light.

"No, you don't," someone said. It was Makai, walking toward us.

"No. We need to find Aliyah. They wouldn't have taken her if they weren't trying to get to me!"

"The mmo are in the Palacia," Makai said. "We fight from the center and hope it's not overrun." To Halifa he said, "Take Cameron and Zion somewhere they will be safe. We can search for Aliyah as we secure the Palacia."

There was that snakelike sound again, coming from above. Makai was wrong. It was too late—we couldn't secure the Palacia. The ceiling in our chambers had caved; who knew how many mmo had gotten in? We were surrounded.

Makai pulled out his sword, and the rest of the soldiers followed him. I noticed something moving next to a statue in an alcove to the left of the hall. A sound met my ears. I felt no fear this time, only anger at losing Aliyah and at Amina sending her mmo for me. I wanted to fight, and if the movement in the shadows was any indication, we all were about to.

"I think that—" I began to say as the shadows moved closer to us. I didn't get to finish. The smoke blacked everything out as the mmo blasted into the great hall. The Palacia door Makai had just come through burst open.

I went to stand beside Zion. "We fight our way through and we find Aliyah." I stared at him intently. "We do it together."

He nodded. I couldn't tell if he was scared or determined. As soon as the mmo solidified, all sound seemed to cease, and time slowed as we entered Dambe. Then chaos erupted.

As soon as I jumped into the air, I was knocked down from above. Two mmo grabbed me under my shoulders as I started to fall. They lifted me upward, repeating the same word.

"Akwukwo, akwukwo, akwukwo," they said as they carried me. I reached upward with my sword, slicing wherever I could. I heard a cry of pain and dropped to my feet before rolling over to blunt the impact. The last mmo that carried me was on top of me almost immediately. I scrambled to the side, but it caught me by my dashiki and threw me to the opposite wall. I coughed and looked at the carnage around me. Soldiers and mmo moved so fast that I could barely see. My sword had almost fallen from my hand. I gripped it as the mmo continued to advance.

Another one joined it and they stalked me. An object hit the wall to my right, but I did not turn to look. I needed to be calm, just as Nneka and Agbala had said. I launched into Dambe and ran forward to meet both the mmo, keeping all thoughts of the fight around me at bay. Zion seemed to step through thin air right in front of me. I turned and touched his back with mine, almost as if we were one person. Both of our swords came up at the same time as we met the mmo with full force.

We fought together, our swords fast and sure. The mmo I was fighting blocked my weapon with its arm and pushed outward with its fist, connecting with my face. I groaned but kept my balance. I swiped upward with my sword, and it clanged against its arm, almost like it was a stone brick standing in my way. Every sword jab was blocked and parried, so I moved away from Zion to give myself more room. Going low, I watched as my sword was stopped by its feet. I jumped high and was pushed back downward. Sweat began to pour from my forehead, almost blinding me. I swiped one arm over my eyes just in time to see the mmo swipe at me in slow motion.

I moved to the side and sliced down, cutting its arm off. It screamed as the appendage turned to dust and fell to the floor. Before it could regain its composure, I sliced straight through its chest. I turned just in time to see Zion killing his mmo, too. I went to stand beside him in the confusion.

"Maybe they took her outside where Amina is?" he asked.

I cut down another one as it rounded upon us.

We continued to fight as we made our way to the open doors. I caught a glimpse of Halifa and Bakari moving toward us. They fought with us, barreling through the mmo as if they were mere annoyances.

By the time the four of us got to the Palacia doors, more mmo were streaming in the great hall, from the ceiling and through the crack in the floor. Before they could make it to the center of the space, a bolt of lightning struck and killed the rest of them. I took a deep breath, grateful for the reprieve, and left Dambe. Ramala walked through the Palacia doors, holding her scepter high.

Everyone grew silent, although the snarling growls of the mmo could be heard from all over the castle. Ramala took a look at the broken floor, tensing before speaking. "They are in the castle. Where is the *Book*?"

Zion and I walked forward.

She pointed at us. "Protect them."

Her words were drowned out by smoke gathering in the great hall once again.

I heard fighting noises, swords slashing through the air, and voices. Before I could think, something punched me in the side of the face, sending me flying across the room. My back hit a statue, and it smashed as I fell. The head of it dropped on my leg, trapping me.

"*Book*, book, book," a voice said. As my heart started to race, a mmo scrambled over to me and landed right on top of the rubble trapping my foot, crouching as it did. I tried to stifle a scream, but I wasn't successful. The mmo looked at me with its bright red eyes, and something like a smile lighted its horrible face.

"Akwukwo, akwukwo, akwukwo," it repeated.

"Zion? Makai?" I managed to say, but nobody heard me. The mmo stared at me one last time and then stood. With a swift movement, the creature swiped at the marble that was trapping me yet again.

The mmo reached down and grabbed me by the throat, choking me. I struggled for breath and tried to remove the creature's hands from my neck, but I wasn't strong enough. It picked me up from the floor and held me high in the air, then tore the sword from my grasp and threw it to the ground. The pain was too much; I drifted in and out of consciousness. I tried to call for help again, but every time I opened my mouth, I felt myself choking on dust. The mmo jumped through the hole in the floor, and we tumbled down into darkness.

I tried to fight it, to claw away from the mmo, but it held me tightly. After falling for a few seconds, we reached the rocky underground. It stood and ran down one of the tunnels, turned right, ran down another tunnel, and stopped in a type of clearing. There, groups of mmo were walking around, talking in their own language. Once they saw me, though, they rounded on me, screaming, "Akwukwo, akwukwo, akwukwo."

The mmo holding me threw me against a side wall of the tunnel. I stumbled down to the ground, unable to move. The mmo stalked around me, grunting to one another. The mmo carrying me grunted again, pointed at me, and shook its fingers. Two of them stepped forward and held me firmly while binding me with a rope. I tried not to let the tears fall. Not only had I lost Aliyah, but I was also caught by the mmo, and now I'd lost Zion, too. I felt so much guilt. It was because of me that the mmo had attacked the Palacia to begin with.

One of them clearly said, "Amina." Now it all made sense. I was being taken to her. So she could kill me.

The mmo standing beside me started to make a noise. The other one holding me made the same noise, too, until the entire group of mmo milling about me had joined in. A bright red light appeared around their bodies.

They're calling for Amina.

As they did, my chest began to ache again, and my eyes clouded until I was in darkness. I heard crying first. Then I saw her, saw a vision of Aliyah. She was shivering underground, and tears shone on her cheeks. A mmo walked in front of her, shrouding her from my view. I opened my eyes again, and the vision of Aliyah was gone.

I needed to get out of here.

Something moved in the darkness as the mmo continued to call for Amina.

"Cameron?" someone whispered. It was a familiar voice. *Bakari.*

"Duck," someone else said. *Zion.*

I did what I was told. A sword flew through the air, cutting down the two mmo holding me. The group screamed and scrambled around the area, looking for the owner of the sword. Zion appeared at my side and sliced at the ties binding my hands. It was my sword; he must've picked it up after the mmo dropped it.

"Let's go," he said, pulling me to my feet. Bakari rounded the corner, retrieved his thrown sword, and fought the group of mmo until I was free. Once we stumbled away, Bakari joined us.

"There're so many of them," he said. We heard stomping as the mmo ran after us, but Bakari took us down a narrow pathway and then crawled into a small space, just big enough for us to crouch in the darkness. We watched as the mmo ran past us.

Zion hugged me. I hugged him back.

"Aliyah was captured, but I think they were supposed to find me and not her. She's down here. I saw her in a vision."

"We should climb back to the great hall," Bakari whispered. "There're too many of them to beat them alone."

"Listen," I hissed. "I'm not leaving Aliyah."

"What do you need us to do?" Zion said.

"We use Dambe, we go fast, and we rescue her."

I grabbed both of their hands. As soon as I did, time seemed to slow, like we were walking through thick molasses. They followed me down the tunnels. We walked slowly and hid behind walls and partitions. Every time we got to a curve, we peeked around it. The creatures seemed to be shadows growing from the walls, the floor, and the dirt.

We ran deeper into the tunnels, keeping our eyes peeled in the darkness. We heard a noise as the ground sloped downward. We could hear the clashing of swords just behind us as the Queensguard finally were able to breach the hole to stop the mmo from advancing through it.

We turned our attention back to the slithering noises coming from down the hall.

"Is . . . that what they sound like when they talk to each other?" Zion said, his voice shaking.

Putting a finger to my lips, I nodded and pointed forward. We continued to run, hoping none of the creatures would be coming back and forth—there were no other pathways, corners, or curves but this one. We continued to walk through the darkness until our eyes were able to adjust to it. The slithering noises grew louder and louder until we heard a clink of a metal door sliding shut.

The three of us moved to a small corner built into the walls. In front of us mmo walked back and forth in front of what looked like a jail cell. In it, there was Aliyah, sitting on the floor, her knees bunched up to her chest. I moved forward, but Bakari held me back.

"What if it's a trap?" he whispered.

"We just need to get closer," I insisted.

"No. Think about it. You said they called for Amina. We'll need help to fight her."

The sharp pain appeared in my chest again, causing me to stoop over and hold on to the corner of the wall.

"I think she's here," I managed to say.

CHAPTER THIRTY-FOUR

In a burst of red light, Amina appeared in front of us. The mmo bowed. The princess kissed her sword and whispered, "Thank you, Ekwensu, for your power."

She rattled it against the prison bars.

"Do you know me?" Amina asked.

Aliyah nodded but said nothing.

Amina sniffed the air. "Where is the Descendant? I can sense that he's close by. Ramala wouldn't be foolish enough to let him fight."

"I . . . I don't know," Aliyah said.

"Are you being truthful?" Amina's voice darkened. "All I need to do is open this cell, and the mmo will take care of you."

"I—I really am telling the truth," Aliyah stuttered. "We got split up. Th-the ceiling caved in, and someone captured me before I could fight back."

Amina turned around to the mmo and spoke to them in their guttural and hissing language. Her hands became animated, and she narrowed her eyes. I could hear the words "Descendant" and "Ekwensu" being spoken a number of times before Amina raised her sword and killed two of them as they spoke. They exploded in black shadows. The others stood straighter, but Amina turned back to Aliyah.

"Why do I always have to do everything myself?" Amina said, but I could tell that her voice was shaking. She muttered under her breath, "They are right. Ekwensu will kill me if I don't make sure the Descendant dies, once and for all."

She signaled to a mmo and spoke louder. "Release the prisoner. We will use her as leverage. I'll take her to the skies if I have to."

"Let's go," Bakari said. "We can't save Aliyah if we're caught, too."

Reluctantly, I followed them back through the tunnels so that we weren't caught. I wanted so badly to save Aliyah, but I didn't know how. We needed a plan.

"We have to draw Amina to the main floor," I whispered to Zion. "Then maybe we'll have a chance of getting Aliyah back."

"But what about you?" he asked. "You can't just give yourself up to her!"

I smiled at him. "Who said I was thinking about doing anything like that? Look, we need information on how to find the ring, right? If I can surrender just long enough to figure out its location, I can escape somehow and get back to you."

Bakari groaned. "That's not a good idea. I'm not going to let you do that."

"I agree, Cam. Amina will never let you escape her after she captures you."

"Well, we're just going to have to come up with another plan, then. You and Aliyah can't die because of me. I brought you guys into this. I'm the Descendant, so it's my job to end this, once and for all."

Fear crossed Zion's expression.

"We have to get Aliyah back. I think it's the only way." We moved on, still clinging to the walls and running into corners whenever a threat presented itself.

The hole was crowded with mmo trying to climb into the great hall, but the creatures were losing badly. The soldiers had overtaken that section of the castle, and they were now milling around the blast site, some of them standing at the top and some of them down inside the tunnels, their swords continuing to clash with the advancing mmo. We continued upward, trying to find another way back to the great hall.

We walked up two floors until we came to another blast site. I helped Zion through the opening, then climbed up behind him. We followed the passage back to the great hall. Black blood and dust covered every surface; it shrouded the walls, the broken statues, the destroyed paintings, and the floors.

Standing in the middle of the hall was Makai. He breathed a sigh of relief when he saw us approaching. "Good, you found Cameron."

"We found Aliyah, too," I said. "Amina is here underneath the Palacia—we saw her with our own eyes—but she won't be there for long."

"Then we need to send soldiers even farther into the tunnels," Makai said.

I grabbed his arm. "If Amina sees that we know where she is, she might kill Aliyah. She's using her to find me."

Makai signaled for a group of soldiers. He whispered to them, pointed at the hole in the floor, and then spoke to me. "And if we do nothing? Look, listen to me and stay with us. It's safer this way."

We all followed him as he walked into the courtyard. Another explosion rocked the sky, opening the deep line in the clouds again. More mmo spilled from it and started to fall toward the ground, but something stopped them in midair. Halifa jogged through the crowd of soldiers and joined us.

I scanned the sky for any sign of Ekwensu or Amina, but there were only mmo. They turned in the air, unleashing their guttural sounds. I held on tightly to my sword.

There was a flash of red light.

Above us, floating in the air with the rest of her army of mmo, was Amina, holding a struggling Aliyah by her dashiki. I held my hand up and called wordlessly for Ugo as an idea came to me.

"I really do not want to kill a child, but I will do so if the Descendant does not present himself," Amina said.

The queen stepped forward. "You don't need to do this, sister. Mother and Father left us a legacy of sacrifice and resilience. We have given up too much to have this place be a paradise and a safe haven for the Igbo."

"Make no mistake, sister," Amina said, "I *will* kill the child if that is what it comes to. *Give* me the Descendant. I can smell the stench of the magic radiating from his body even now." Amina's eyes found mine and pointed at me. "Hmm. He *is* here."

I walked toward the queen, still hoping and praying that my help would come.

"What are you doing?" Ramala whispered. The court-yard had grown completely quiet.

"I'm here," I said to Amina in a soft voice. "Please let my friend go. She has nothing to do with any of this."

Even from where I was standing, I could see Amina's face brighten with an evil smile.

"So you finally show yourself to me. Wonderful. You will open the barrier for me now."

She pushed Aliyah forward.

"Don't hurt her!" I yelled. "Please, I will do anything you want. Just don't kill my friend."

"I don't know. Maybe I've changed my mind. I asked you to surrender before all of this started, but you chose otherwise.

Now I have lost most of my mmo army. There has to be consequences."

"Please, just let her go."

Ramala sensed what I was going to do. She grabbed my shoulder, hard. "Cameron, no!"

I shrugged her off. I was done allowing them to tell me what to do. "I will give you what you want if you just let her go."

"Let her go?" Amina asked, smiling sweetly. "Well . . . if that's what you want."

Amina opened her hand.

Aliyah screamed as she started to fall.

CHAPTER THIRTY-FIVE

I launched myself into Dambe. Before anyone could catch me, I was running across the courtyard toward the mountain's edge. A flap of wings greeted my ears.

Time slowed as soon as I reached the edge of the mountain and threw myself into the air. I didn't know if I would survive this, but I heard Agbala's words in my head: *Remember, you have the Book, which means you have power. Use it.*

For the first time, I finally did feel like the Descendant—I knew exactly what I had to do. I rose to meet Aliyah's falling body. Ugo screeched and floated beneath me. I landed on him and dug my heels into his sides, directing him in the direction of the still-falling Aliyah. A flash of lightning almost blinded me, but I kept my eyes open. I was so close to her now that I could see tears streaking her cheeks.

Aliyah screamed again as I maneuvered Ugo close enough to catch her. She fell onto his back with a groan.

Amina appeared in midair in an explosion of ruby light, her teeth bared, her cape and braided hair flowing behind her. She raised her hands. "Give me the *Book*, Descendant."

I turned from her and urged Ugo toward the mountain's edge. Another flash of light told me she was following me at full speed. With all my strength, I pushed us both to the Palacia grounds, and we landed right on the cobblestones.

I jumped down from Ugo and helped Aliyah to dismount. We both ran back to the Palacia doors as Ugo flapped his wings, screeched, and then flew into the air. Another explosion sounded. Amina was running across the courtyard, directing her anger right at me. She cut down multitudes of soldiers as she ran. I watched in horror as they rose again as shadow, as mmo.

I turned to meet her attack head-on as Aliyah ran ahead, and I thrust my sword forward. Amina's strength was formidable, augmented by the death god. Her sword came down in an arc, and I stumbled, missing her strike by mere inches. She moved quickly, but I moved just as fast. But then as I backed up from one of her sword swipes, I tripped on a rock and fell. She grasped me by my neck and raised me in the air. As her sword came up to meet my chest, I summoned Dambe and kicked her stomach, and her hand slipped from my neck. She was quick and moved into Dambe, too.

I hit the ground and scrambled away as she raised her sword to strike me again. She moved so quickly that I could barely turn from her sword attacks in time. A small crater appeared every time her weapon struck the ground. She raised her sword again, an evil smile brightening her face. "I will get the *Book* even if I have to cut it out of you."

As she raised her arm again, a figure barreled through a group of mmo and connected with her side, sending her flying across the courtyard. *Zion.* He reached down, grabbed my hand, and pulled me to my feet. Before I could open my mouth, Amina was back, murder in her eyes. We both battled her now. I heard another sound and saw Ramala, running through the crowd. Amina fought all three of us with precision, trying her hardest to get to me.

Zion tripped, and when she slashed at his cheek, he stumbled backward, causing her to advance on him. I reached out and kicked her in the back. She turned to me, and the dance began again, Zion, Ramala, and me weaving around one another, striking at her with our swords whenever we could, taking small hits, and retaliating with our own. Amina jumped in the air and twirled in a deadly arc. Ramala jumped after her.

Zion raised his sword as she came down, clipping her right in the stomach. Ramala struck her from above. Amina fell to the ground, while Ramala rolled to her feet.

I delivered the last blow, right through her left shoulder. Amina grunted as she stared upward at me in pure hatred.

She sputtered and looked over to her shoulder as blood spurted out onto the ground.

"It's over, Amina," I whispered, removing my sword and placing it near her throat.

She sneered. "Boy, it's never over." Red light exploded around her and launched itself into the sky.

As I turned to look at the clouds, Zion and Ramala kept their eyes and swords trained on the princess.

The clouds parted, and a lone figure floated in the air, falling down closer and closer to the edge of the mountain. It was a mmo, the last one remaining in Amina's army.

I raised my sword to face the creature shrouded in black and shadows.

"Would you give me the *Book* now if I give it life again?" Amina said in a low voice, coughing up blood.

I looked at the mmo. Another bright red light spread all over the creature's body, removing the black of its visage, the gray of its skin, the ruby in its eyes, and the yellow of its long nails.

The figure struggled as the creature's outer layer blew away in the wind.

"Cam, what's going on?" Zion said.

The figure emerged from the mmo like a butterfly from a chrysalis, its hair blowing in the wind, its brown skin shining in the light that surrounded it, its dark-brown eyes trained on me. It was dressed in a flowing gown, almost angelic, but its face was contorted in unbearable and unmistakable pain.

"Mama?"

CHAPTER THIRTY-SIX

"Cameron, no!" someone screamed. I ran across the court-yard to my mama. Amina emitted a monstrous laugh from behind me, but I kept running.

Mama looked at me and blinked. Then her face turned ashen, her nose slanted downward, and her skin was covered in gray once again.

"Mama!" I yelled as I got to the edge of the cliff. But the mmo only struggled in the air, releasing guttural noises. I turned to see Makai and a couple of the other soldiers pick-ing up Amina from the ground and tying her with heavy rope so she couldn't move. They pulled her onto their shoul-ders and walked with her inside the Palacia.

When I turned back around, my mama had disappeared. Amina continued to scream and laugh maniacally as she was carried inside. "I have your mother! And I won't let her go until the *Book* is in my hands!"

I twirled my sword in the air, faster and faster, so that I could launch it at Amina. "I'll kill you!" I yelled. She should have to suffer the way my mama had.

Something strong clamped down on my shoulder, stopping the momentum of the sword. "No, Cameron," Ramala said. "We have captured Amina. We need to figure out where the ring is. We can't do that if she's dead."

I shrugged her arm off me. "Leave me alone," I growled. "Zion! Aliyah!" I trudged up the Palacia steps and into the destroyed great hall. I did my best to stop the tears from falling down my face. Not now, not in front of everyone. Soldiers watched us as we picked through the debris and climbed the steps to our chambers.

"Grab your stuff," I managed to say. "We're going home."

I took off my armor and my dirty clothes, placed them on the large bed, and grabbed the repaired clothes I had worn when I came to Chidani. I retrieved Zion's clothes, too, and threw them at him.

"Cam?" he said.

I held up a hand. "No. Just put on your clothes and let's go."

I could feel the tension in the room as I finished dressing, but Zion didn't say anything. When we got back into the sitting area, Aliyah was waiting for us.

"How are we going to get home?" she asked.

"Agbala said I have the ability to open portals to both worlds," I said.

"Are you sure?"

"I've made up my mind," I said, glancing back and forth between them as I stood by the fire. "Look, I'm tired of this. My mama has been a mmo for I don't know how long, and who knows what really happened to my daddy? I just need to go home. Please?" I managed to squeak out.

As soon as they touched me, I started to cry. I wiped my tears away and concentrated on the opposite wall. I knew what to do. I called with all my strength for the portal to open.

There was a boom of light and a rumbling, and then the portal opened, right along the wall, shining blue and tinged with lightning.

"Cameron—" Agbala said, coming into the sitting room.

"Too late," I said, and I pulled Zion and Aliyah with me as I ran toward the portal. We leaped through the hole in the wall and disappeared.

CHAPTER THIRTY-SEVEN

We spiraled through darkness once again before we landed on a hard surface. I looked around and saw that we were back in Grandma's attic. Moonlight poured in through the skylight above us.

"Mama, Daddy," I whispered. I wasn't sure who I was talking to, but the words kept spewing from my mouth on repeat.

I felt a sharp pang in my stomach that made me double over and almost fall to the ground. Aliyah and Zion picked me up. These were the tears I had been saving for so long, tears that I needed to shed at the loss of my parents. I didn't know what to think or what to believe. I just knew that my mama was undead and that my daddy was nowhere.

A growl came from behind us. Before we could turn around, the attic door burst open. Grandma was standing right in front of us, holding a kitchen knife. "Cameron, move!"

Whatever the thing was behind us growled louder, so close to us that goose bumps rose on my neck.

Grandma reeled back and threw the knife with all her strength. We ducked out of the way, then heard a scream. I stood up to see a mmo standing near the attic's window. The knife was protruding from its chest. It screamed again before falling to the ground and turning to dust.

"It finally shows itself," Grandma said, walking through the attic door.

"Wait, what?" I said.

"That . . . *thing* has been prowling around here for years, Cameron; that's why I didn't want you coming up here. When the pictures changed . . . I had to protect you somehow."

"I *knew* there was something wrong with our house!"

Grandma opened and closed her mouth, as if she didn't know what to say. Then she sighed. "I used to be the Descendant before your mama, so I noticed the changes. I tried my best to . . . to shield you from everything. There has simply been too much pain."

"You know about everything?" Zion said.

"Of course I know!" Grandma said, pulling herself to her full height. "I'm a Battle. The *Book* is part of our family."

"How long have we been gone?" Aliyah asked. "When we were in Chidani, it felt like we had been there for months."

"I'm glad it wasn't months for me, or I wouldn't have known what to say to your parents. It has only been three days' time in our world."

The mention of parents caused tears to roll down my cheeks again. I ran to Grandma, enfolding myself in her arms. "She's a mmo," I said, rocking back and forth, more tears falling. "And I don't even know what happened to Daddy. What if he's one of them, too?"

Grandma could do nothing but rub my back and hold me close in her warm embrace. I couldn't believe how badly I had missed everything about her, from her smell to the way she yelled at me for not cleaning my room when she told me. I even missed all the times she'd barred me from the attic. Maybe if I'd listened to her, none of this would have happened.

"Come on, let's go to your room," she said. We all walked down the attic steps and back to my room, where she helped me to sit on the edge of my bed. She sat down with me and pulled me close to her. "I didn't want you to go to Chidani, didn't want that life for you. But once I felt the changes, once I was certain that the mmo were trying to get to our world, once one showed up in our house, I knew it was only a matter of time before we had to fight back. I just didn't want you to go over there so young, baby."

"I saw her," I finally admitted. "I saw them both in a vision from the day they died. It was my last test before I mastered my fear of fighting. I'm not scared anymore, but . . . seeing them one last time . . . seeing them . . . die . . . was too much for me."

Aliyah patted my shoulder. "Cam, I'm so sorry."

Zion gripped my hand and squeezed. "You shouldn't have had to go through that."

I didn't know what else to say. It was all just so unfair. It seemed like everyone around me had loving parents and I didn't. Fresh tears stung my eyes.

"She's a mmo, Grandma," I repeated. "When she died, that's what she became, and Amina won't let her go."

Grandma rocked me back and forth, her own tears falling onto my shoulders. "That should've never happened. We can't let her stay a mmo, Cameron. We must do something."

"I tried, Grandma. I tried," I said, feeling as if the tears would never stop.

"But what do we do now?" Aliyah asked. "We can't just leave Chidani the way it is."

"Amina has been captured, but the ring is still hidden somewhere," Zion said. "I don't know about y'all, but we can't have the barrier overrun with demons."

I faced them. "Don't you get it? I don't care about Chidani anymore! They took everything from me. They can solve their own problems!" Even as I was saying those words, I knew I didn't mean anything I said. Mama and Daddy hadn't seen it that way. They had seen Amina and Ekwensu as a threat and had wanted to do everything in their power to stop them, to save everyone in both worlds. Even if it meant that they might never see me again. Daddy didn't even have ties to Chidani, and he had chosen to help because he loved Mama and he loved me, and they both loved our people and our world.

I couldn't allow their memory to be tarnished because I

didn't want to fight back. I had to fight back because they had fought for me. Mama and Grandma's legacy lived through me, and it was a role I had no choice but to accept. And now, after everything I'd seen, after everything I'd done, I actually *wanted* to accept that role.

Grandma brushed the tears from my face. "Amina did this, *not* the people of Chidani. You have to stop her. *We* are your family now. Zion and Aliyah and me, and all the people of Chidani. I am sorry about what happened to your mama and daddy, more than you know, and heaven knows I've tried to keep you from harm. But y'all are smarter than I thought. I can't keep the legacy of our family from you—the *Book* won't allow me to anymore. When you left, I realized that I can't protect you the way I want to. I'm . . . I'm not meant to."

They *were* my family now. Amina had captured Mama, so I couldn't talk to her. But I could talk to my best friends. Seeing them staring at me only made me cry even more.

"It's your call what we do," Zion said.

I gazed at them all. "We need a good night's sleep, and some of Grandma's chicken soup, and a shower that doesn't involve magic. Then we can make a new plan. I know I have to go back. I can find the ring, figure out what happened to my daddy, and then . . . I can try to see if it's possible to save my mama."

Zion grabbed Aliyah's and my hands. "Okay. We do it together."

EPILOGUE

The Supreme Mother, Ala, appeared in a shower of light outside the gates of the Sun Kingdom's palace. She took out her scepter, knocked on the gates, and waited.

A servant appeared, took one look at her, and bowed.

"I need to see my son," she said. "Now."

"Yes, Mother," the servant said, beckoning her forward. She followed him into the Burning Palace until they came to a long room. At the foot of it sat Anyanwu on his Sun Throne. He was staring through an opening in the palace ceiling at the sun in the sky. His skin was dark brown, his hair was red flame, his eyes were the color of roaring embers, and the cloak he wore dripped fire down to the floor. He was a tall god, taller than any of the other children she had birthed.

"Anyanwu," Ala whispered.

The sun god dipped his head toward her in a slow

movement, as if it had been the first time he had moved in centuries.

"Hello, Mother," he said in a surprisingly soft voice, one that didn't match the magnificence of the sun's warmth.

"Have you seen what has happened in Chidani?" she asked, moving forward.

He stepped down from his throne, his entire body engulfed in flames, and caught his mother in an embrace. The flames did not harm her. "No, I have not. I have not watched Chidani since the queen denied me."

Ala moved her hand. A scene appeared in the air, and they looked down at the ruined Palacia, the mmo dead in the courtyards, and the carnage in Asaba.

Anyanwu gasped.

"Do you know where your ring is, my son?" Ala asked.

"No, Mother, I do not."

"The princess stole it from Ramala. The Descendant came back to Chidani, but now he's gone."

Anyanwu narrowed his eyes. "We must find that ring. If we don't, I fear that all we know will be lost."

She touched his face as the scene in front of them disappeared. "We will, my son. We will."

"What should we do?" Anyanwu said.

She stared into his eyes of fire.

"We started this, so we must end it for good. We must rejoin the world, my son. The people need the gods once again. All the people. But one little boy in particular."

ACKNOWLEDGMENTS

When I first started writing this book, I wasn't sure if it would ever find an audience, but I knew that I had to keep trying, no matter what the outcome would be. *Cameron Battle* wouldn't be here without a group of people helping to make it happen. I thank you for thinking, critiquing, and standing with me as I wrote something so revolutionary.

To Nia (N.E.) Davenport, thank you for everything you have done in helping me come up with the concept for this book, becoming my first friend in this industry (and now my best friend). We spent numerous hours texting and talking about this book, dreaming up scenarios and scenes, and laughing our way through it. Our friendship means a lot to me, and I can't wait until your own words are out in the world. We need them.

To Sara Crowe, you saw the potential in this novel before an editor or a publisher did. Thank you for sticking with me through numerous manuscripts to get this ready to become my debut novel. To Rena Rossner, you truly are an agent extraordinaire. You took the bare bones of this novel and really shaped it into something spectacular, something that would garner the attention it needed when we sent it to publishers. Thank you for sticking by and with me and always telling me, "Jamar, it only takes one person to say yes." To Mary Kate Castellani—you are a dream editor. Thank you so much for seeing the potential in *Cameron Battle* from the beginning and guiding me along this journey when no one else would. Your editing prowess has made this work the best book it can possibly be, and I don't know how I can ever thank you enough.

To Amber McBride, thank you for being my rock in a hard place, for being the person to understand me on a deeper level than anyone ever has. I had so many doubts while writing this book, and you told me over and over again, "Jamar, this book will mean a lot. Celebrate your wins when they come." I'll always thank you for your generous and genuine support through brainstorming this novel and helping me with its numerous edits.

To Oswaldo (Journey) Reyes—man, we've been in this since the beginning. You have been nothing short of a lifesaver, and the time you spent reading my manuscripts and offering feedback has been amazing. I am so glad to call you my brother for life.

ACKNOWLEDGMENTS

To Maiya Ibrahim, what an amazing person and friend you have been to me during these times. You have read this book multiple times, offered your help when I was struggling through edits, and made sure I felt loved and supported through it all. Thank you for everything, sis.

I would also like to thank all the people who stood by me through the writing and publication of this novel; your support of me filled my spiritual well in ways that I can't quite understand yet. To George Jreije, Ryan Douglass, Justine Lee, Emily Timbol, Michael Strother, Marquis Dixon, Ayana Grey, Katie Zhao, Amanda Joy, Daniel Best, Claribel Ortega, K.E. Lewis, Caitie Flum, Peter Knapp, Isaac Fitzsimons, and Amélie Zhao, thank you for being there for me on the days that I couldn't be there for myself, when I no longer believed in my writing. Your support for me—through reading my work, conversations about the book over the phone, small acts of kindness, and giving me feedback on the cover—has allowed me to pursue this work in a way that was authentic to me and my experiences as a Black man.

To queer Black boys/men, I love you, I hear you, I see you. Thank you for standing with me through this justice journey. I hope you especially love Cameron Battle.

He loves you, too.